Dreaming of Florence

Dreaming of Florence

T.A. Williams

CANELO

First published in the United Kingdom in 2018 by Canelo

This edition published in the United Kingdom in 2018 by

Canelo Digital Publishing Limited
57 Shepherds Lane
Beaconsfield, Bucks HP9 2DU
United Kingdom

A CIP catalogue record for this book is available from the British Library.

Print ISBN 978 1 78863 139 6
Ebook ISBN 978 1 911591 92 4

Look for more great books at www.canelo.co

Printed and bound in Great Britain by Clays Ltd, Elcograf S.p.A.

To Mariangela and Christina as always with love

Chapter 1

Debbie was feeling good.

It was a lovely English summer's day as she cycled through the streets of Cambridge on her way home from work. She was humming to herself, her eyes on the cycle path ahead, but her mind was far away in her happy place. Ever since her teens, this special secret place in the hidden recesses of her mind had been her refuge from everyday life and worries about school, family, work, or, more recently, Paul. It was a place to relax and unwind, to rest and recuperate, and she loved it dearly. She had seen it in her daydreams so many times over the years that by now she felt she knew every blade of grass and every single petal on the rose bushes, even though she had never actually been there.

'Ouch.'

She winced as she bumped across a pothole in the tarmac, and felt the sharp jab as a spring poked up through the battered old saddle of her battered old bike. Doing her best to ignore her stinging backside, she returned her thoughts to her place of solace. Instead of the uncomfortable saddle, she imagined the soothing feel of the wooden bench, its surface warmed by the Tuscan sun, the scent of the flowers around her, the singing of the birds and, of course, the breathtaking views over the magical city of Florence. To her, this place spelt peace, quiet and safety.

'Look out!'

Even as she shouted, she realised it was too late. A tall man had just stepped off the pavement directly into her path, his head turned the other way, totally unaware of her presence. She swerved desperately, lost control and found herself flying headlong at him. As the bike crashed to the ground beneath her feet and slid out into the road, she made contact with the man's shoulders and felled him as effectively as a rugby player making a tackle. He was thrown sideways by the impact and landed heavily on the ground, followed, a split second later, by Debbie herself. She felt the breath crushed out of her lungs as she ended up sprawled across him, her left elbow making heavy contact with the tarmac as she did so. She would have squealed in pain, except that she was completely winded. She lay there for a few seconds, gasping like a freshly-landed fish, trying to catch her breath, before movement from beneath her shook her out of her trance-like state.

'*Maremma cane! Che cacchio…?*'

She immediately recognized the language as Italian, although her Italian teacher hadn't taught her either of these expressions. They were followed by what were in all probability another few choice expletives before he turned his head to look at her. Their faces were only a few inches away from one another and she found herself looking straight down into his eyes – rather nice deep brown eyes. She suddenly became embarrassingly aware that she was lying on top of him, her left hand somehow jammed into his crotch. She shifted slightly so as to remove it before risking a few words.

'I'm very sorry. You just stepped right out at me.' She had to pause to suck in some air. 'I just didn't have time to stop. Are you all right?'

He raised a tentative hand to his head and probed a bit through his thick mass of black hair, before nodding cautiously. 'Yes, I think so, but I'm the one who's sorry. That was totally my fault. I looked left, instead of right.' He managed a faint smile. 'I've been here a month, but I still haven't got back into the habit of everybody driving on the wrong side of the road. What about you? Are you sure you're OK?'

Unexpectedly reluctantly, Debbie rolled off him and raised herself into a sitting position on the edge of the cycle path. A couple of concerned bystanders had stopped alongside them, as had a bus full of people in the road, all now peering down at them curiously. She felt her cheeks flush as she realised her skirt had ended up around her waist, and she scrabbled to pull it down again. Once reassured she was decent once more, she checked herself for damage. Her right knee was a bit sore, her left elbow badly scraped, and one of the nails on her left hand broken, but otherwise, she seemed to be all right. She transferred her attention back to the man she had hit, who was resting back on his elbows on the pavement. By now, the smile on his face had broadened. She did her best to chase away her blushes, but wasn't completely successful.

'I think I'm fine, thanks. Your body broke my fall.' Her eyes contemplated his body for a few moments, rather liking what she saw. He looked as if he were around her age, maybe a year or two older, say thirty or so, and he

3

clearly looked after himself. His shoulders were broad, his chest strong, and she had already felt his hard stomach muscles for herself. His tanned face was classically handsome, and his bright eyes strangely magnetic. In spite of the circumstances, she felt a distinct shiver of attraction.

'Well, I'm glad I did.' With an athletic movement, he climbed to his feet, grimacing slightly as he straightened up, rubbing his side. After a few seconds, he bent towards her and offered her his hands. 'Here, can I help you up?'

Debbie caught hold of his hands and let him help her to her feet. She winced as she put weight onto her right leg and gave a little squeak as she straightened her left arm. Her elbow worked, but it hurt a lot. She took a better look at it and saw it running with fresh blood where contact with the road surface had scraped away a big patch of skin. She was searching for a tissue in her pocket when he handed her a clean, white handkerchief.

'Here, take this. It's clean, I promise.' He pressed it into her hand. 'I took it out of the suitcase only this morning.'

Debbie took it gratefully as the bus driver appeared beside them, a sympathetic expression on his face.

'Are you all right, love?'

Debbie nodded.

'I saw the whole thing: there wasn't anything you could do. This gentleman just walked right out in front of you. If you need a witness statement, you can get me at the bus company. My badge number's CAM3276.'

'Thank you very much, but I'm fine. Just a few scratches and a bruise or two.' As she spoke, she felt fingers on her elbow and she let the man with the brown eyes take over bandaging her cuts. As he did so, she heard him explain to the bus driver.

'I've already told her it was all my fault. Completely. I've come over from Italy and I wasn't concentrating.'

'All right, then. Well, I'm glad you're both OK.' The bus driver looked relieved and Debbie was quick to thank him for his concern. As the bus full of people set off again and the two pedestrian onlookers followed their example, Debbie found herself alone with the brown-eyed man. As he finished tying a knot securing the makeshift bandage, Debbie couldn't help noticing how neatly he had done it.

'Thank you so much. That looks great. Are you a first-aider?'

He smiled again; it lit up his face. 'Actually, I'm a doctor, and I'm glad there aren't any trained nurses watching. I've never been very good at bandaging and I'm sure I could have done it better.' He glanced down at her knee. 'Want me to take a look at that?' Without waiting for a reply, he crouched down and she felt his hands on her skin. She found herself looking down on the top of his head, as he surveyed the damage.

'Steady yourself against me and try bending your leg for me, would you?'

She did as ordered, resting her hands on his shoulders and, although the knee hurt a bit as she moved it, she could feel that it wasn't too bad. The doctor agreed.

'Just a bit of bruising, I'm glad to say. Take a couple of painkillers when you get home and it should be fine by tomorrow – just a bit stiff and sore for a day or two, I expect.' He stood up again and stretched out his hand. 'By the way, my name's Pierluigi Masino. I'm very pleased to meet you, although I apologise once again for the circumstances.'

Debbie took his hand and shook it formally. 'I'm Deborah Waterson. Everybody calls me Debbie. Thank you so much.'

'For knocking you off your bike and almost under a bus?' He was smiling and she found herself smiling back.

'That was an accident. No, I mean thank you for bandaging my cuts and for breaking my fall.'

'That was the least I could do under the circumstances.'

'Are you Italian? Your English is fantastic.' It really was. She saw him nod to acknowledge the compliment.

'Yes, I'm Italian, but I did my medical training here in the UK, so I've had to learn to speak your language reasonably fluently. In fact, I'm over this summer for a course at King's, here in Cambridge.'

'So, you'll be here for a while?' For some reason Debbie knew that this was important for her to know.

He shook his head and she felt surprisingly disappointed. 'Not really. I've been here since early July, but now I've only got another two weeks before I go home again. Just until the middle of August.' He glanced across at her bike that some kind soul had rescued from the roadside and propped against the railings at the side of the cycle track. Her eyes followed his and it became immediately apparent that she wasn't going to be riding it, even if her elbow and her knee allowed. The handlebars were twisted, the front tyre was flat and, worst of all, the front forks were bent out of shape.

'I'm afraid your bike isn't looking too good. Why don't I call a taxi to get you and it home?'

'There's no need for that really, thank you.' Debbie tapped his arm to stop him reaching into his pocket. 'My house is quite close by. I'll just push the bike home. It won't take long.'

'Well, at least let me push it for you. That elbow of yours needs to be rested.'

Debbie protested, but he insisted, and she was secretly rather glad of his company. There was something very appealing about this kind and handsome Good Samaritan. Together, they set off and she noticed that he had to lift the front wheel right off the ground as the forks had buried themselves in the spokes. As they walked, they chatted and she told him a bit about herself. When he heard what she did for a living, he was unsurprised.

'An English language teacher, eh? There must be lots around here. I've seen so many schools of English all over the place since I got here. It must be big business in Cambridge. Everywhere I go, there are swarms of teenagers – and a lot of them are Italians.'

Debbie nodded cautiously. 'It's been quite a busy summer, but everybody says student numbers are down. I've even heard of some schools closing.'

He looked surprised. 'You'd never know it from the numbers of kids all over the place. So, do you enjoy your job?'

'Yes, I do, I really do. I've been working here now in the same place for almost five years and I love it. What about you – are you a happy doctor?'

'A reasonably happy doctor.' He smiled across at her as they turned the corner and she led him into the cul-de-sac where her little flat was situated. Now that Paul had left, it was proving to be pretty expensive, and she was struggling to keep it on by herself as well as try to pay off some of her student loan debt. Her alternative, she knew, would be to move back into a room in a house with other people, but she had got used to her independence and was loath to give it up. But it wasn't easy making ends meet. They hadn't had a pay rise at the school for almost three years now and it was tough.

As they reached the garden gate, she showed him where to put the bike behind the dustbins, reflecting that this might well turn out to be its final resting place. It was a very old bike she had bought for just forty pounds several years earlier, but it had done its job and she had grown attached to it. Now, looking at it, she felt fairly sure it would cost more to repair than to replace. She resolved to look into getting another one as a matter of urgency, although, from the way her knee felt, it might be a few days before she tried riding again.

'There, the bike's out of the way.' He came out from behind the dustbin and wiped his hands on the legs of his jeans. They were new-looking jeans and he looked very smart, or he should have done. For the first time she noticed the tear just above the left knee.

'I'm really sorry about your jeans.'

He smiled at her. 'Don't even think about it. Who knows? Maybe they've suddenly become fashionable.' There was a brief pause before he stuck out his hand. 'Well, Deborah Waterson, my apologies once more. If you need me to take a look at your elbow or your knee, here's my card. You'll have to stick 0039 in front of the mobile number, but do call if you need me. If I were you, I'd put that arm in a sling for support for a day or two.'

'Thank you, Doctor Masino. You're very kind.' As she shook his hand, Debbie was seriously considering inviting him in for a cup of tea, but he had already turned away before she could reach a decision. As he closed the little metal gate behind him, he half-turned towards her.

'*Arrivederci, Debbie.*'

'*Arrivederci, Pierluigi.*'

And he was gone, leaving her feeling quite unexpectedly sorry to see him go.

–

It was about six o'clock when she heard the doorbell. For a moment she felt an irrational surge of hope that it might be her Italian doctor friend, come to invite her out for dinner, but no sooner had the thought crossed her mind than she dismissed it. After what had happened with Paul, she had absolutely no interest in starting a relationship with another man any time soon. Besides, her Italian doctor friend had said he was only here for a few more weeks and she certainly wasn't looking for a casual holiday romance, even though she had to admit that he had been rather dishy. Shaking her head, she went out into the hall and opened the front door. It was Alice.

'Hi, Debs, how's things?' Alice stopped and gawped. 'What's wrong with your arm?'

'Fell off my bike.'

Following the orders of her newly-acquired personal physician, Debbie had fashioned a primitive sling out of a scarf to support her sore elbow.

'Is it broken?'

Debbie shook her head. 'No, just scraped and bruised. Thank goodness.'

She led Alice into the flat and told her the story as she made them both some tea. As she recounted the events of that afternoon, she omitted to mention that the man

9

who had caused the accident had been really rather good-looking.

There was a reason for this. Had she indicated in any way that she had found him attractive, Alice would have been at her heels like a little terrier, doing her best to put the two of them together. Alice had been quite unable to understand Debbie's decision to take a timeout from men for the foreseeable future, after the four-year relationship with Paul had been so rudely interrupted back in the spring. Ever since then, Alice had been constantly on the lookout for suitable replacements, deaf to Debbie's protests. So caution was the watchword as far as Alice was concerned.

'He was Italian, you say?'

'Yes.'

'And a doctor?'

'Yes.'

'Age?'

'Oh, I don't know. Maybe early thirties.' Debbie did her best to sound disinterested.

'Really? That's perfect. So, tell me, what did he look like? Buck teeth, bald, scrawny, smelly, scruffy?'

'Yes, all of those, definitely.' Debbie concentrated on the tea.

'Was he tall or short?'

'Tallish, I suppose.'

She handed her friend a mug of tea and they both sat down at the kitchen table. Gingerly, Debbie rested her damaged elbow on the table and let the sling fall from her shoulder. She stretched her arm cautiously, pleased to be able to move it more easily. The paracetamol had definitely begun to do its work.

'Taller than you, then?'

'Erm, yes.'

'Well, that's bloody tall. Look at you, Debs. Your legs are just about as long as my whole body. So, he's tall, Italian and a doctor. Tasty!'

'Don't forget the smelly, scruffy thing.'

She heard Alice snort.

'What's wrong with a bit of a pong? I went out with a boy a couple of years back who smelt like an elk, but it didn't bother me.'

'How on earth do you know what an elk smells like, Al?' Debbie found herself smiling.

'Trust me. He smelt like an elk. Or a moose, or a buffalo, or one of those big hairy things.'

'So why did you go out with him if he smelt like some form of wildlife?'

Alice winked. 'The smell wasn't the only thing about him that reminded me of a big, hairy beast, if you catch my drift.'

Debbie sighed theatrically. 'I always catch your drift, Al. Anyway, this guy didn't smell like any kind of quadruped.' She could see that Alice still wasn't satisfied but, fortunately, she changed the subject and Debbie was able to relax, at least for now.

'Anyway, Debs, you really need to do something about your hair and your clothes if you're on the lookout for a man.'

'For the thousandth time, I'm not on the lookout for a man. Besides, what's wrong with my hair?'

'Well, have you ever thought about going to a hairdresser, for instance? Your hair's a mess and you know it. If you let it grow much longer, it'll get caught in the chain of your bike, and you'll have another accident even without some hunky man bumping into you. Look at yourself. Your split ends are developing their own split ends by now. If you put it off much longer, you're going to start looking like some scruffy old bag-lady.'

'I'm not bothered, Al. I'm quite happy like this.'

'I know you are, and you shouldn't be. You're a twenty-eight-year-old girl with long legs and the sort of bottom us mere mortals can only dream of. For crying out loud, Debs, smarten yourself up. Cambridge is full of handsome men just dying to get their hands on you.'

'Well, if it is, I haven't seen many of them.' Apart from her Italian doctor, of course, but she wasn't going to voice that thought to Alice. 'And as for letting them get their hands on me, I don't think so, somehow.' Debbie deliberately stifled any more thought of her Italian doctor and grinned across the table. 'Besides, I've got my job, my Italian class and my bike. What do I need some big hairy, possibly smelly, bloke for?'

'I'll have to buy you a book all about the birds and the bees, Debs. Surely you haven't forgotten already?'

'Trust me, Al, I'm just fine as I am. As for the visit to the hairdresser, that'll have to wait anyway now, as first of all I'm going to have to find the cash to get myself a new bike. In case you hadn't noticed, I'm skint.'

They sipped their tea and Debbie was pleased to get the topic of conversation away from the doctor and onto Alice's ever-changing panoply of boyfriends. As ever, Debbie felt amazement and maybe even a pang of envy at her friend's ability to jump seamlessly from one rela-tionship to another, with hardly a pause for breath in between. Every one started out as the real thing and rapidly deteriorated into old news. Her latest conquest, if that was the word, was a forty-year-old astrophysicist at Cavendish, called Dave. By the time Alice finally left, Debbie had received a full and frank appraisal of him as a man, scientist and lover. Debbie's gut feeling was that this was yet another relationship destined for the scrapheap, not least because Dave spent most of his nights glued to a telescope, rather than to Alice.

She took a long, hot bath to ease her aches and pains before going to bed and, inevitably, her subconscious drifted away from Cambridge, across Europe, to her happy place once more. She imagined herself sitting on the wooden bench, the smell of roses and the hum of bees in the air. Down below her, beyond the muddy brown waters of the river Arno, the massive red dome of the Duomo and the shining white marble of the Campanile di Giotto towered above the mass of terracotta tiles that formed the roofs of Florence. She knew almost all the buildings by name by now, after hours spent as a girl in the local library in Bristol where she had grown up and, in more recent years, on the computer. The picture of the place she had built up in her mind was fascinating, tantalising and very, very comforting. Some day, she knew, she would have to go there and see it for herself.

As her sore limbs responded to the soothing touch of the water, her mind relaxed under the spell of this magical place and she felt the cares of the day recede. The British Council inspection had gone well, she was pretty sure. These inspections of every aspect of the school and all the staff were always stressful and she, like the rest of her colleagues, was relieved it had passed without incident. The lesson on the conditional tense she had trotted out for the inspectors had felt like it had been a success and, of course, on her way home she had met her Italian doctor.

She thought a lot about him as she lay in the warm water, half of her here in Cambridge, the other half somewhere in the ether above Florence. She could still remember the feel of his body beneath hers as they lay on the pavement. She remembered his eyes, his mouth and even his smell. As she finally opened her own eyes and pulled herself upright, she found herself smiling. No, he definitely hadn't smelt of elk.

Chapter 2

She took the bus to work the next day. As Pierluigi had predicted, she woke up feeling pretty stiff and sore, but the discomfort began to wear off as the day progressed. At lunchtime Simon, the principal, put a smile on her face when he told her in confidence that the British Council inspectors had singled her out for a special mention.

'They said it was one of the best lessons they'd ever seen.'

'Terrific, Simon. Let's hope they tell lots of people, and we get more students as a result.'

He grimaced.

'Well we certainly need them!'

'It'll work out, I'm sure. We're a good school and people always need English.'

He looked more worried than usual.

'I hope you're right. Enrolments for the autumn and winter are dire.'

She gave him an encouraging smile. 'It'll be fine. You'll see.'

She was still smiling as she walked back along the road from the bus stop at half past four and turned into the cul-de-sac. Her smile broadened as she saw she had a visitor waiting for her.

'Pierluigi, hi.' She realised she was very pleased to see him again and, from the smile on his face, she got the impression he felt the same way. He jumped up from the wall where he had been sitting and held out his hand.

'Hello, Debbie. I was hoping you'd be coming home around the same time as yesterday. I thought I'd drop by and see how you're feeling today.'

'I'm feeling fine, thanks. Still a little bit sore, but nothing terrible.' She shook his hand and then glanced at her watch. 'Would you like a cup of tea?' Remembering that he was, after all, Italian, she immediately qualified her offer. 'Or coffee? It's only instant, but it's not too bad.'

'I'd love a cup of tea. That's very kind.'

He opened the gate for her and followed her up the path. As they reached the dustbins, she felt his hand tap her on the shoulder. She turned and her eyes followed his pointing finger.

'I also came to make amends. Your old bike looked pretty terminal yesterday, so I've taken the liberty of replacing it for you. Will this do?'

Debbie stared at the shiny new bike resting against the wall. Unlike her old one, there was no sign of rust anywhere and the saddle was flawless and smooth, without even a hint of a spring poking through. The tyres were still clean and fresh from the shop and the wicker basket on the front was clearly making its first outing in the open air. A tiny Italian flag hanging from the handlebars completed the look. She heard his voice again, sounding slightly unsure.

'Will it do? I chose a blue one, but I didn't know your tastes. They've got a green one exactly the same if you prefer. The man said he'd just swap them over if you want.'

'It's wonderful, Pierluigi, but I can't accept that. What happened yesterday was an accident.' Debbie returned her eyes to him. 'Really, it's not fair. There's no need for you to go and do something like this.'

'There's every need. Yes, it was an accident, but it was caused by me.' He smiled more broadly. 'Anyway, it was a happy accident because it gave me the opportunity to meet you. So, blue's all right? Sure?'

'Blue's perfect, but like I say, there was no need.' On an impulse, she leant towards him and kissed him on the cheek, breathing in his scent again. 'This is really, really kind of you. And, yes, it was a happy accident. I'm really glad to have met you, too.' She turned and led him inside.

Some kind of sixth sense had caused her to get up earlier than usual that morning so as to wash the dishes and tidy the house before leaving for school. Maybe it had been some kind of premonition, or at least wishful thinking, that he might come by. As a result, she was now able to offer him a seat at the table that was, for once, unusually uncluttered. But not completely. As he sat down, his eyes alighted on her Italian textbook.

'Are you studying Italian?'

She blushed slightly. 'Yes, but my Italian's nothing like as good as your English.'

'*Però! Guarda, guarda...* So, do you want to speak Italian?'

Debbie shook her head as she decided not to attempt a reply in Italian.

'I've been studying it for six years now, but I'm certainly not what you might call fluent. So it's probably

best if we stick to English.' She gave a shy cough. 'I did
A level a few years ago and I go to an Italian class once a
week, but it's not enough.'

'Well, any time you want to speak Italian, just say the
word. So, have you been to Italy?'

Debbie was relieved he wasn't insisting on speaking
Italian to her. It was odd enough to have a man here
in the house, without making it worse by conducting
the conversation in a foreign language. In fact, thinking
about it, he was the first man to set foot in here since
Paul's departure in March. She put the kettle on and took
the two least battered mugs out of the cupboard before
replying.

'No, never. I almost went when I was at school. There
was a school trip to Florence, but my mum and dad didn't
have the money for me to go.'

'I'm very sorry to hear that, Debbie. What a terrible
shame.'

She nodded slowly. 'That's life.' She shook her head
at the memory as she put tea bags in the two mugs while
the kettle came to the boil. 'Milk and sugar?'

'Just milk, please. I never used to drink tea until I came
over here to university. Now I can't get through the day
without it.' He flicked through the Italian textbook. 'So,
when the time comes for you to go to Italy, where's the
first place you want to visit?'

'Florence.' The answer came out spontaneously. No
thought was necessary.

'Well, well. I bet you'll never guess where I come
from.' He was smiling more broadly now.

'Not Florence, *Firenze* in Italian, by any chance?'

'That's right. *Firenze* is my home town. I live bang in the middle.'

'Wow, that's amazing. Florence is my number one favourite place in the whole world. Wait a minute, can I show you something? Hang on, will you?'

She set the two mugs of tea down on the table and hurried through to the bedroom. There, as ever, on her bedside table, was the little picture frame she had found in a junk shop in Bristol and, inside it, protected behind glass, her precious postcard. She picked it up and took it back to the kitchen.

'Here, do you know where this is?' She watched his face intently as he took it from her and studied it at close quarters.

'Well, the Duomo's pretty unmistakable, isn't it? It's obviously Florence and the photo's taken from the other side of the Arno, probably from Piazzale Michelangelo or maybe the Boboli Gardens. What is it? Is it a postcard? It looks like you've had it for a good long while.'

Debbie nodded. 'Yes, it's a postcard. My friends who went on the school trip sent it to me from Florence and I've kept it ever since.' Tearing her eyes away from the photo, she glanced up at him. 'I've been on Google Earth and I think it must have been taken from Piazzale Michelangelo, just like you said. It's funny though. Somehow, although I've never been to Italy before, I get the feeling I know this place intimately. It feels so familiar and I can imagine the scene so clearly.'

He caught hold of her hand on the tabletop and gave it a squeeze before releasing it again. She found she enjoyed his touch. 'Maybe you were a *fiorentina* in a previous life – say, one of the beautiful Medici princesses. Who knows?'

'More likely the housemaid who emptied the Medici chamber pots. I come from a very poor background.' She laughed to conceal her secret pleasure at being compared to a beautiful princess. 'So is that where you live and work – Florence?'

He nodded. 'Yes, although for my speciality – I'm an oncologist, but I won't bore you with the details – the place to be at the moment is in the US. That's where so much new work's being done, and I'd love to be part of it. So I'm doing this course this summer in the hope that it'll help me get a position over there.'

'But your home's in Florence?'

'Yes. I'm afraid I'm a stereotypical Italian, in that I still live at home with my parents at the ripe old age of thirty-three.'

Somehow Debbie felt relieved to hear that he wasn't married or living with a girlfriend. She tried to keep the satisfaction off her face as she replied.

'I was reading an article in *La Stampa* only a month or two ago. Apparently, two-thirds of all Italians our age still live at home.'

'Our age? Surely you're a lot younger than me?'

'I'm twenty-eight, but only for a few weeks more. I'll be twenty-nine on the twenty-ninth. Not so different.'

'You look younger.' He studied her appreciatively. 'I suppose if you put your hair up, you might look a bit older, but like you've got it now, tied in a ponytail, you look ten years younger than me.'

'I certainly didn't feel it when I got out of bed this morning. I was creaking like an old crock.'

'Anyway, old crock or not, the other reason I came round to see you was to ask if I could be allowed to take you out for dinner some time.' He waved his hand to stop her replying immediately. 'And this has got nothing to do with my trying to atone for my stupidity yesterday. This is because one of the best things in life is to eat good food in a good restaurant in the company of a beautiful woman.'

'I'm afraid I'm not the best person to ask about good restaurants.' Debbie did her best to stop her cheeks from flushing. Even with Paul, she had rarely been out to any "good" restaurants and, if she were totally honest, she found those sort of places a bit intimidating.

'Well, I've found the beautiful woman, so I'm already halfway there. Now, surely there must be a good restaurant somewhere in Cambridge.'

This time she couldn't help blushing. 'Well, the answer is that I'd love to come out for dinner with you, but I don't really know anywhere chic. I know the pubs down by the river reasonably well, and I sometimes go to the Angler's Rest. The food there's normally OK. Besides, it's got a terrace overlooking the river and if the weather stays like this, we could probably eat outside. When were you thinking of?'

'Whenever you like. I'm free tonight, tomorrow – you name it.'

'Tonight's good for me. Tomorrow's my Italian class.'

'Very good. Let's make it tonight. We can speak Italian if you like. That way, you'll be able to impress your teacher tomorrow with your increased fluency.'

Debbie shook her head. 'I think I'd be happier keeping it in English for now. Maybe if we get to know each other a bit better, we could try a bit of Italian.' As she spoke, she realised that she really did hope she would get to know him better.

Debbie got to the Angler's Rest at eight o'clock and was impressed to see Pierluigi already there, waiting for her. He gave her a big smile when he saw her and it seemed the most natural thing in the world for her to catch hold of his hands and kiss him on both cheeks, taking a surreptitious inward breath as she did so – definitely not elk.

He had phoned ahead and booked a table out on the terrace, overlooking the river. Further up, in the distance, a group of people were doing their unsuccessful best to squeeze three or four punts underneath a low bridge and, even from here, she could hear the shouts and screams of laughter as attempt after attempt failed. The river was so slow-moving as to look stationary, although the water itself was far clearer than the River Arno in Debbie's postcard of Florence. She and Pierluigi stood there for a moment, enjoying the scene as the sun dropped towards the pink horizon, until Pierluigi turned his attention from the river to her.

'You look marvellous. I was right, you know. Pinning your hair up has made you look a bit older, but it's also made you look even more gorgeous. And you've got such lovely hair.' He reached over and ran the back of his fingers up the side of her head and she thrilled at the sensation. She thought back to a few hours earlier when she had summoned up the courage to brush her hair out in front of her and then, with the good scissors from the sewing box, she had trimmed almost a foot off it. As the auburn locks dropped to the floor, she had repressed a feeling of regret but now, here, listening to him, she knew that it had been worth it.

'Thank you for the compliment. I must say you're looking pretty good yourself.' And he was. He was still wearing jeans, but these were light grey and didn't have a tear at the knee. His shirt with a little crocodile logo on the chest was light pink, open at the neck, and it showed off his tan to advantage. For the first time she noticed the very expensive-looking gold watch on his wrist. He looked smart, stylish and affluent. As always, she began to feel a sensation of discomfort. Coming, as she did, from a very ordinary background, she wasn't used to being in the company of wealthy people.

She would have settled for a salad of some kind, but the pub was doing a Spanish night, so she let herself be persuaded to join him in tapas and red wine. This all turned out to be unexpectedly good. As darkness fell, they chatted and she gradually began to learn more about him and his life. He was an entertaining companion and she felt herself becoming ever more attracted to this generous, intelligent man who also just happened to look like a film star. It was just a pity that he would only be in Cambridge for a few more days.

Inevitably, the conversation came round to her favourite city, his home town.

'So, what's it like, living in Florence, Pierluigi?' She had just helped him finish a plateful of ham. He had explained to her that this was wonderful, tasty *jamón ibérico*, produced from a special breed of black pigs whose diet included acorns. Debbie wasn't a great ham connoisseur, but she had to admit that it was some of the best she had ever tasted – acorns or no acorns. She was feeling pleasantly full – maybe not so full as to be unable to manage a dessert in a little while, but pretty full all the same.

'Florence is hot in summer, cold in winter, the traffic's awful and the place is full to bursting with tourists. Otherwise, it's great.' She could see the smile on his face illuminated by the orange glow of the light on the wall above them.

'Yes, but, apart from all that, it must have its good sides.'

He took a mouthful of Tempranillo wine before answering. 'Oh yes, it has its good sides all right. There's the food. Don't let anybody from anywhere else in Italy try to tell you otherwise – the food in Florence is the best. The olive oil's amazing, the meat's to die for, and the wines are excellent. And the bread is just the best anywhere. And then there's the setting – squeezed into the valley of the Arno, with Fiesole up to the north, the Apennines beyond, and the Chianti hills rising up on the other side.' She could see a faraway look in his eyes.

'And, above all, there's an overwhelming sense of history. The shops, the offices, even McDonald's, are set in buildings that are three, four, five hundred years old. Sometimes, coming home from a night shift in the early hours, it feels as if you could turn a corner and meet Machiavelli himself, swaggering along the pavement towards you.'

Debbie was conscious of the longing in her voice as she replied. 'That's exactly how I dream of Florence, you know. And the Duomo, is it as magnificent as they say?'

'The Cathedral of Santa Maria del Fiore, to give it its full name, is one of the seven wonders of the world.' He smiled. 'All right, I'm biased, like all Florentines, but you've really got to see it. When you do, just remind yourself that when it was built, back in the Middle Ages, most of the people in Europe were still living in single-storey houses, most of them built of wood, bricks or even mud. If you just stand in front of the Duomo and look up, it goes on forever. It's a symphony of white marble, punctuated by lines of green and red stone, the colours of the Italian flag.'

'And the bell tower alongside it?'

'The Campanile di Giotto shares the same colour scheme and it's a wonderfully elegant structure. And of course, there's the Baptistery as well.' His eyes flashed in the lamplight. 'I guarantee Florence will blow you away when you see the place for yourself.'

Debbie smiled across the table at him.

'You make it sound so amazing.'

'It is amazing, Debbie. There's no other word for it. No surprise that millions and millions of people every year flock to Florence. That's just about the major disadvantage of living there: the crowds.'

'I can imagine! I'm sure there must be all sorts of disadvantages to living in a tourist hub, but there are so many compensations.'

'So why have you never been? Surely, now that you're working, you could afford to take a holiday.'

Debbie nodded hesitantly. 'I'm not so sure about that. I've only just started paying off the debts I built up at university, but I've thought about it a lot, although I've never summoned up the courage to go over there to see it for myself. I know, it's going to sound so silly, but, somehow, I didn't want to spoil the image I've built up of it. You know – like meeting one of your childhood heroes and finding he's got bad breath. Do you understand what I mean?'

'I do, but I still think you should bite the bullet and give it a try. Mind you, you're not too far off the mark with the bad breath thing – when it gets hot, the drains can certainly smell a bit. But, overall, I'm sure you'd find it as wonderful as you imagine.'

'There's something else as well.' She hesitated, the idea that had been lying in her subconscious now stirring just about for the first time. 'Student numbers at the school where I work have been dropping and I was wondering whether I might do well to start sussing out the chances of getting a teaching job elsewhere. And, if I decide to go abroad, naturally the first place for me to look would be Florence. Do you think there are many schools of English over there?'

He smiled broadly. 'That would be amazing. And, yes, there are quite a few schools, I'm sure. With so many tourists from all over the world, knowledge of English is essential nowadays. You should come over for a few days and look around. I'd be glad to act as your guide.'

'That's really sweet of you, but I don't know...' Before she could carry on, she heard a familiar voice.

'Debs? Fancy seeing you here.' There was genuine surprise in Alice's voice. 'So, are you going to introduce me to your friend?'

'Hi, Al.' Debbie's heart fell – not at the sight of her best friend, but at the follow-up she knew was now going to have to endure over the coming days. Reluctantly, she pointed to Pierluigi, noticing his eyes focused on Alice's bust. Mind you, she thought to herself, most men seemed to do that when they first met her. 'Alice, this is Pierluigi.

He's from Italy and we bumped into each other yesterday. Pierluigi, this is Alice, my best friend, who always knows what's best for me.'

'So you're the man who's been knocking my friend about?'

Pierluigi stood up politely and held out his hand, gallantly raising his eyes from her cleavage as he did so.

'It was a fortunate accident. I'm very pleased to meet you, Alice.'

Alice took his hand in both of hers and shook it. As he sat back down again, she shot a clandestine glance across at Debbie and raised both thumbs for a second, unseen by him. Clearly, she approved of Pierluigi. As she did so, Debbie saw her mouth the words "scruffy and smelly?".

'So, what about introducing us to your friend, Al?' It was on the tip of Debbie's tongue to ask whether the man with the black beard behind her friend was Dave the astrophysicist, but she knew Alice too well. It was lucky she did.

'This is Jean-Claude. He's a teacher from Lyon and he's over here with a group of kids at a language school – not yours.' She turned to her companion. 'Debbie's one of my oldest, and tallest, friends. She teaches English at one of the other schools in Cambridge.'

They all shook hands and there was a slightly uncomfortable pause while Debbie tried to make up her mind whether politeness decreed that she invite them to sit down. But Alice was far too streetwise. Debbie saw at once that she had already worked out that two was company and four definitely a crowd in this case. Taking a proprietary grip on Jean-Claude's forearm, Alice waved with her free hand.

'Well, you young people have fun.' For a second or two, her eyes met Debbie's. 'Don't do anything I wouldn't do.'

'That gives me a lot of scope, Al. I'll remember that.' As the others disappeared into the door of the pub, she gave Pierluigi a two-line précis of her relationship with Alice.

'Alice and I have known each other since I first moved to Cambridge. We lived in the same house for a couple of years before I moved out. She's a sweetie.'

'She looks very nice. So, why did you move out?'

Debbie hadn't wanted to bring Paul into the conversation this evening, or any time soon, but she didn't have much option. 'I moved in with my boyfriend. In the same flat you've been to.'

She spotted more than idle curiosity in his eyes as he asked his next question. 'And your boyfriend, where's he now?'

'My ex is in the United States. Last time I heard about him, he was in San Francisco.'

'So you broke up?'

Debbie nodded.

'Long ago?'

'Just over four months ago, at the end of March.'

'I see.' He didn't query her any more and she was grateful to him for that. Instead, after a polite pause, he returned the subject to food. 'So, would you like some dessert?'

–

They walked home together under the light of the streetlamps. She very nearly took his hand or his arm, but then

28

thought twice about it. After all, she had only met him the previous day and she didn't want him to think she was out of the same mould as Alice. Besides, what was the point of even considering a new relationship with somebody who would be disappearing to Italy, if not the USA, in a few days' time? Even so, she couldn't miss the feeling of attraction growing inside her for this lovely man and she had no hesitation in inviting him in for coffee when they reached her gate. To her disappointment, he declined the offer.

'I'd really like to, Debbie, but I promised a colleague I'd help her with an assignment that has to be handed in tomorrow. Besides, coffee at this time of night might stop me sleeping.'

She took a closer look at him. Either he was naïve enough to believe that an invitation to coffee just meant an invitation to coffee – and nothing he had said or done so far had given any hint of naivety – or something was holding him back. For a moment, she spared a thought for just who this female "colleague" might be who demanded his presence at almost midnight, but she steered clear of the subject. After all, as she had been telling herself all along, they had only just met and he was only going to be here for a week or two.

'Well, goodnight, Pierluigi, and thanks for a lovely meal. Next time, I'm paying.' One thing was for sure. She knew she wanted there to be a next time.

'Absolutely not! But I do hope we can do this again. Could I maybe have your phone number? You've already got mine, unless you lost the card.'

The card was safely tucked into the frame holding the precious postcard beside her bed.

'Of course I've still got it.'

Debbie gave him her number and wondered when she would hear from him again. After tucking the phone back into his pocket, he held out his hand towards her.

'*Buona notte*, Debbie.'

'*Buona notte*, Pierluigi.'

As he took her hand, he pulled her gently towards him and kissed her softly on the cheeks.

'This has been a lovely evening.'

'It certainly has.'

She stood by the gate and watched him walk back up the street again until he turned the corner onto the main road and she lost sight of him. Only then did she open the gate and go up the path to the front door, stopping to check that her lovely new bike was still safely chained up behind the dustbins.

Inside her flat, she headed straight for bed, knowing that she had to be up early next morning for work.

As she lay in bed, her eyelids heavy, her thoughts, as ever, turned once more to her happy place on the hillside above the magical city of Florence. For the first time she sensed a presence on the sun-warmed bench beside her. She couldn't see who it was, but she felt comforted to know she wasn't alone. She drifted off to sleep with a smile on her face.

Chapter 3

It was three days before she heard from him again. This came in the form of a text message and it simply read, *Hi Debbie. Can I see you again? P.*

They had been three surprisingly long days. Debbie had found herself thinking about him a lot and she had come close to calling or texting him herself on a couple of occasions, but had resisted the temptation. All the time she had found herself questioning why he had refused to come in for coffee, or whatever else she might have ended up offering. Who was this female colleague who required his help? Was he holding back because he wasn't interested, or was there somebody else? Was there maybe a girlfriend back in Italy?

At the same time, she had also been doing a good bit of self-analysis.

Four months had now passed since Paul had left, and so far she had remained true to her resolve to steer clear of men. Did this sudden attraction to the handsome Italian mean she was over Paul and ready to move on?

Inevitably, this was also the question uppermost in Alice's mind. On the way home from school on the day after their encounter at the Angler's Rest, Debbie had been pretty sure she could expect a visit from Alice as soon as she got out of work. Consequently, she was totally unsurprised to hear the doorbell ring at six o'clock that evening. The questions started the moment Alice walked in the door.

'Scruffy and smelly, eh? Are you sure, Debs?'

'Well, maybe not smelly.'

'He's a total hunk, your Pierluigi, and you know it. So why deny it?'

Debbie took advantage of a few seconds' thinking time as she filled the kettle and dug out two clean mugs, but, in spite of this, her answer sounded weak even to her.

'I suppose he is quite good-looking really.'

'He's like something out of a catalogue and you know it. So, does this mean you've finally taken my advice and put that slime ball Paul behind you and decided to get on with the rest of your life?'

Debbie did her best to answer her friend as honestly as possible.

'I really don't know, Al. You're right, of course, Pierluigi *is* very good-looking and he's also kind, generous and intelligent. I suppose the answer to your question is probably a qualified yes. I think I may be over Paul, or at least getting there.'

'Why qualified?' Alice's tone was now less confrontational and more sympathetic.

'I mean this is the first time since Paul that I've felt attracted to another man, but I know nothing about him, really. He's Italian. He's a doctor. He lives in Florence with his parents and he's going home in little more than a week's time. That's about it.'

'Did you say Florence?' Alice was one of the few people in whom Debbie had confided about her dreams of Florence. 'Surely that has to be a sign? The universe is telling you this man's the one for you, Debs.' As ever, Alice had come close to reading Debbie's mind.

'I know, Al, it *is* a coincidence, but maybe that's all it is.'

'I'm not so sure, but anyway, what're you going to do about him? Have you got his phone number? Do you know where he's staying?'

'Yes, and no. I think he said he was in one of the halls of residence, but I don't know which.'

'Well, call him and find out.'

Debbie shook her head.

'To be honest, Al, he's out of my league. His shirt alone probably cost more than everything I was wearing last night, and I'm pretty sure his watch would be worth more than the entire contents of this flat. He's from another world. He even knew what the bloody pigs we were eating had been fed on, for crying out loud. He wouldn't be interested in me.'

She saw Alice roll her eyes. 'Do you hear yourself? What are you – little orphan Annie? You're a grown woman with a good degree, a responsible job, and did I mention your bum? Of course he's interested in you.'

Debbie wasn't so sure. She would wait for him to make the next move.

So when the text message arrived, she hesitated before replying. There was no denying the fact that she would love to see him again, but she also knew she wanted to take things slowly, even though he would be leaving all too soon. The break-up with Paul had scarred her deeply and she wasn't about to make the same mistake twice. After a lot of thought, and taking a deep breath, she texted back: *Love to. Where and when? D.* She resisted the temptation to add a little x before her initial. 'Take it slow,' she murmured to herself.

Seconds later, her phone rang. It was his number. She was in the kitchen at the time, so she sat down at the table as she answered.

'Hi, Pierluigi, how are you?'

'Debbie, hi.' He sounded very pleased to hear her voice. 'Today's Friday. I was thinking about renting a car tomorrow and taking a little tour of the area. Would you feel like joining me?'

'That sounds lovely. The forecast's good, too.'

'Shall I pick you up at ten?'

'It's a date.'

As she put the phone down on the table, she reviewed her terminology. She had called it a date. Was that really what it was?

–

It was a beautiful day and their tour of the countryside around Cambridge was equally beautiful. There was just one problem. Pierluigi had arrived wearing shorts, and the problem for Debbie was that his long, tanned legs were very, very distracting. Time and again, she found herself having to consciously raise her eyes from his brown knees to the scenery outside. In the course of the day, they visited most of Cambridgeshire as well as quite a bit of Norfolk and Suffolk. Although she had lived in the area for five years, she had rarely ventured outside of Cambridge itself, and she thoroughly enjoyed discovering the surrounding countryside. And of course, she had a wonderful guide.

They stopped for midmorning coffee at a table outside a sixteenth-century inn by the side of the river Ouse. As they nibbled biscuits and sipped their drinks, they watched the antics of a family of mallard ducks with their tiny, fluffy young, as they threaded their way among the pleasure craft of all shapes and sizes that chugged up and down before them. Lunchtime was spent in Ely, visiting the wonderful cathedral, so incongruously enormous in such a little town. She wondered how it would rate alongside the Duomo in Florence.

It was after a pub lunch, while they were sitting on a bench in the shade of a massive old oak tree, that they gradually began to find out more about each other. Debbie was the first to pluck up the courage.

'So, Pierluigi, is there a special lady in your life?'

'Apart from my mother, my sister and the person sitting beside me?'

His tone was gentle. She nodded and waited until he gave his answer.

'No, I'm afraid not.'

There was something in his voice that made Debbie decide not to pry. However, after a few moments, he elaborated.

'Working shifts in Careggi Hospital doesn't do a lot for your social life.' He gave her a little smile. 'On those nights when I am free, I'm normally too tired to want to go out. But, what about you? You said you'd broken up with your boyfriend some time ago. Surely a beautiful girl like you has got a queue of men at the door.'

Maybe it was because she knew he would be gone in a matter of days, maybe it was because she felt he was something a bit special, but unusually for her, she decided to go for full disclosure. Even so, she didn't have the strength to look him in the face. Instead, she stared across at the intricate towers of the cathedral as she told him all about it. Her eyes followed the vertical lines upwards as she explained what had happened.

'I was engaged to be married. His name was – is – Paul. We'd been living together for four years and we were planning to get married next summer. Originally it was going to be this summer – this month in fact.' She stopped for a moment, composing herself. 'But Paul insisted on putting it off, and I suppose I should have realised then that something was wrong. Anyway, to cut a long, sad story short, this winter wasn't much fun and finally, at the end of March, we broke up and he moved out.' She was relieved to have been able to deliver her speech without her voice betraying her. 'And since then, I haven't really felt interested in getting involved with anybody else.'

'How awful for you. Why did you break up, if you don't mind me asking?'

Debbie sighed inwardly, loath to revisit old, unpleasant memories that she had been trying so hard to suppress for months now. Reluctantly, she decided that, having started to talk, she might as well go the whole hog.

'He worked for a company that owns English language schools, some of the biggest in the country, and even worldwide. They've got branches all over the place and he spent a lot of his time travelling, trying to promote the schools and get students. The trouble we had was that his busiest time was during the winter, while my busiest time in the classroom was the summer. As a result we really saw very little of each other and it was almost impossible even to arrange to go on holiday together. It was a mess.'

'So is that why you broke up? Just logistics?'

Debbie steeled herself and looked up, turning towards him.

'No, I could have lived with that. In fact, I did live with it. It wasn't ideal, but I thought we could make it work. That is until I heard a chance comment from the group leader of a big group of Brazilians over in Cambridge for a course this winter. It turns out he and the travel agent in São Paolo had been having an affair for two years, on and off.'

'And you tackled him about it?'

'Yes.'

'And he admitted it?'

'At first he tried to deny it, but then, finally, he admitted it. Not only that. It transpired that there was also a woman in Mexico, one in Paris, one in Spain... you get the picture.'

'Did you love him?'

'Yes... yes I did.'

'And when did you stop loving him?'

For a moment she hesitated, unsure of the true answer.

'I don't know really. I suppose I did sort of love him right up until I heard the whole story.'

'I'm so sorry for you.' He reached across and took her hands in his and squeezed. She looked up at him gratefully.

'Thanks, Pierluigi. I'm sorry to burden you with that.'

'Not at all. It's good to talk.'

That afternoon they visited Thetford and, finally, Bury St Edmunds, stopping to visit the stunning old abbey in the middle of the historic town. The weather remained fine and it was a lovely drive. They spent their time chatting, getting to know each other better and, although she knew it was crazy, seeing as he would be out of her life in a week or so, she felt closer to him than ever. When he delivered her back to her home at half past five, she had no hesitation in inviting him in.

This time, he accepted the invitation.

He finally left her house, and her bed, just before midnight, telling her he had to be up early to concentrate on the paper he had to write before the end of his course. As she closed the door after him and returned to the still warm sheets, she had no regrets. He was a lovely man and, although she knew it couldn't and wouldn't last, she told herself she didn't mind. She lay there, staring up at the ceiling, smiling at her memories.

'Carpe diem,' she murmured to herself as she fell asleep. That night she dreamt about Florence once again, but the figure on the bench beside her now had a form, a face and a name.

Chapter 4

When she woke up next morning, it was to the sound of rain dripping from the broken gutter above the front door. She peered out of the curtains and saw that it was raining hard and, seeing as it was a Sunday morning, she had no hesitation in climbing back into bed again. She could still smell Pierluigi's scent on the pillow and she deliberately rolled her face into it, snuffling happily.

As she lay there, she thought a lot about him. He had told her that he would be leaving the following Friday, so that gave them barely five more days, and nights, together. Last night had been fun, but she was honest enough to admit to herself, if not to him, that it had meant more to her than that. If only things had been different, she felt sure she could see a relationship developing with him that could become every bit as deep as the one she had shared with Paul. Or at least until it had fallen apart.

That Sunday morning she also found herself reflecting on something Pierluigi had said. When she had told him of her hesitation about going to visit the site of her most personal of dreams, his advice had been to take a chance and go. Now, the more she thought about it, the more she found herself coming round to thinking he was right. After all, she now had three good reasons to go over there: to see him, to check out teaching opportunities in

English language schools and, of course, to look for her secret magical spot. Maybe the time had come to take her courage in both hands and head to Florence.

She knew she had to be realistic. It wouldn't always be warm and sunny in Florence. There would be grey, wet days like this over there as well. Cambridge got pretty full of visitors in the summer, and she felt sure Florence would be even busier. But, nevertheless, it would be gorgeous – of that she had no doubt. It was Florence, after all. The more she thought about it, the more the idea grew.

Over the following days, she spent as much time as she could with Pierluigi, and her feelings towards him didn't change. In fact, they deepened. As the days leading up to his departure counted down, she struggled hard to control her feelings, but it wasn't easy. Scared of making a scene, she told him she wouldn't come to the station with him on Friday morning, so the last time she saw him was at midnight on Thursday.

It had been an idyllic evening and she had managed to keep a tight rein on her emotions right to the end. She even contrived to produce a smile as she kissed him goodbye, but as she closed the door behind him, the dam finally burst and she cried her eyes out. "Tis better to have loved and lost, than never to have loved at all," might sound all right in a poem, but she seriously questioned whether Alfred Lord Tennyson had felt the pain she was feeling. She made herself a mug of camomile tea and reached for the tissues.

As the next hours and days dragged by and, the more she thought about it, the determination to go to Florence to check out the city for herself developed in her head. This would also give her the chance to see him again and she knew that was something she dearly desired. Of course, he lived with his parents, so she would need a hotel. She knew it was likely to be very expensive, so she did her sums and worked out that with a cheap flight and a cheap hotel, she might just about be able to stay there for three nights or so. Her twenty-ninth birthday was coming up at the end of August and, because of the bank holiday in England on the Monday, this would give her a three-day weekend, so she started seriously looking into just how much it would cost to make a flying visit to the city of her dreams.

She sent Pierluigi a text message, telling him of her plans, but they were immediately shot down in flames. His reply came as a serious disappointment, and she gritted her teeth as she read it. *So sorry. Have got an interview in Boston that Monday and ticket booked to fly to the States the Friday before. X. Pierluigi.*

She tried to make up her mind whether to delay her visit until she knew he would be there, or to go anyway. From what Simon at work had told her of student numbers here in Cambridge, the idea of looking for teaching opportunities elsewhere appeared to be ever more urgent. Maybe she shouldn't delay. In the end, what swung it was Alice. When Debbie told her she was thinking of going over to Florence for a quick visit at the end of the month, Alice immediately agreed and announced her intention of coming along. Apart from halving the costs of a hotel room, Debbie knew she would be really pleased to have the company of her best friend, so, together, they decided to go for it. The fact that Pierluigi wouldn't be there was a blow, but at least she would be able to look into employment opportunities, as well as searching out and tracking down the mysterious spot that had inhabited her dreams for so long.

They booked cheap flights from Stansted to Bologna and a room in the cheapest pensione they could find, not far from Florence main station. From there, Debbie knew from all the hours she had spent poring over Google Earth, they would find most of the main sights, including her happy place, within walking distance.

As the day of their departure approached, Debbie found herself more and more apprehensive. Would the city of her dreams match up to her expectations? Would she find the place she had dreamt of for so long? Alice did her best to convince her she was doing the right thing, but by the time they got to the airport, Debbie was having serious second thoughts. By now it was too late.

The flight was on time, but the aircraft was predictably packed and their hand luggage had to go in the hold. As a result, they were delayed at Bologna airport, waiting for the bags to arrive on the carousel, and had to take a taxi into the city centre station, rather than the bus as planned, for their train to Florence. She gave the taxi driver a tip and he seemed surprised, thanking her profusely. They got there with ten minutes to spare, but almost missed the train as they got lost in the maze of escalators as they plunged deep underground into the hi-tech new station. They finally arrived on the platform just in time to see the swish orange nose of the high-speed train come purring towards them.

The train ride took little more than half an hour and almost all of that was inside tunnels carved through the chain of the Apennines. When they finally emerged into the daylight again, just before half past five, they found themselves already entering the outskirts of Florence, and Debbie's first impression of this magical city wasn't very encouraging. There was no sign of anything historic – just apartment blocks lining the streets, and graffiti all over the walls alongside the railway tracks. She glanced across at Alice and wrinkled up her nose.

'Not quite what I was expecting, Al.'

'Don't worry, Debs. The historic bit's bound to be in the centre. Here, we're just in the suburbs. Everywhere looks grotty from a train.'

Debbie could hear that she was trying to sound reassuring, but her anxiety that her special place might turn out to be not so special didn't go away.

Things didn't really improve as they left the crowded station in search of their pensione. As they came out into the full heat of the late afternoon, it was like being flung into a sauna. Even the air Debbie breathed into her lungs felt hot. She and Alice exchanged glances and hugged the shady side of the road as a steady stream of traffic roared by. After a hundred yards and a perilous crossing, they turned off into a side street that was, thankfully, completely in the shade, although the heat still radiating from the walls as they passed was testament to the power of the sun earlier on.

It was a very narrow street and a constant stream of cars, bikes and scooters ensured that they had to be wary as they picked their way along the busy pavement. The buildings here were noticeably older than those out on the main square, with shops and cafés punctuating the ground floor of most of the houses. However, in spite of it all looking older than the station, Debbie still couldn't really see any signs of the wealth of medieval or Renaissance history she had been expecting. She did her best to keep her spirits up, but she was struggling to stay positive. Had she made a serious mistake?

The pensione was situated in a nondescript building and didn't immediately look too promising. They pressed one of a battery of polished brass buttons set into the wall and immediately heard a buzzing sound as the heavy wooden door opened. Inside, things began to improve. The entrance hall was pleasantly cool and, at the far end, it opened out into a courtyard with colourful flowers and plants on display. To one side of the hall, they found a modern-looking lift that took them up to the third floor. When they got there, they received a warm welcome and Debbie started to relax a bit more.

'*Signorine, buona sera.* Good evening.'

The receptionist was a man around their age with a meticulously trimmed black beard and a d'Artagnan-style moustache with waxed ends pointing skywards. He was smiling broadly and Debbie found herself smiling back.

In spite of having rehearsed what she was going to say in Italian over and over again, she took advantage of the fact that he had said 'good evening' to speak English with him. It was immediately clear that he both under- stood and spoke it without difficulty and she felt relieved. Although she had studied his language for a good few years now, she was suddenly overcome with an uncharacteristic attack of shyness at the prospect of finally using it for real.

She was surprised when the receptionist took and copied their passports, but he returned them immediately with a map of the city and their key.

'Room seven is at the end of the corridor. If there's anything you need, please don't hesitate. My name is Ronaldo, like the footballer.'

Debbie wasn't too sure who Ronaldo the footballer was, but Alice more than compensated by giving him a broad smile. She admitted later to having "a thing for moustaches".

Their room was a lovely large space with high ceilings and a private bathroom. Everything, while not in the first flush of youth, was spotlessly clean and it was blissfully cool in there. It was interesting to see that there was a big radiator on one wall. It was hard to believe on a day like this that it could ever be cold enough in Florence to warrant extra heating.

'Take a look at this, Debs.' Alice had managed to pull the blind up and light flooded into the room. Debbie went across to join her and followed Alice's eyes across the rooftops in front of them. Before them, rising up in all its majesty, was the unmistakable cupola of the Duomo, its red terracotta roof divided by white stone ribbing into segments like an orange. At the very top, tiny figures could be seen moving about the viewing platform that dominated the city. Debbie's anxiety levels began to drop. She was here. This was really Florence.

'So, what's the plan, Debs? Start hunting round for schools of English, or head straight across the river to look for that place you've been telling me about?'

Debbie hesitated, but only for a moment. Today was Saturday and they only had this evening and all of Sunday. Their flight home was on Monday morning and would mean leaving on an early train for Bologna, so time was of the essence. She nodded decisively.

'As far as schools are concerned, I've got a list I found on the internet. Although I imagine they'll be closed at the weekend, I'd quite like to take a look at some of them from the outside, but that's not so urgent. Yes, definitely, if you're up for it, let's start with trying to locate my spot. It looks like quite a climb up to Piazzale Michelangelo – that's the viewing point with a stunning panorama over the city – but I was reading that we can take the number 12 bus from the station to get up there. In this heat, it could be a bit uncomfortable climbing a socking great hill on foot. How about we take the bus and then, if we feel like it, we can walk back downhill from there into the centre afterwards. OK with you?'

'Fine by me. You're the boss. I'm only here for the sights, the food and drink – and maybe a taste of our friend Ronaldo out there.'

'Alice, really...'

Ronaldo turned out to be very helpful, explaining that they could buy bus tickets from the local tobacconist and showing them on the map where the number 12 bus stop was. Alice rewarded him with a blistering smile and Debbie thought she saw the pointed tips of his moustache twirl.

It took less than ten minutes to get to the bus stop via the tobacconist on the corner, where Debbie successfully used her Italian to buy them a couple of bus tickets. They then had to wait another ten minutes in the burning sun – still hot even though it was now six o'clock – until their bus arrived. As they were waiting, Debbie spotted a bus with *Careggi* on the front. She remembered that this was the hospital where Pierluigi worked and she felt another stab of regret that she had chosen to come here the very weekend he was thousands of miles away.

When their bus arrived, it took them along a circuitous route, crossing the river and then winding up the tree-lined road that led to Piazzale Michelangelo above them on the hillside. Either the driver had obviously been watching a few too many Grand Prix, or he was just very eager to reach his destination and he raced up the hill. He threw the heavy vehicle round the succession of sharp corners with obvious enthusiasm and skill while Debbie and Alice, along with the other passengers, had to hang on for dear life. They were relieved when the bus finally drew up with a jolt and the doors hissed open.

They crossed the road towards the wide-open space of Piazzale Michelangelo. This flat area dominated the city and provided a natural viewing point from which to admire the full magnificent beauty of Florence. Threading their way through a crowd of people and stalls selling souvenirs, postcards and T-shirts, they reached the edge of the piazza and stopped.

The view was indeed spectacular.

The ground sloped steeply from where they were standing, right down to the river Arno below. All along the far bank of the river, four- or five-storey ochre-coloured buildings marked the edge of the old town, and a jumble of red-tiled roofs extended back beyond these. In the middle, the Duomo and its famous bell tower were unmistakable. A bit further over was the elegant fortified tower that Debbie recognized as belonging to the Palazzo Vecchio, with the imposing bulk of the Uffizi Gallery beside it. All around, spires of other churches pushed up among the red roofs, creating a totally unique and unmistakable skyline. On the far side of the city, across the valley, the hills rose steeply to Fiesole and beyond. They both stood and breathed it in. It was magnificent.

After a while, Alice popped the question. 'So, is this it? Is this the place you've been dreaming about? What kind of vibe is it giving you?'

Debbie had been asking herself the same thing. The view was almost identical to her old postcard, apart from a couple of massive cranes doing some sort of building work, but something just wasn't quite right.

'We're too high up, Al. The roofs are at the wrong angle. Somehow, we need to be lower down.'

Although the photo had definitely been taken from here or somewhere around here, she felt sure it had to be further down the hillside. The other thing was that although her dreams definitely involved this view, they also included a rose garden and a wooden bench. Although neither of these things were shown on the post-card, over the years, her mental image of her special place had evolved to include them.

However hard she told herself that this was probably just the product of her imagination and there was no reason to believe such a place existed in reality, part of her still felt convinced it did. Up here, looking round over the broad expanse of Piazzale Michelangelo, with its stone slabs, hordes of tourists and street traders, there wasn't anything remotely resembling a rose garden.

Her musings were interrupted by Alice tugging urgently at her arm. 'Look, Debs, over there to the left. Down below, can you see? There's another terrace with what look like rose bushes. Could that be it?'

Debbie followed Alice's pointing finger and felt fresh hope spring up inside her. Yes, down below the piazza, reached by a wide stone stairway, was what looked like a garden. She couldn't see a wooden bench, but she felt sure this had to be the place. She paused long enough to take a number of photographs and then almost ran across to the steps and down to the lower level, followed by Alice. As they descended the steep flight of steps – now more slowly and carefully – they both began to get a fuller view of this lower terrace.

'They're definitely roses, Debs, along with all sorts of other flowers. Do you think this is it?'

Debbie stopped as they reached the foot of the steps and took a good look round. This terrace was a lot smaller than the piazza above and a well-trimmed hedge bordered the left side of it. She immediately saw that this area also contained a bar, built into the hillside. Tables with smart red and white tablecloths ran down the right-hand side, most of them taken by tourists relaxing as the sun began to set. The umbrellas provided shade that was very welcome, even though the shadows were lengthening. In the middle was a raised garden with a patch of neatly mown lawn and a variety of plants and bushes, among them white and pink roses. Ahead of them was the viewing area and Debbie hurried across to the edge.

She leant on the railings and looked down, reaching for her phone to take some photos. The view was almost identical to the panorama from above but, gradually, as she stared and stared, she began to realise that this still didn't feel right. The view was just like the postcard, but the feeling she got – what Alice had called the "vibe" – wasn't right. Her special place was smaller, more private and more personal, and she felt sure it didn't contain a bar or tables. Somehow she just knew this wasn't it. She gave a little snort of frustration.

'This isn't it, Al. It just isn't.' Her voice echoed her frustration and Alice was quick to come up with a solution – at least a temporary one.

'There's an empty table over there. Come on. I'll buy you a drink.'

'It'll cost a fortune up here.'

'We're on holiday, Debs. Come on. My treat.'

'Do we buy drinks at the bar or do we sit down?'

'I can't see a bar, so let's sit down and see.'

Debbie let herself be led across to a table, slid the surprisingly heavy iron chair back and slumped down in the shade of the umbrella alongside Alice.

'Bugger!'

'You sure this isn't your place?'

Debbie nodded wearily. 'Afraid not. It's just too big, too different.'

At that moment a waiter appeared. Without consulting Debbie, Alice raised two fingers. 'Could we have two glasses of Prosecco please?'

Debbie was about to translate when she saw him nod and heard him reply in pretty good English. 'Two glasses of Prosecco. Of course.' He gave them both a smile and turned away. The penny was beginning to drop in Debbie's head that Pierluigi had been right when he had said that knowledge of English was essential to almost anybody working here in Florence, seeing as it was full of visitors from all over the globe.

'Debs…' Alice sounded a bit hesitant. 'It *is* only a dream, after all, isn't it? You've probably just imagined it, sort of built up an image in your head that isn't reflected on the ground. Besides, things change over the years, after all.'

Debbie nodded. 'I suppose I'm coming round to thinking you're right, Al.' She did her best to sound positive. 'Ah, well, at least we're here and we've found where the photo was taken from. Maybe this spot'll grow on me.'

The wine arrived with a little ticket, indicating that these two small glasses came to a total of fourteen euros. Alice reached for her purse, but the smiling waiter waved it away 'Later, later.'

Debbie looked across at her. 'Getting drunk here could be an expensive business.'

'We're on holiday. Relax.'

They took their time over their wine, feeding pieces of the accompanying crisps to a fearless little sparrow who returned time and time again to their table and departed with morsels in her beak, no doubt to feed her family. It was past seven o'clock and the sun approaching the horizon when they decided to head off again. Debbie called the waiter and Alice paid. As they were about to leave, the waiter indicated that they should take their receipt with them. Debbie had been reading about this before coming away. Anti-tax-fraud laws introduced a few years previously demanded that every transaction be accompanied by a receipt. She wondered how effective this was proving.

As their bus tickets were valid for an hour and a half from first use, they decided to take the bus back down into the town again rather than walk. It was almost dark by now and by the time the bus deposited them back at the station, all the street lights were on, even though the sky was still a royal blue colour and birds were still wheeling about in the clear evening air.

'What about something to eat, Debs? I'm starving.'

For the first time Debbie realised she was really rather hungry. Lunch had been a bag of crisps on the plane, so something more substantial seemed like a good idea. Food would also cheer her up. The disappointment of not seeing Pierluigi and now not finding her special spot had been weighing heavily on her, in spite of the indisputable pleasure of finally visiting the city of her dreams.

'Definitely. What do you fancy?'

'Seeing as we're in Italy, shouldn't we have pasta, or a pizza?'

'Sounds good to me. I tell you what, let's head away from the old centre of town where all the tourists are, and see if we can find somewhere *genuino*. My teacher said that's what the Italians call The Real McCoy, whether it's food or drink or whatever.'

They walked for about fifteen minutes until they found themselves at Porta al Prato. Almost on the corner, they spotted a trattoria that looked as if it might fit the bill. There was no sign of pizza on the menu outside, but the prices were a bit lower than those down by the station, so they decided to try it.

It turned out to be an excellent choice. The restaurant wasn't big, made up as it was of a series of smallish rooms, with just three or four tables in each, but it had high ceilings and it was cool in there. As they walked in, they passed a glass cabinet full of dishes containing the night's specialities, from stuffed tomatoes to octopus salad, along with a number of plates the contents of which Debbie just couldn't identify. It all definitely looked distinctly *genuino*.

The local speciality here in Florence appeared to be massive steaks, some almost the size of a dustbin lid, with eye-watering prices. Instead, they opted for a plate of mixed ham and salami to share as a starter, followed by spaghetti for Alice, who stuck to her original decision to have pasta. Debbie fancied some fish and, on the waiter's advice, opted for a plate of fried prawns and squid in a very light batter, accompanied by a green salad.

The antipasti platter arrived without delay and they were both very pleased they had opted to share a single portion between the two of them. It was absolutely huge. There was freshly sliced ham – both cooked and raw, salami-flavoured with fennel, smaller *salamini* that the waiter revealed as wild boar, and *crostini* – slices of toasted bread rubbed with garlic and sprinkled with wonderful green olive oil. It was delicious, as was their main course. They drank mineral water and a carafe of good local red wine with it. For dessert, they shared a bowl of lovely big red grapes, split the bill and remembered to take the receipt, and walked back home feeling pleasantly full.

When they reached the door of the pensione, Debbie checked her watch. It was only ten o'clock and, in English time, that was merely nine o'clock. She glanced at Alice. 'Shall we head for the centre of town and have a drink before bed? This time, I'm paying.'

'That's the best idea you've had all day, Debs. Definitely.'

With the aid of the map Ronaldo had given them, they made their way through the increasingly narrow streets, having to squeeze out of the way of cars and scooters as they did so. Most of the taxis appeared to be virtually silent electrical cars and they weren't surprised to find that a lot of them had fitted bleepers to warn pedestrians of their arrival. Even so, they had to stay alert and it was a relief to reach the pedestrian zone around the Duomo, although the armed soldiers and police posted in the square were a sad sign of the times.

They mingled with the crowds, keeping a wary hand on their bags, listening to the countless different languages being spoken around them, and looking up in wonder at the magnificent façade of the Duomo on one side and the Baptistery's golden doors on the other. To Debbie, it was like seeing the pages of a guidebook laid out before her and she was greatly impressed.

They gradually worked their way around the cathedral until they were right at the rear of it. Here they found a table in a pavement café and she ordered two glasses of Prosecco. One thing led to another and they ended up ordering two wonderful ice cream sundaes as well, although the prices indicated on the menus were not for the faint-hearted.

Alice did her best to calm Debbie's scruples. 'We may never come back again, Debs. We owe it to ourselves to make sure we make this visit memorable.' She was checking out the nearby tables and her eyes had alighted on three tall, suntanned and muscular men drinking beer.

'Now I know what could make this night even more memorable...' She glanced at Debbie and giggled at the look of disapproval on her face. 'It's all right, Debs, I'm just joking. I don't think I could handle even just one of them after that meal and all this ice cream.'

Debbie grinned back at her. The temperature, even at this time of night, was still high, but the stifling heat they had experienced upon their arrival in Florence that afternoon had moderated Both of them were just wearing thin tops and shorts and they now felt more comfortable. She sat back and watched the never-ending stream of humanity walk by, trying to guess the nationalities of the people before they came close enough for her to hear what language they were speaking. She had reached seventeen different languages when a tall, Italian-looking man walked past, and she sat bolt upright. For a moment, she really thought it might be him. Could it be Pierluigi? But he was supposed to be in Boston.

Her thoughts were interrupted by Alice.

'You know who that guy reminds me of?'

'Yes, I know. I was just thinking the same thing.'

'Mind you, if it is him, he's grown that moustache pretty quickly.' As Alice was speaking, the man glanced sideways for a second and Debbie immediately realised that this was a completely different person. Her pulse began to slow and she turned towards her friend with a smile.

'Well, at least I wasn't the only one to be seeing things.'

'I wonder how his interview on Monday's going to go.' She glanced at Debbie. 'Do you hope he gets it?'

Debbie nodded. 'Of course I do – for his sake at least. I suppose if I'm in Cambridge, it doesn't make a lot of difference whether he's in Italy or the States.'

'Give or take a few hundred pounds extra on the air fare.'

'I know.' She turned to Alice. 'It was always destined for disaster, Al. We both knew that when we started it.

'Like I say, we're worlds apart, even without him going off to the States. It was an amazing week, but, in all probability, there's not really any future in it.'

'Who knows? Maybe he'll stay in Florence and you really can get a teaching job here, so as to be with him.' She caught Debbie's eye. 'I wouldn't want to lose you, but from what you've been saying about student numbers back home...'

'I'm not sure that's going to be so easy. I found a good number of schools listed here, but nothing much in the way of situations vacant.'

'It's still August, Debs. Didn't your Italian teacher say everywhere closes down in Italy in August? You wait. There'll probably be loads of jobs appearing over the next few weeks when it all starts up again after the holidays. So what's the plan for tomorrow? Checking out schools or are you still thinking about your spot?'

'Schools, definitely, but first, I think I'm going to give it one more go. It should be cool enough early on for me to walk up to Piazzale Michelangelo, rather than taking the bus. You never know, I may still happen upon the place from my dreams.' Deep down, she felt pretty sure she was only kidding herself, but she felt she had to give it one last try. 'But you don't need to come unless you feel like it. Besides,' she grinned at Alice, 'if Ronaldo's on the morning shift, you might be otherwise engaged.'

Alice shook her head. 'Too hot, too much food, too tired. No, a man-free weekend is probably a good idea. I'll let you know in the morning whether I feel like climbing the hill with you.' She finished her drink. 'You know what? I feel quite tired.'

'We both need a good night's sleep. And tomorrow evening, by the way, I'm taking you out for dinner, seeing as it's my birthday. My treat.'

'That sounds brilliant. Any ideas about a restaurant?'

'Yes, I have, actually, but I won't tell you. It can be a surprise.'

Chapter 5

Next morning, Debbie woke up early, feeling rested and refreshed after sleeping remarkably soundly. Alice was still fast asleep in the other bed so she crept quietly into the bathroom, showered, and changed without waking her. She had an initial moment of confusion when hot water started coming out of the tap marked with a C. Only then did she remember that C stood for *caldo*, hot and F for *freddo*, cold. When she was ready, she let herself out silently so as not to disturb Alice, and went through to the breakfast room. Two cups of coffee, two glasses of orange juice and two croissants filled with apricot jam, and she was ready for the day.

She went out past the reception desk that was now staffed by a matronly lady, reflecting that this boded well for Alice's self-imposed temporary vow of abstinence. Outside, she checked her watch and saw that it was still only a quarter past seven. She really had got up early. It wasn't cold, but it was certainly much cooler than the previous afternoon and evening. The sky was a clear, cloudless blue so doubtless the temperature would soon rise again in the course of the morning. But at least for now, she was reassured that she should be able to climb the hill on the other side of the river without too much discomfort.

Apart from teams of street sweepers and noisy little trucks going round washing the streets with whirring brushes, there weren't many other people about this early on a Sunday morning. Debbie was able to make her way with ease up to the cathedral, finding that it looked even more impressive in the daylight – the early morning sun reflecting off the shiny white marble, highlighting the exquisite sculptures set into the façade and the bands of green and red stone cutting across it at regular intervals. She remembered Pierluigi's description of it and had to agree with him. It really was amazing. After standing in silent appreciation for several minutes, she crossed the piazza and followed the little arrows along the main shopping streets until she came to the Ponte Vecchio.

Debbie had often seen photos of the Ponte Vecchio – probably one of the most photographed bridges in the world – leading over the river Arno. She could see that, as well as serving as a means of getting across the river, the bridge was also a shopping mall in miniature, with tiny shops lining both sides of it. At this time of the morning these shops, mostly selling jewellery, were all still boarded up, but she could imagine how busy this thoroughfare would become later in the day. Above the shops to the left of her was a long line of windows at first-floor level, protected by hefty iron gratings. This, she knew, was the fortified passage that had been built to serve as a private walkway for the dukes of Florence from the Palazzo Vecchio across to the Pitti Palace on the other side of the river.

But she didn't stop to consider the history of the bridge or to admire the view up and down the Arno from there. She had other things on her mind this morning. She turned left at the end of the bridge and walked parallel to the river until she saw a sign to the right pointing up the hill towards Piazzale Michelangelo. This started as a gently sloping road, leading to one of the old gates in the original walls of the town and, beyond that, it then became rapidly steeper until it turned into a wide flight of stone steps leading ever upwards.

Debbie climbed at a steady pace, trying to count the steps as she did so, but she lost count somewhere around a hundred. However, even with a pause for a breather halfway, she was delighted to find herself at the top much sooner than she had expected. She turned left and walked along the road as far as the terrace where she and Alice had fed the little sparrow the previous day. She went across to the railings, breathing hard, but not too badly out of breath. All the cycling she had been doing in Cambridge had obviously been to good effect.

At this time of the morning, she was the only person here and, for a few minutes, she found herself able to relax and survey the full beauty of Florence without an accompanying background hubbub of voices. It was a lovely, still morning and the heat haze hadn't yet built up. Opposite her, in the far distance, the outline of the tree-clad hills and the mountains beyond was crystal clear. She stood there for a few minutes, breathing in the view and the atmosphere until she was disturbed by the grating noise of metal chairs being pulled across the paving slabs behind her. She turned to see the staff of the café starting to get ready for the daily onslaught. Spotting the waiter who had served them the previous day, on impulse, she went over to him.

'*Buongiorno.*' She was determined to practice her Italian.

'*Buongiorno, signorina. Ben tornata.*'

'You remember me?' She was impressed. *Ben tornata* meant welcome back.

'A tall, beautiful English girl who speaks Italian – of course I remember you.' He gave her a cheeky grin and she smiled back, trying not to blush.

'This is probably going to sound like a silly question.' She was delighted to find the words coming out pretty easily in Italian and to see comprehension on his face. 'But do you know of another spot like this up here somewhere?'

He looked a bit puzzled. 'You mean another café?'

'No, a place like this with roses and benches, with a view over the city.' She decided to tell a little white lie. 'A friend of mine was telling me about it.'

He hesitated, resting on the back of the chair beside him. 'Roses, you say? What about the *Giardino delle Rose*? That's close by.'

A place called the Rose Garden? Debbie nodded eagerly. 'That sounds perfect. Where's that?'

'Have you just come up the steps on foot?'

She nodded again. 'Yes.'

'Well, you've walked right past it. It's just down the hill from us. Go back to the steps, start going down and you'll see it on the right. Big iron gates.' He hesitated. 'It might still be closed at this time of day, but you can try.'

'Thank you so much. That's wonderful.'

She hurried off back to the steps and started descending, delighted her Italian had been up to the task, and excited that the friendly waiter might have actually pointed her in the direction of her special place. Certainly, the name was auspicious.

Before long, she came to a pair of rusty iron gates on her right. Earlier, she had been concentrating so hard on climbing the never-ending steps on the way up that she must have trudged right past without noticing. Attached to the gates was a transparent plastic sign, clearly marked *Giardino delle Rose*. The bad news was that the gates were secured with a chain and a padlock and the sign indicated that the garden would only be open to the public from 10 a.m. on Sundays. Debbie glanced at her watch. It was still only just after eight o'clock.

She peered through the bars of the gate and immediately noticed two things. First were the numerous plants, among them rose bushes, and second, two solid wooden benches. The closer of the two, set in the shade of a clump of trees, was empty, but the other looked as though it had somebody sitting on it. From behind, it looked like a man wearing a funny, flat-topped hat. After a moment's hesitation, Debbie called out to him.

'*Buongiorno. Posso entrare?* Can I come in?' It was a long shot, but he might just be able to open the gate. There was no response from him, so she tried again, a bit louder, still without any result. Then, to her surprise, there was the sound of footsteps and a woman appeared from the right, holding the end of a hosepipe.

'Can I help you?' She looked friendly enough. By her accent, Debbie reckoned she was local to these parts.

'Yes, I'm very sorry, but I've come all the way from England to see this garden and I'm only here today. I don't suppose you could let me in, could you?'

The gardener dropped the hose and walked across to the locked gate, glanced around, then shook her head. 'We're closed until ten, and I'm afraid I don't have the key to this padlock.' She hesitated, checking once more that Debbie was on her own. 'Listen, if you go on down the steps, you'll come to a door set in the wall, right at the corner. That's the way I came in and I've a feeling I may have forgotten to lock it behind me.' She gave Debbie a wink. 'I suppose if you were to find it open and wander in, nobody would blame you. Just don't tell my boss I let you in.'

'That's terrific. Thank you so much. I promise I'll be very quiet and I won't say a word. After all, I'm foreign and I don't speak Italian, do I?'

'Of course you don't.' The lady smiled and then lowered her voice. 'Actually, you speak very good Italian. My compliments. Now don't hurry. I'll need a couple of minutes to go down and check that I did forget to lock it.' She grinned at Debbie. 'And, by the way, when you come in, close it behind you, would you?'

'You're really, really kind. Thank you so much.'

Debbie watched the gardener turn and set off across the cobbles and on down a narrow path until she disappeared from sight. She waited by the gate for a minute or so, breathing in the atmosphere, increasingly convinced that this might finally be the place of her dreams. Then, after a bit of time had passed, she set off down the steps and easily found the sturdy wooden door set in the stone wall. She pushed it with the palm of her hand and it opened. After going in, she pressed it closed behind her until she heard it click, and then climbed up half a dozen steep steps into the garden.

She walked slowly up the path towards the benches she had seen. The path led her through the rose garden and along the side of a lawned area, surrounded by trees, shrubs and flowers. The scent of roses filled the air and she could hear the twittering of birds in the branches. It felt peaceful, relaxing and somehow very, very familiar. As the path levelled out onto the cobbled area, she found herself confronted by two statues. The first was a massive metal outline of a suitcase, complete with a handle that formed a frame through which to view the roofs of Florence below.

The second was more unsettling. There, right ahead of her, was the wooden bench she felt increasingly sure she had seen so often in her dreams. But sitting on it was the man in the funny hat she had viewed from the gate – only it wasn't a real man. In fact, it wasn't necessarily even a man. Like the suitcase, this was also a statue, this time of an androgynous being, made of what looked like bronze. The figure was sitting on the bench, with its left arm resting along the back of the bench, as if waiting for somebody to sit down alongside. She found herself gawping as she approached it.

She stood for a good few minutes, just staring down at the figure, before slowly, almost reluctantly, taking a seat on the bench. The feel of the sun-warmed wood beneath her was unmistakable, as was the scent of roses in the air. She raised her eyes and looked straight ahead, the panorama of the rooftops of Florence matching up exactly with her mental image formed over so many years. She relaxed against the statue's bronze arm running along the back of the bench, and her right hand quite naturally landed in the statue's other hand, resting on its bronze knees. As she took hold of the metal hand with her fingers, she distinctly felt the hairs on the back of her neck stand on end.

This was it. This was her spot, her special place.

She felt her eyes burn and first one, and then a flood of tears began to run freely down her cheeks. Years of pent-up emotions spilled over and she sobbed her heart out. The disappointment she had felt as a teenager, when her mum and dad hadn't been able to scrape up the money to send her on the school trip, rose up and was washed away. Even as she wept, she knew that she wasn't weeping out of sadness. Instead, she was crying with relief, with joy, with a sense of belonging she hadn't felt before.

'Are you all right, *signorina*? I couldn't help noticing that you were crying.'

Debbie looked up, reaching into her pocket for a tissue with her free hand. It was the gardener from before, standing in front of the bench, looking concerned. After blowing her nose and wiping her eyes, Debbie took a big breath before replying.

'Thank you, but I'm fine.' She took another deep breath. 'I'm sorry about this. It's hard to explain. I've been dreaming of this place ever since I was a little girl and now I've finally found it, it's had more of an influence upon me than I expected.'

She glanced sideways at the bronze figure. She was still gripping the hand tightly and it felt comforting. So comforting, in fact, that she felt the beginnings of a smile forming on her face.

'I'm fine, honestly. Thank you so much for your concern.'

The gardener didn't look convinced.

'You're not the first person to have a funny turn with this statue, you know. We had a lady here a month or two ago who grabbed hold and wouldn't let go. We almost had to prise her away.'

The image made the smile on Debbie's face broaden. With sudden decision, she released the hand and stood up. To her relief, there was no sense of loss and the feel of the warm metal against her palm stayed with her even after she had thanked the kind gardener and made her way back down through the garden and out onto the steps once more, remembering to pull the door closed behind her.

She walked slowly back across the Ponte Vecchio, which was already filling up with people, and through the backstreets to the pensione. All the way home, she could feel the smile still on her face.

–

After an exhausting walking tour of the sights that day, and a whistle-stop tour of half a dozen English language schools that didn't really produce much more than the recognition that they existed and that they boasted signs screwed to the walls of buildings advertising their presence, Debbie and Alice took the number 7 bus to Fiesole. This was on the hill, the other side of town from Piazzale Michelangelo, but the bus driver, a woman this time, demonstrated the same racing and rallying skills as her colleague the previous evening.

As the bus climbed the hill out of Florence and they were thrown from side to side round the corners, the views got better and better. Debbie saw that the hillside was peppered with magnificent villas, most surrounded by imposing cypress trees, presumably planted centuries ago to provide some shade against the heat of the sun. Some of the villas were the size of small castles and no doubt cost as much. For a moment she found herself wondering if Pierluigi came from somewhere as opulent as this. The realisation that he and she were from very different worlds struck her yet again.

The bus came to a halt in the main square of Fiesole and the doors hissed open. This paved area was just about the only relatively flat space they had seen since beginning the climb up from the outskirts of Florence. Over to the left was an imposing church, and the square was ringed by what they now recognized as typical Florentine buildings – sturdy façades, the plaster a creamy, light ochre colour, with green shutters and pink terracotta roofs. There was what looked like a craft fair going on and the centre of the square was full of stalls offering handmade objects for sale.

As they strolled through the crowd, admiring the paintings, pottery and woodcarvings, Alice returned to the subject that had occupied both of them on and off for most of the day.

'You say yourself that you've read lots of books about Florence and you've spent hours on the internet, researching the place. That postcard you've got only shows the view, not the place from where it was taken. That rose garden is something you've dreamed up – you most probably saw it in a book somewhere and, although you don't remember, the image must have lodged in your head.' Alice glanced across at her. 'Or are we talking something supernatural here? You don't really think you were there in a previous existence?' Debbie could hear from her tone what she thought of that idea and she agreed with her.

'Nothing like that. I'm not totally bonkers, you know.' She remembered Pierluigi asking her if she had been a Medici princess in a previous life and discounted it now, as she had then. 'I'm sure you're right. I must have seen a photo or something and it affected me subliminally.'

'And your reaction to it, crying your eyes out?'

'I invented, or found, or remembered, this special place years ago when I was a girl at school. Sitting there today with that statue's arm round me brought back memories, that's all.'

Alice nodded approvingly. 'So it all goes back to when you were a teenager. It's probably all tied up with hormones and sex and stuff like that.' She grinned. 'So, talking of sex, did the hand you were holding remind you of anybody? Like a certain tall, handsome doctor, by any chance?"

'I don't know if it reminded me of him, but I certainly thought about him.' Debbie felt another little stab of regret that he wasn't here with her, but the joy of having found the solution to her longstanding mystery more than compensated for his absence. At least for now. 'Anyway, now's the time to reveal where we're eating tonight. It's a little restaurant that got great reviews on the internet and, unless I'm mistaken, that's it over there.'

They were shown to a table outside on a roof terrace, with a stunning view over Florence. From up here, the whole city was laid out before them and Debbie could easily make out Piazzale Michelangelo, with the hills towards Siena beyond. It was too far away for her to spot her rose garden, but she didn't mind. Now that she knew the place was real, she intended to return as often as she could.

Once Debbie had overcome her fear that this restaurant might turn out to be too pricey and pretentious, she began to enjoy herself. It certainly wasn't pretentious. Yes, most of the other diners most probably had more money than the two of them put together, but it didn't matter. They were all there for the view, and the food – and both were excellent. Quite a few of the tables contained children alongside the adults, and a number of the kids spent the evening running about and playing. The waiters and other diners didn't bat an eyelid and Debbie found herself comparing their reaction to similar places in the UK, where she felt sure a very dim view would have been taken.

They started with glasses of Prosecco to celebrate Debbie's birthday then moved on to Chianti Classico while they ate ham, fresh pasta, and then wonderful little lamb chops, cooked over a charcoal grill. At the end they were too full to manage dessert, but the waitress brought them some cantuccini – rock-hard almond biscuits that they dipped in their red wine to soften before nibbling them. It was a memorable meal.

By the time they finished, the sun had set and darkness had fallen. The lights of Florence twinkled down below them in the distance and a light breeze had brought the temperature down to a comfortable level. Debbie felt very full, very happy, and very pleased that she had accomplished what she had set out to do.

'So, how does this birthday match up to others you've had?' Alice sounded equally content.

'Brilliant. Yes, I know it's all been a bit of a mad rush, but I'm so very pleased I came. And I'm pleased you came with me, Al.'

'I've enjoyed it as well. I really have. So, can we say Florence has lived up to your expectations?'

Debbie nodded decisively. 'Very much so.'

'And when are you coming back again?'

'Just as soon as I can.'

Chapter 6

When Debbie went into work on Tuesday, she found that Simon had called a staff meeting for that afternoon. The announcement he made took a lot of people almost totally by surprise. Although Debbie had been half-expecting it, it still came as a shock to the system. After a brief preamble, he very rapidly came to the point. And it didn't make for pleasant listening.

'I'm very sorry to have to tell you that the school's in financial trouble. Although we've had a good number of students here this summer, enrolments for the autumn and winter terms are dire. The way things are looking, we could go under, unless we do something about it.'

The teachers and admin staff looked around nervously. Most of them had been aware that student numbers had been dropping over the past few years, but after a busy summer, they had been hoping things were improving. Clearly, however, this was not the case.

'Anyway, the situation dictates that we cut costs as soon as possible. I'm hoping we can do this without any of you having to lose your jobs, but if anybody feels like resigning, we've put together some pretty good redundancy packages, so do give it some thought, please. We'll be very sorry to lose you, but if you're interested, please come and speak to me.'

That evening Debbie called Alice, who came over for a council of war. Debbie had been at the school for most of her working life, she loved her job, and she was saddened at the thought of losing it. Alice, as always, was determined to look at things positively and reminded her of their recent discussions.

'This is the opportunity you've been waiting for, Debs. Surely this is the moment for you to make that change we were talking about. Like I told you, I wouldn't want to lose you, but the universe could hardly be making it any clearer. I reckon you need to think seriously about Florence.'

Debbie had been thinking the same thing, ever since returning home. 'I know. It's almost as if it's a sign.'

The previous night, when they got back from their trip, she hadn't slept particularly well, her mind still filled with images of her special spot and the wonderful city of Florence. She knew she wanted to go back and she had been feeling quite bereft at the thought that it would be months, or maybe even years, before she would be able to return. The three days in Italy had seriously depleted her savings, such as they were, and she knew it would take a good while to find enough to allow her to go back again. And from what Pierluigi had said, he might well be off to the States before long and it would have been so good to see him one more time first. If she could find a job there...

'So how do you go about getting a job, and what about the Brexit thing? Might they sling you out again in a year or two?'

Debbie shook her head. 'I doubt it. I imagine there'll always be a need for English speakers. As for finding a job, I've been looking on the internet and it's like I said – there aren't many jobs on offer. But I've just come across this. What do you think?'

She opened her laptop and handed it across. The advert, on a TEFL website, was short and to the point.

> Wanted, native speaker to teach English as a Foreign Language at reputable, long-established school in Florence, Italy. Must be well qualified and experienced. Flexible hours. Good salary. To start early October. Apply with full CV to Box 1472.

'Not a lot of detail, is there?' Alice sounded a bit doubtful. 'And they want somebody to start in only just over a month. Could you get out of your current job as soon as that?'

'I imagine, as far as the school here's concerned, the sooner they can stop paying me, the better.'

'Well, it does say *good salary* so why not give it a try? I'd hate to see you move away but, to make up for it, there's always the knowledge that I'd be able to come over for holidays in Italy.'

Together, they drafted a reply, asking for more details about the school and the position on offer. At Alice's suggestion, Debbie included a query about accommodation. Somehow, she got the feeling that could be very pricey in a place like Florence. She dug out her old CV, updated it and sent the whole thing off.

After Alice left, she sent a text message to Pierluigi, asking him how the interview had gone and telling him the latest developments, hoping he would be enthusiastic at the possibility of her coming to Florence. Maybe, she told herself, if this job materialised, she might see him again in less than a month.

That night, as she lay in bed, turning over in her head the developments of the past few days, she felt herself gently slipping into the warm embrace of her special place once more. As her eyes closed, she could hear the birds singing and smell the roses. As she drifted off to sleep, she could feel the touch of the bronze arm against her shoulder and the warm fingers clasping hers. It was relaxing and reassuring and very, very familiar.

–

It all happened very quickly after that. She got a reply to her application the very next day. This came from a man called Steven Burrage, who described himself as Principal and Director of Studies of the Florence Institute of English Studies, FIES for short. This school was situated right in the very centre of the city, only a matter of yards from where Debbie and Alice had sat drinking very expensive Prosecco and eating even more expensive ice cream at the rear of the Duomo. Debbie and Alice had walked past it on their quick tour of inspection, but she remembered little about it apart from its proximity to the cathedral. The email informed her that the school had a population of three hundred students and had been in operation for over thirty years. It all sounded very promising.

Steven Burrage informed her that he would be in London to interview potential candidates the following Friday and Saturday, and invited her to come and meet him. She replied immediately, asking if the interview could be on the Saturday as she was working on the

Friday, and the appointment was set for Saturday noon at an address in Soho that sounded like a travel agency. Presumably the agency had some arrangement with the school.

She spoke to Simon at work, who told her how sorry he would be to lose her and promising her a glowing reference if she did decide to move on. As she had expected, he saw no problem in her leaving at the end of September, even though this was now less than a month away.

There was no response to her text message to Pierluigi, but this was most probably because he was still in the USA. She decided to delay contacting him again until after her interview in London when she would hopefully have something more definite to tell him.

She travelled down to King's Cross by train on Saturday and made her way across to Soho. She arrived well in advance and found the travel agency without difficulty. She went in, introduced herself, and was ushered into a back office where she waited for Mr Burrage.

It was a long wait.

It was almost one o'clock before Mr Burrage put in an appearance. He arrived in a state of considerable agitation, apologising profusely for the delay, which had been due to a problem on the line that had held up his train in from the suburbs. He was a short, middle-aged man, with a scarily red complexion, wearing a heavy tweed jacket in spite of the warm early September weather. His accent was unfathomable, completely without any regional inflections, no doubt as a result of years spent abroad, teaching foreigners.

The interview took Debbie by surprise. It went like this:

'Your name's Deborah Waterson?'

'Yes.'

'And you've been working in one of the best schools in Cambridge for the past five years or so?'

'Yes.'

'Can you start on the fourth of October?'

'Yes.'

'Excellent. Have you had lunch?'

'No.'

'Let's go and have a curry.'

Slightly bemused, Debbie followed him out through the travel agency and into a narrow street directly opposite. Halfway down there they turned right, and then left again, or that may have been right. By this time Debbie was beginning to lose her bearings. Then, abruptly, he stopped and the unmistakable smell of Indian food filled their nostrils. She glanced at him. The expression on his face was not dissimilar to their old spaniel when he smelt his tin of food being opened.

'Excellent. I'll lead the way, shall I?' Without waiting for a reply, he pushed the door and led her up a flight of red-carpeted stairs to another door. Beyond this, Debbie found herself in a huge dining hall filled with tables and decorated in a dramatic combination of black, red and gold. A tall, bearded head waiter approached, bowed, and escorted them to a table in the far corner. He deposited two menus, the thickness of telephone directories, on the tabletop and hovered while they sat down.

'Can I get you anything to drink, sir, madam?'

The hungry dog expression on Mr Burrage's face broadened. 'A pint of lager, please. No, better make that two pints.' Remembering his manners, he glanced at Debbie. 'What would you like to drink, Deborah?'

'Just water, please.' Debbie had no intention of letting alcohol interfere with her better judgement in what was, after all, a job interview.

The waiter bowed once more and retired. By this time, Mr Burrage's head was buried in the menu. Debbie followed suit and soon realised she was out of her depth. Never a great curry eater, her field of expertise didn't really extend much beyond chicken tikka masala. She let her eyes run along the multitude of dishes that filled page after page until she felt them start to glaze over. She set it down and looked across the table, just as Mr Burrage looked up.

'Decided what you're having?'

Crossing her fingers, hoping she wouldn't regret it, she shook her head and told him, 'I'll have what you're having.'

'Excellent.'

A young waiter arrived at that moment with two pints of beer, a jug of water and two water glasses. From the speed with which Mr Burrage reached for his lager, Debbie got the impression he wouldn't be using his water glass any time soon.

'Cheers, and welcome aboard.'

As Debbie was still digesting whether this represented a job offer, Mr Burrage proceeded to empty two-thirds of his first pint down his throat. He replaced the glass, wiped his forehead with his napkin, and gave a sigh of satisfaction, before beaming across the table at her.

'So, anything you'd like to ask me, Deborah?'

She poured some water into her glass and tentatively enquired about what appeared to be her new job. 'Can you tell me who I'd be teaching? Adults, kids, whatever?'

'Adults, for the most part. We don't do a lot with kids these days. The Italian state school system's working pretty well for languages nowadays, more's the pity. Most of our clients are adults.'

'Working adults?'

He nodded. 'Indeed. That means most of the teaching takes place in the afternoons and evenings, after the students finish work.'

Just then the head waiter returned to take their order and Debbie sat in silent apprehension as she heard Mr Burrage order a frightening number of dishes, only one of which she recognized – naan. Well, she thought to herself, at least she could eat some bread if all else failed. As the waiter turned to leave, Mr Burrage drained the remains of his first beer and proffered the empty glass.

'And another one of these, if you would.'

The food arrived very swiftly and in such profusion that another small table had to be set alongside theirs to hold it all. Debbie took a tiny helping of each of the dishes, in the hope of finding something she liked. Opposite her, Mr Burrage worked his way assiduously through all of them, washed down with liberal quantities of beer.

The food proved to be excellent and Debbie found herself taking second helpings of almost everything. As they ate, she continued to ask questions about the job and received remarkably clear answers. In short, it looked as though her working week would mainly take place between the hours of five and ten o'clock on weekday evenings. Accommodation was apparently no problem. A room would be found for her "at an affordable rent" in a flat shared by other teachers.

Mr Burrage was on his fourth, or that might have been his fifth, pint of lager when he dropped an unexpected bombshell.

'You say in your CV that you speak Italian. How well do you speak it?' To Debbie's surprise, the question was directed at her in very fluent, unaccented Italian. She took a deep breath and tried her hardest to reply in her best Italian.

'I've studied it for almost ten years. Just evening classes recently. I think I'm reasonably fluent, but I badly need practice.'

To her surprise and relief, she heard him grunt approvingly. 'Excellent. That sounds great.' He carried on in Italian as if it was the most natural thing in the world. As she listened, she rather wished she had ordered a pint or two of lager herself. This was turning out to be quite nerve-wracking.

'What we really need, Deborah, is a Director of Studies. I've been doing it all for a good few months now, ever since Angela left, and I need somebody who can interview students and teachers, decide on syllabus, provide training for less experienced teachers. You know – all that sort of stuff. With your background, qualifications and experience, I think you're the right person for the job.'

'You want me to be Director of Studies?' Debbie was still trying to work out just what might constitute *tutta quella roba lì* – "all that sort of stuff".

'That's right. You'd still be doing some teaching, but a reduced timetable of course. The pay would be quite a bit better than a normal teacher's pay.' He produced a pen from his pocket, took the paper napkin from underneath the water jug, and scribbled the bare bones of the job offer for her. She squinted across the table, reading upside down. On the face of it, this would mean fewer contact hours in the classroom, a lot more responsibility and, after a brief calculation, a salary that would work out to quite a bit more than she was getting at present. She felt her spirits rise.

He finished scribbling and spun the napkin round so she could read it without craning her neck.

'So, what do you think?' She barely noticed that he had reverted to English.

'I'm very interested.' She gave it some thought. 'Yes, I really am *very* interested.'

'Excellent. Deborah, do you dislike alcohol? You're not teetotal or anything?'

Bemused at the change of direction to his questioning, she shook her head. 'No, I'm not teetotal. I just thought I'd better stay sober, seeing as this is a job interview.'

He beamed. 'Excellent. That's exactly what I need. I want somebody serious. Terrific attitude.' To reinforce his remark, he drained the last of the beer in his glass. 'Do you like Prosecco, by any chance?'

'Um, yes, yes I do.'

'Excellent.' He raised his arm and waved it in the air. The head waiter was at his shoulder within seconds. 'Could I see the wine list, please?'

Conversation lapsed as Mr Burrage studied a wine list that looked as comprehensive as the menu. While he did so, Debbie's mind was racing. Here she was, being offered what sounded like a challenging new job in the city of her dreams. Much as she enjoyed teaching, she had always hankered for a bit more responsibility, but she knew full well that in English language schools, you either taught in them or ran them. There was little in the way of a pyramidal career structure. It had famously been described as being like a plateau with a radio mast. Now she was being offered the chance to leapfrog up to the next level.

A bottle of Prosecco arrived and Mr Burrage subjected the label to close scrutiny, removing his glasses in order to read the small print. Finally satisfied, he handed it to the waiter to open while he replaced his glasses and explained to Debbie. 'Valdobbiadene.'

'Val… what?' This was a new word for her.

'The best Prosecco comes from Valdobbiadene, up to the north of Venice. I had to be sure.'

Debbie filed the information away, alongside the information that Mr Burrage knew his wines. And liked them.

The wine was poured and Mr Burrage looked across the table towards Debbie. 'Well, what do you say? Are you joining the good ship FIES? We'd love to have you.'

Debbie stared down into her wineglass for a few more seconds. It would mean a major upheaval in her life. It would take her further away from her parents and her friends, particularly Alice, and it would mean making a new start a thousand miles away from here. Was she really ready for this? Her eyes strayed to the top of the wine bottle, protruding from the ice bucket, a crisp white cloth folded across it. The Prosecco had come all the way from Italy to here, so why couldn't she do the same in reverse? Surely a new life in Florence was all she had ever dreamt of. Taking her courage in both hands, she made her decision, looked up, and smiled.

'Yes, please. Thank you so much. I'm delighted to accept the offer.'

She wondered if she should offer Mr Burrage a hand-shake, but he had other ideas. Unsurprisingly, his wine glass was already in his hand and he held it out towards her. Once she had raised hers, he reached across and banged the two glasses together sufficiently hard to attract the attention of nearby diners. Luckily, the glasses were strong enough to withstand the impact, although a trickle of Prosecco ended up on the back of her hand.

'Excellent, Deborah, excellent. Your very good health.' And he drained his glass in one.

He was already reaching for the bottle in the bucket as she was still licking the Prosecco off her hand, wondering just how much her life was going to change as a result of this decision.

Chapter 7

The very next day, Debbie was relieved, and slightly surprised, to receive a detailed and comprehensive email confirming the offer of the position of Director of Studies at the school in Florence, along with a contract to sign and return. Clearly, when he wasn't eating and drinking, Mr Burrage was very businesslike, and she took that as a very good sign. She replied formally, accepting the offer, and printed off the contract to return by post. She also received a reply to her text message to Pierluigi, telling him of her decision. It was encouraging and disappointing at the same time.

> Great news. Am going on holiday to Greece for a few weeks (no mobile signal) and will be in touch when I get back. No news about US job yet. X. Pierluigi.

Being selfish, the idea that he might not get the American job and so might be there with her in Florence was exciting. On the other, the fact that he was likely to be in Greece at least initially when she arrived in Florence was disappointing, but she felt sure she would see him before long.

She handed in her notice at work and, with the land-lord's blessing, managed to dispose of her flat very quickly to a friend. Alice volunteered to look after her excess belongings, including her brand new bike, for the time being.

The following weekend Debbie took the train to Bristol and broke the news to her parents.

Her father, not unexpectedly, was a bit suspicious. 'That all sounds fine, but just you make sure you get your social security and pension and all that kind of thing fully paid up.'

All his life, her father had been deeply suspicious of employers. He wasn't likely to change now, only a few years short of retirement. Debbie gave him a smile.

'I'm sure it's all above board, Dad. I've got a written contract and everything. It's all spelt out.'

He nodded. 'That's good, but you just keep an eye on them. Foreigners don't always have the same respect for the rule of law as we do.' Debbie was about to protest, but he changed the subject. 'Anyway, this way we'll be able to come and see Florence for ourselves when you're settled. There are flights from Bristol to all manner of places all over Europe. We'll probably be able to get over to see you just as quickly as trying to get from here to Cambridge.'

The previous year her mum and dad had got caught up in a massive traffic jam on the M25 on their way back from a weekend in Cambridge with Debbie, and had few illusions as to how long the journey could take.

Her mother was also concerned, not so much for her daughter's pay and conditions, but for her personal happiness. 'As long as it's what you want.' She caught Debbie's eye. 'But are you sure you feel like moving to another country?'

'I think I could do with a bit of a challenge, and the job sounds perfect for me. I'd get to practice my Italian, do a bit of teaching, and move on to something with a bit more responsibility at the same time.'

'And money-wise, will you be able to manage?' Money had always been tight in their household and it was inevitable her father should focus on that.

Debbie nodded. 'Yes, I think so. I'll get a few thousand from Cambridge when I leave, and with that I should have enough to buy my air ticket, pay a deposit for accommodation and so on. I should even have a bit left to pay off some more of my student loan.'

They went through the details of the job together until Debbie felt confident they were both reassured. She had gone through the same exercise with Alice a few nights earlier and the result had been the same. Given the uncertainty of her position in the school in Cambridge, the offer of a better-paid, more varied position in the city of her dreams was too good to miss. And, of course, with the man of her dreams waiting for her over there as well, the prospect was enticing. For now, she didn't mention Pierluigi to her parents. There would be a time for that later on.

'I'm glad you both think it's a good idea. I feel I need a bit of a challenge and this Director of Studies thing might be just what I need. And a change of air should be good for me.'

Her mother reached out and patted her hand. 'You deserve it, after the year you've had, I must say. I'm delighted to see you looking and sounding so positive. It's good to see you with a smile on your face again.'

Debbie felt the same way. One thing was for sure: she was definitely over Paul now.

She bade farewell to all her friends in Cambridge, realising she was going to miss them and the city. Alice was in floods of tears as they said goodbye, but promised to try to fly over for a few days some time before Christmas. Debbie was equally emotional, knowing that she was leaving a very good friend behind. However, the prospect of her new job, and the knowledge that she would be meeting up with Pierluigi again, meant that she left Cambridge in a buoyant mood.

She took a morning flight across to Bologna on the first Sunday of October and manhandled her big suitcase on and off the train to Florence with a bit of a struggle. Knowing that autumn had arrived and that winter here was likely to be cold, she had included a load of warm clothes, even though the temperature upon arrival was like a balmy summer day in England. She took a taxi and went straight round to the accommodation promised by Mr Burrage, her fingers firmly crossed that it wouldn't be too Spartan.

She already knew from checking online that the block of flats was outside the historic centre, not that far from Porta al Prato, where she and Alice had had dinner on the first evening of their flying visit that summer. From there to the school would be a half-hour walk, but there were buses and, of course, she could always buy herself a bike. The outside of the building looked a bit tired, but the area seemed reasonably smart. She paid off the taxi and rang the bell for flat 5.

'Yes, hello?' It was a man's voice and for a moment she thought it might be Mr Burrage himself, until a distinct Scottish accent proved her wrong. 'Who's that?' Debbie noticed that he made no attempt to speak Italian.

'Hello, I'm Debbie Waterson. I'm coming to work at FIES. Mr Burrage told me to come here.'

'Oh, right, good. I'll let you in.' He sounded friendly enough and Debbie felt a sensation of relief. There was a buzzing sound and she leant on the door. It opened to reveal a slightly cluttered entrance hall, half-full of bikes and scooters, and, to one side, a flight of stairs. Flat 5 was on the second floor, so she started to haul her suitcase up, one step at a time. Before she reached the first landing, however, she heard footsteps running down towards her and the cavalry arrived in the shape of a tall man with broad shoulders and a smile on his face.

'Debbie? I'm Rory. Welcome to Florence. I'll take that for you.' Waving aside her protests, he picked up her bag in one massive hand and led her up the stairs as if he was carrying nothing heavier than a briefcase.

When they reached the second floor, he indicated a half-open door. 'Go on in. It's open.'

Debbie walked in and was immediately struck by a wonderful smell. Somebody had clearly been baking a cake and she suddenly realised how hungry she was feeling. Behind her, she heard Rory's voice.

'Yours is the room at the end on the left.'

Debbie walked down the short corridor and opened the door as instructed, bracing herself for the worst. In fact, the first impression was very positive. The room was empty, clean and bright. The bed was made up, with pristine white sheets and pillowcases. A small pile of towels had been laid on the bed in readiness for her, with keys to the front door, the flat, and her room on a key ring on top. The view from the window was out over a courtyard to a blank wall – not very panoramic, but unobtrusive. Altogether a lot better than she had feared.

'The room's been empty for a good few months now, ever since Angela left.' Rory set her suitcase down on the floor beside the bed. 'You might need to air it a bit.'

Debbie turned towards him. 'Thank you so much, Rory. This looks fine.' She gave him a smile as she studied him. He was probably five or six years younger than her, with close-cropped fair hair and, in spite of his hulking frame, he looked a little bit shy. He appeared friendly, which was just as well, as he was very big indeed. In fact, his shoulders only just made it in through the door. 'And thank you so much for carrying the case up for me. I'm sorry it was so heavy.'

'No problem. By the way, I've made a cake, so if you want to come along to the kitchen, you can have a slice if you like, and I'll make you some tea.'

'That's the best thing I've heard all day. Thank you so much. Just show me where the bathroom is, and I'll go and wash my hands first.'

The bathroom was quite a large room, which was just as well. The shelf unit in there was absolutely packed with toiletries, from shampoos to perfumes, deodorants, and a box of make-up surely large enough to service a family of clowns. Debbie wondered who on earth the owner of all this stuff might be. Presumably the occupant of one of the other rooms. Still, it was clean and functional. She washed her hands, went back out into the corridor and found Rory standing at an open door.

'The kitchen's in here.'

Debbie walked in and was impressed by the cleanliness of this room as well. Unlike the house she had shared in her first year in Cambridge, where the occupants of the different rooms appeared to be competing to see who could leave the ever-growing pile of dirty dishes the longest, this place was pretty well spotless. She gave Rory an appreciative glance.

'Who's responsible for keeping this place so clean and tidy?'

'There's a lady, Antonella, who comes in three times a week. She's amazing.'

That sounded like very good news. Debbie sat down with Rory and had a mug of tea and a big slice of his excellent Victoria sponge cake. He told her, rather sheepishly, that his hobby was "baking – baking and rugby". He wasn't playing this weekend as he had strained a ligament – not that this had prevented him from carrying her suitcase around like a feather – and so he had baked instead.

Debbie enquired about the other occupants of the flat and discovered that these were two girls called Virginia and Claire. They were "away for the weekend" and Debbie didn't pry as to where they had gone or when they would return.

Rory asked her if she wanted to join him for dinner, but she knew where she wanted to go. She glanced at her watch and saw that it was already three o'clock. Thanking him, she told him she had an appointment and headed straight out. She had texted Pierluigi from Cambridge the previous day, telling him her travel plans, but had received no reply. Presumably this meant he was still in Greece, but she knew she wanted to check to be sure. After all, mobile phones could always break down, get broken or stolen.

Although she had never asked him for his home address, he had told her he worked at Careggi Hospital, and her map showed her this was only a bus ride away. She walked down to the main road, relishing the fact that the temperature was pretty well perfect, so different from the stifling heat of August. She walked through the massive stone arch of Porta al Prato and down past the restaurant where she and Alice had eaten. The menu looked reassuringly unchanged and she vowed to come back for a meal one of these days. After a brief wait, she saw her bus approaching. She had to change once, so it was almost four o'clock by the time she arrived at the very smart modern hospital.

She went up to the reception desk, feeling a surge of excitement, and told them she was looking for Doctor Pierluigi Masino. The busy lady seated there pointed towards Oncology and Debbie followed the signs along corridors and up stairs until she got to the cancer department. There was a queue at the counter, and as she was waiting to speak to the receptionist, she spotted two young doctors over to one side of the room and decided to take a chance. She went across, gave them her friendliest smile, and launched into Italian.

'I'm very sorry to bother you, but I wondered if you knew a friend of mine: Pierluigi Masino… Doctor Masino.'

The younger of the two men smiled back and nodded. 'Yes, of course, we know Pierluigi. He's on holiday in Greece with his fiancée at the moment. They should be back next week, I think. Maybe the week after.'

As Debbie stood there, feeling stunned, the other doctor confirmed what his colleague had said.

'I got a message from him yesterday saying they were having a great time in Santorini. They've rented a villa with a pool along with another couple and he sent me a photo.' He glanced across at his colleague. 'Just to rub it in. What with the course in England, he's been away more than he's been here this summer. It's all right for some. Here we are – working on a Sunday.' He smiled at Debbie. 'Your Italian's very good. Where are you from?'

'Um, England.' Debbie looked round desperately, knowing she had to get away. Her mind was churning, her emotions in free fall, as she tried to digest what she had just heard. Drawing upon hitherto unsuspected acting talents, she summoned an even brighter smile. 'Oh well, I was just passing through, and I thought I'd call by just in case I caught him.'

'Would you like us to give him a message when we see him next?'

There were lots of messages Debbie could think of giving to Pierluigi, but she decided to keep these to herself. Instead, the smile still plastered on, she thanked them and turned away, heading back down the corridor towards the exit. She made her way back out onto the pavement and started walking blindly back the way the bus had come. All the time she found herself thinking what a fool she had been – a fool who had let herself believe that a casual holiday fling could mean anything to a man like Pierluigi. She didn't cry, but she felt a pall of gloom descend upon her as she came to terms with the fact that here she was now, all alone in a strange city.

After plodding aimlessly along for a good long while, she came to a bus stop just as a bus arrived. Without really thinking, she stepped on board and sat down, lost in her thoughts. It was only ten minutes later, when the bus arrived at the main station that she came to her senses and got off. She stood on the pavement for quite a few minutes, before she finally began to get a grip on her emotions. As her brain cleared, she knew exactly where she wanted to go next. She took a few deep breaths and set off on foot towards the historic centre of the city.

There were fewer tourists around, compared to August, but the city wasn't empty by any means. It still took a good while to walk up the crowded pavement, past the Duomo and into the side streets until she reached the Ponte Vecchio. Squeezing through the noisy mass of tourists, she crossed the bridge and turned left. A few hundred metres later, she turned right and headed up the hill.

She climbed up the last few steps to the rose garden at just after five o'clock and was relieved to find the gates still wide open. Inside, she found she was just about the only visitor, so she walked across to the bench she knew so well and took a seat alongside the bronze statue, instinctively reaching over to take hold of the figure's hand. The bench and its statue were already in the shade, as the sun dropped towards the horizon, but the metal fingers were still warm, and felt very comforting. She settled down, her eyes barely registering the roofs of Florence laid out below, and thought back over the events of that summer, up to and including her brief visit to the hospital.

Somehow, deep down inside, she realised that she wasn't totally surprised by what she had just discovered.

The lack of communication from Pierluigi since leaving Cambridge had been suspicious. Surely a tourist destination like Santorini would have good mobile phone connections, after all? Also, since he had left, she had only received three brief text messages from him – also suspicious. She saw now she had been so completely infatuated by him that she had blinded herself to the facts. Now, there was no doubt. Pierluigi was a rat, and he and she were history.

She ran through it all in her head, her fingers still clasping the bronze hand alongside her, and gradually she felt her head clear. Along with this newfound clarity came a gradual resurgence of her sense of excitement at her new life that was beginning over here in Italy. By the time a gaggle of American college kids arrived and she got up and moved off, back down the steps towards the old town, she was definitely feeling better. Not great, but better.

The initial pain she had felt at the news of Pierluigi's true colours had now been replaced by a sense of irritation with herself. In spite of her best intentions in the wake of the whole sad mess with Paul, she had fallen into just exactly the trap she had sought to avoid. Yes, Pierluigi was a rat, but she had been too trusting – pretty damn stupid. Well, she told herself firmly, as she walked past the Uffizi gallery into Piazza della Signoria, she definitely wasn't going to make that sort of mistake again with any man, any time soon.

Repressing her annoyance, she went over to a statue of David, took a couple of photos of the famous naked man, and sent them to Alice. Half a minute later, her phone rang.

'Debs, hi.'

'Hi, Al. Got the photo?'

'Certainly have. It's a beautiful bit of sculpture and he's a handsome chap, but...' Her voice tailed off in disappointment. She didn't say more, but Debbie knew full well what was on her friend's mind. She would have expected no less of her.

'Maybe it was a cold day when he posed for the sculpture, Alice. Give the poor man the benefit of the doubt.'

'If you say so. Anyway, how was the journey, and how's it going over there in Florence? Any sign of your lover man?'

Debbie went over and took a seat on the stone steps at the side of the square and related the conversation she had had with the two doctors in the hospital. Alice waited until Debbie reached the end of her tale before responding. When she did, she sounded disgusted and furious – but maybe not really totally surprised either. Debbie prodded her a bit.

'Should I have known, Al? Have I been a total idiot?'

'No, of course not.' But Alice didn't sound too convincing. After a short pause, she qualified her reply. 'The fact is that he *was* bloody gorgeous. In my limited experience, gorgeous men are the most likely to turn out to be bastards.'

Limited experience? Debbie bit her tongue and managed to suppress the exclamation before it came out. 'So, you're saying that all good–looking men aren't to be trusted?'

'No, not all of them obviously, but the two do sort of seem to go hand in hand. Take your Paul, for example: whatever else he was, he was one of the best-looking men I've ever seen.'

Debbie nodded to herself. Alice was right about that. She took a couple of deep breaths. 'Anyway, Al, I've well and truly learnt my lesson now. I'm staying off men, particularly good-looking men, Italians, and doctors, for the foreseeable future. If you hear me say different, jump on a plane, come over here and give me a smack, will you?'

'That's sort of what I was calling about – the jumping on a plane thing, not the smacking thing. It looks as though I might be able to swing another visit to Florence some time in November. Do you think you'll be able to put me up?'

'Brilliant, Al, of course I'll be able to sort something out. That's really great. I'll look forward to it.'

They chatted some more and Alice must have picked something up from her voice.

'You sound as if you're taking it pretty well, Debs. I'm glad to hear it. Just forget about him now and move on. Remember, half the world's male. Sooner or later, you'll find one who's got a brain and a conscience as well as the other interesting bits. Trust me, it'll happen.'

'Not for a good long while, if I've got anything to do with it.'

After the call ended, Debbie stood there for a few minutes, reflecting on what Alice had said. Yes, she thought to herself, she *was* taking it fairly well – but then, what else could she do? Always a pragmatic person, she gave herself a mental shaking. Pierluigi was out of her life, but she was about to start a new life here in Florence, the city of her dreams. Maybe things weren't so bad, after all.

To underline her conviction that things were irreparably broken between her and him, she took out her phone and sent him a short, sharp text message. *Enjoy your holiday in Santorini with your fiancée.* She didn't sign it.

She was admiring the architecture around her, watching the crowds go by, when her phone whistled. It was a text from Steven Burrage. *Welcome to Florence, Deborah. If you're free, can I buy you a drink? Dinner?*

She stood there for a few seconds, looking down stupidly at the phone, not really feeling like being sociable, before common sense kicked in. It wasn't a question of being sociable. This was work. Taking a deep breath, she texted right back. *Thank you. I'd like that. Where do we meet? I'm near the Palazzo Vecchio now.*

His reply was immediate. *Excellent. See you in the Giubbe Rosse in Piazza della Repubblica.*

Even without consulting her map, Debbie knew where this piazza was. It was barely a five-minute walk away, but to allow Mr Burrage time to get to the café, if he wasn't already there, and to get a better grip on her emotions, she dawdled a bit longer, taking a photo of the Palazzo Vecchio in the dusk and sending it, with a short message, to her parents. Needless to say, the message made no mention of Pierluigi. By the time she got to the café, she was still feeling pretty hollow inside, but she was once more functioning rationally.

Mr Burrage was already there, standing in the middle of a crowd of people at the bar, nursing a half-empty glass of beer. The noise level was high and Debbie had to squeeze her way up to him and tap him on the shoulder before he saw her.

'Deborah, excellent. Welcome.' He took her hand and pumped it vigorously. 'What can I get you? A glass of Prosecco?'

She forced herself to smile. 'That would be lovely, thank you.'

'Excellent.' Mr Burrage disappeared into the crowd, to reappear a minute later carrying a bottle of Prosecco and two glasses, his beer no doubt already swallowed. While he was away, Debbie had been surveying the scene. Clearly, this was a well-known and historic place, with paintings all round the walls, and it looked pretty much as it would have done a hundred years ago, with dark wood, mirrors and chandeliers. When he reached her side, Mr Burrage splashed some wine into both glasses and was just handing one to her as a voice cut in.

'Aren't you going to introduce me to the lovely lady, Stefano? She's the most beautiful woman I've seen all day.' To reinforce the point, the Italian man alongside Mr Burrage brought his thumb and fingers to his mouth and kissed them theatrically. He was probably a few years older than Mr Burrage, maybe in his early or mid-sixties, and he had a strong Tuscan accent, but Debbie would have got the message quite easily even without understanding a word. The glint in his eyes and the fact that he was doing his best to look down her front were a dead giveaway. Her opinion of men was at an all-time low and she had to suppress the urge to fling her Prosecco in his face. Gritting her teeth, she summoned another smile, straightened her back and stood her ground confidently, pleased to see that she was a good few inches taller than him.

'This is our new Director of Studies: Deborah Waterson.' Mr Burrage transferred his attention to Debbie. 'And this is Doctor Montevarchi, Fausto Montevarchi.'

In spite of herself, Debbie's ears pricked up. 'Doctor? Do you work at the hospital?' She had had quite enough of Italian doctors.

For some reason this question struck both men as amusing and Debbie had to wait for Doctor Monte-varchi to be distracted by a telephone call before her new employer was able to explain, sotto voce, in English.

'Everybody's a doctor over here. It just means he went to university.' He lowered his voice even more. 'Or not. It's often just a general term of respect. Fausto's a businessman with a finger in a lot of pies. As far as I know, the closest he's come to the hospital is when he had his prostate checked.'

Debbie found herself with the beginnings of a smile on her face. 'Ah, I see. So, does that mean that I'm a doctor, too?'

'Absolutely. You're not only a female doctor – a *dottoressa* – but a *professoressa* as well. It's a bit of a mouthful, but you can legitimately sign yourself *Dott. Prof.* Waterson if you like. Now, let's go and find a seat in the back room where it's a bit quieter.'

He led her through to a larger room at the back. The tables were set for dinner and a number of customers were already in there. Clearly Mr Burrage was a well-known face, as one of the waiters waved to him and pointed to a table in the corner.

'Your usual table's free.'

Mr Burrage led Debbie across the room and glanced at her as they sat down.

'Have you eaten?'

Food wasn't high on Debbie's agenda for now. 'I'm OK. I've just had a slice of cake with Rory.'

'Ah, yes, our rugby-playing chef. He's a damn good teacher, too. Shame about the Scottish accent, but you can't have everything. But you need to eat, you know. We've got a busy week ahead of us. If you have time, we could have something to eat while we talk.'

Debbie nodded her agreement, even though she didn't really feel hungry. Food would, at least, soak up the alcohol he seemed intent upon pressing upon her, although the bottle of Prosecco was by now barely a quarter full and she had only had a single glass. As if to correct the imbalance, as they sat down, Mr Burrage filled her glass to the brim and tipped the remainder into his.

'We should probably move onto some red with the meal, or would you like to stay on the fizz?'

'Um, just a little drop of red would be lovely, Mr Burrage. And some water, please. I don't want to drink too much wine.'

'Of course you don't. And call me Steven, will you? Everybody does. Or Stefano, my Italian alter ego. Anyway, tell me, how's the flat? Is it all right?'

'It's fine, thank you, Steven. It's clean and very tidy. I'm impressed.' She decided to get onto business matters as soon as possible and, certainly, before the next bottle arrived. 'So, when do I start? Nine o'clock tomorrow morning?'

'Yes, or ten o'clock. Not much happens in the mornings and Giancarla's there from nine to look after things. She's a mine of information.'

'Giancarla?'

'She's the school secretary. Don't be fooled by the title. She near enough runs the place. She's been there for the best part of twenty-five years, even longer than me, and she knows everything that goes on at the school.'

Debbie nodded. It sounded as though her first priority should be to get into Giancarla's good books. Clearly, she was a lady of great influence and Debbie had no desire to make an enemy of the school's longest-standing employee. She carried on asking questions about work and noted the replies. Although some lessons had taken place in September, it sounded as though most of the courses would start this week. It looked like she was in for a baptism of fire.

The waiter who had recognized Mr Burrage came to take their order. Once again, Debbie put herself in her boss's hands as far as ordering was concerned, but she added a plea for small portions. She didn't understand the names of all of the dishes that were discussed, but she agreed with relief that they would just have a starter and a main course, deciding against including a pasta course as well. After a summer of cycling around Cambridge, and the stress of packing and moving house, her jeans didn't fit too snugly at the moment and she wanted to keep things like that.

She took advantage of his obvious expertise to ask him about Italian food. 'Do Italians really eat a starter, a pasta dish and then a main course, followed by cheese and dessert, every meal? And if they do, why aren't they enormous?'

Mr Burrage smiled. 'You'd be surprised how many Italians still insist upon having pasta at least once, if not twice a day. But no, I would think very few have the full works every meal.'

'So, it's all right to come into a restaurant and just order, say, a plate of pasta?'

'Absolutely. Mind you, you'd probably need a carafe of red to go with it.'

The meal was very good and, to her surprise, Debbie discovered she did, in fact, feel like some food after all. The Chianti Classico arrived and she accepted a glassful, while Mr Burrage, aka Steven, made short work of disposing of the rest. They had *crostini* along with raw ham and fresh figs, followed by a mixed grill of lamb chops, steak, and sausages, accompanied by a heap of roast potatoes. Not for the first time, Debbie reflected that Tuscany wouldn't necessarily be the best place for a vegetarian. All the way through the meal, she pumped Steven Burrage for information until she felt slightly more confident as to what would be waiting for her the next morning. Remarkably, in spite of the liver-crippling quantity of wine he consumed, he remained lucid to the last. Clearly, this was a man with an iron constitution.

Finally, after politely declining a dessert or an espresso, Debbie rose to leave, pleading tiredness after her journey. She refused his kind offer to walk home with her and left him happily consuming the two glasses of grappa that had come with the compliments of the management. She made her own way down to the station, past the bulk of the basilica of Santa Maria Novella and through the less populated roads to home, arriving just after half past ten.

She let herself in and climbed the stairs, feeling really quite weary. All was quiet inside, so she used the bathroom and then headed for bed. As she laid her head on the pillow, she was relieved to find that the image that entered her head wasn't of Pierluigi, but of her rose garden. It felt comforting and familiar as ever. She could feel the touch of the statue's bronze hand in hers as she drifted off to sleep, wondering what was in store for her in the morning.

Chapter 8

In spite of the news she had received about Pierluigi and his fiancée, Debbie managed to get a pretty good night's sleep, although she was woken around two o'clock in the morning by the sound of female voices in the corridor outside her room. No doubt Virginia and Claire had returned from their weekend away. As the noise diminished and doors closed, she drifted off to sleep again.

She got up early and breakfasted alone. There were no signs of life from the other rooms and she realised that the three teachers were probably having a long lie-in, as they wouldn't be on duty until the afternoon or early evening, so she tried not to disturb them.

She left the house at eight-fifteen and walked to work. Today the sky was grey and a cool wind was blowing, but at least it was dry. As she walked past the station and up the main street towards the cathedral, she found herself predominantly in the company of other working people, recognisable by their smarter clothes and faster pace than the slower tourists.

She glanced in the shop windows as she walked along, marvelling at the choice of items on display and the astronomical prices on some of the clothes and shoes. Some shops didn't even show any indication of price, which she thought was decidedly sinister, and she resolved to stay away from these. She might be getting paid a bit more than before, but she wasn't in the plutocrat bracket by a long way.

The school occupied the second floor of a magnificent Renaissance palazzo in a narrow street directly behind the Duomo. The massive wooden gates that had been closed when she and Alice had done their brief reconnaissance back in the summer were now open. A stone-flagged passage led into a courtyard, which would once have welcomed the horse-drawn coaches of Florentine notables. Doubtless, with her humble background, she would have been lucky to get a job here as a serving wench back in those days. Now the only carriage on display was a Smart car parked in one corner. A door on her left was open and, as she walked past, a head appeared from within.

'*Buongiorno signorina.*' The owner of the head emerged to reveal a man, maybe in his fifties, with meticulously combed grey hair. He was wearing a dark green apron on top of a freshly-ironed white shirt and impeccable black trousers.

'Good morning.' Debbie glanced at her watch. It was still only twenty to nine, so she paused to chat. 'My name's Debbie Waterson and I'm starting work today up at the school.'

The porter smiled in recognition. 'My name's Nando. I'm the porter here. I'm very pleased to meet you. Signor Burrage told me you'd be coming. You're going to be the new Director, I believe.'

'Director of Studies, yes.'

'Angela was a very nice girl.' He caught her eye and explained. 'Your predecessor. I liked her.'

'Was she here long?'

He shook his head. 'Sadly, no. She only started around this time last year and she left this Easter. All very sudden, her departure.'

Debbie wondered what had caused the previous DoS to leave in a hurry and resolved to check with Steven next time she saw him. After a short chat about everyday things, she gave Nando a cheery wave and walked across to the stairs. There was a small, fairly antiquated-looking lift alongside, but she decided to walk up. The stairs themselves were wide enough and tall enough for a rider on horseback to have ridden up them and, for a moment, she found herself wondering if this had ever happened in the dim and distant past. Certainly, she reflected as she climbed steadily upwards, this place was very different from the little terrace house where she had grown up.

As she reached the second-floor landing, she found a pair of arched wooden doors set in the wall in front of her, emblazoned with a highly-polished brass plate bearing the name *Florence Institute of English Studies*. Alongside the doors was an equally shiny brass doorbell. She walked over and pressed it, hearing a dim echo of the bell on the other side of the door. There was no answer so, after a decent wait, she pressed it again. This time, she got a response. There was a jingling of keys and the right hand half of the door opened a crack. A woman's face appeared.

'The school's closed, I'm afraid. The secretary will be here at nine.' The lady's Italian was fluent, but her accent was definitely foreign. She had black hair, dark brown eyes and she was wearing yellow rubber gloves.

'Hello, my name's Debbie Waterson. I'm the new Director of Studies. I wonder if I could come in.'

The woman looked a bit dubious, so Debbie was quick to list her credentials.

'I've been employed by Mr Burrage and I'm here to see Giancarla.'

An expression of comprehension and relief crossed the cleaner's face. She stepped back and ushered Debbie in, first through the wooden door, and then through an internal glass door.

'Of course, *Professoressa*, do come in. I'm Bella.' As Debbie walked in, Bella pushed the door closed behind her. 'I'm just finishing doing the classrooms. Is it all right to leave you here?'

'Of course, do carry on, please.'

As the cleaner disappeared through a doorway in the left corner, Debbie took a good look around. Her first impression was very positive. The reception area was enormous, with a long counter running along the right-hand side. The ceiling was immensely high, with a massive chandelier suspended in the centre of the room, but the star of the show was an obviously ancient fresco on the wall opposite the entrance. This depicted a group of men on horseback, some carrying hawks on their gloved hands, with a gaggle of servants on foot around them, all clearly engaged in a hunt. A pair of unfortunate rabbits could be seen hanging from the hands of one of the servants while another little grey bunny was running for its life, chased by massive hounds. It was quite stunning and Debbie stood in silent contemplation, knowing she was going to enjoy working in such a historic setting.

Her thoughts were interrupted by the sound of a key in the lock and she turned to see the door open. A woman around the same age as the porter downstairs appeared through the door and stopped dead in surprise.

'*Buongiorno.*' Her tone was deeply suspicious. 'And you are?' She was a stern-looking woman with grey hair tied tightly into a bun, and her expression was as wary as her tone.

Debbie launched into a major charm offensive. 'Good morning. My name's Debbie Waterson. I'm the new Director of Studies. You must be Giancarla.'

'Must I?' The woman's tone was glacial.

Debbie hesitated. 'Aren't you Giancarla? Steven told me you run the place.'

The woman's stern expression softened fractionally. 'Yes, my name is Giancarla and yes, I run the school.' With an effort, the secretary walked across, set her handbag and today's post down on the counter and held out her hand, somewhat reluctantly, towards Debbie. 'I'm pleased to meet you. What did you say your name was? I was told it was Deborah.'

'Yes, it is, but my friends call me Debbie, or Debs.' She shook hands, realising as she did so that, daunting as the other woman was, she was quite tiny, her head barely reaching up to Debbie's shoulder. However, clearly she compensated for her lack of physical stature by having the coiled aggression of a cobra.

'I shall call you Deborah.'

'As you wish.' Debbie registered the put-down and felt her hackles begin to rise. Nevertheless, swallowing hard, she plastered a broad smile across her face. 'So, Giancarla, Steven told me you would show me round.' Steven hadn't said any such thing, but Debbie was keen to see what effect their boss's name would have. It didn't take long to discover.

'He can show you round himself. I've got far too much to do.' To reinforce the message, Giancarla marched round the end of the counter and back to her desk, where she began to sift through the letters she had brought in with her. A few moments later, as Debbie was leafing through a pile of textbooks on display, an old grandfather clock against the end wall struck nine and Giancarla strutted across and unlocked the main entrance doors. She pushed them open, back against the outside wall, leaving just the internal glass door. Debbie noticed that this had FIES etched on it in red, white and blue.

'Is it all right if I take a look round, Giancarla?'

'Help yourself, but stay away from my desk. I don't want my things messed up.'

'Of course.' Debbie repeated her friendly smile, albeit while gritting her teeth, and went over to a door along-side the fresco, marked *Principal*. She glanced inside, but immediately heard a disapproving tut-tutting sound from Giancarla behind her and decided to leave Steven's office for another time.

She followed the route taken by Bella the cleaner though the doorway to the left and found herself in another charming, huge room, with doors leading off on all sides. She wandered round, counting six class-rooms, all well-equipped, a little leisure area with a coffee machine and water fountain, and a door with *Staffroom* on it. Inside, there was a pretty comprehensive library of books and teaching manuals, as well as audio materials. There was also an electric kettle and mugs on a tray, freshly washed by Bella, from the look of them.

She stopped for a brief chat with Bella at the staffroom door, and learnt that she was Romanian. Like so many of her compatriots, she spoke very good Italian and Debbie remembered that Romanian was, of course, a Latin-based language and a close cousin of Italian. As Bella seemed happy to chat, Debbie took the opportunity to ask what had happened to the previous DoS. She saw Bella's eyes dart anxiously towards the reception area.

'She had a problem with another member of staff.' She kept her voice low and rolled her eyes in the direction of the front door. Debbie wasn't surprised.

'She and Giancarla didn't get on?'

Bella nodded. 'Ask Signor Stefano. He will tell you better.'

Debbie nodded. 'Thank you, Bella. I will ask him.' Sensing Bella's discomfort, she changed the subject and saw relief on the cleaner's face.

'And have you worked here long?'

'Four years. Signor Stefano is a very nice boss.'

'Well, you keep the place looking very good. Congratulations.'

Beyond the staffroom, at the end of the corridor, there was a door with *Director of Studies* written on it. Debbie opened it and went in. It was smaller than the staffroom, but pleasantly light. Inside stood a desk, three chairs and a bookcase filled with reference books. She walked over to the window and looked out. There, towering right in front, was the massive domed roof of the cathedral, and she took a deep breath. Not many offices could boast a close-up view of the Duomo, and she found herself smiling. However much of a cow Giancarla might turn out to be, this was a pretty amazing place to work. She pulled out her phone and took a photo to send to her mother and Alice.

She was disturbed by a ringing sound. On the desk was a grey-blue phone, bristling with a battery of buttons. One of these was blinking as the phone rang so she picked the receiver up and pressed the lighted button.

'Deborah, there's a lady here who needs a grading test. Please come and collect her.' Giancarla's voice hadn't become any friendlier.

'Of course, Giancarla. I'll be right there.' Steven had spoken to her about these tests. Basically, any potential students who came in had to be tested to establish their level of English, so that those who were advanced didn't end up in a beginners' class or vice versa. Over the course of the next three hours, Debbie carried out four of these brief tests, after which she returned the students to Giancarla in the front office to complete the enrolment formalities and to pay their fees.

At just before noon, Steven arrived and sat down with Debbie to go through the timetable with her. Debbie was interested to see that Giancarla's attitude towards him was even colder than it was with her. The school secretary was clearly an unhappy person and her boss was most definitely not in her good books. At least, Debbie was happy to note, Giancarla's attitude towards the students, while not gushing, was polite and even welcoming. Maybe she just had a problem with authority. Debbie tried to broach the subject of the previous DoS, Angela, but Steven added little to what Bella had told her.

'She got very stressed out and decided to leave at Easter. I've been filling in since then. That's why I'm so glad you're here now.'

Debbie decided there wasn't much point trying to probe any further. It certainly sounded as though Giancarla's prickly personality had been responsible for the DoS's departure. For now, Debbie resolved to treat Giancarla with severe caution. The fact was that she liked the feel of this job, and she had every intention of making it work.

The rest of the day passed quickly. At half past twelve on the dot Giancarla picked up her handbag and left, closing the door behind her without a word, and didn't reappear until three o'clock. Debbie and Steven worked through the lunch break, stopping only for a quick sandwich in a café downstairs in the street. Debbie drank mineral water, but couldn't help noticing that Steven put away three glasses of red wine in the twenty minutes they were down there. Even though he appeared unaffected, Debbie wondered what all this alcohol might be doing to his vital organs.

A few hours later, Rory arrived to start work, accompanied by the two girls – Virginia and Claire. They were both a few years younger than her and it was clear that these two, between them, were the owners and users of the mountain of toiletries back at the flat. Dolled up to the nines as they were, Debbie began to wonder whether they shared man-eating DNA with Alice. Time would tell.

The girls were pleasant enough, although Debbie detected a hint of apprehension, maybe even antagonism, in their attitude towards her. She could understand this. She was, after all, their new boss. She did her best to be friendly and supportive and by the end of the day, she sensed a thaw beginning to take place – which was more than could be said for Giancarla, who remained po-faced all day. Two other teachers also appeared, both were female and both married to Florentine men. They had worked at the school for a number of years and clearly had experienced a number of Directors of Studies, and they accepted her presence without a murmur.

–

That week and the weeks that followed were some of the busiest, and most exhausting, of Debbie's life. She made a point of getting into work before nine every morning – she now had her own key – and often didn't leave until ten o'clock at night. She started teaching, enjoying meeting the students, and gradually managed to wheedle snippets of closely guarded information out of Giancarla's jealous hands. As she learnt more and settled in, she soon started to see ways in which things could be improved. Needless to say, change was not on Giancarla's agenda.

Her first idea came to her one rainy day when, instead of walking, she took the bus to work. Looking round the crowded interior, she saw that there were lots of older people sitting there. This reminded her of the courses her old school ran for so-called Third Age students. When Steven came into work that day, she suggested trying to promote courses for older people and, in spite of a stony wall of non-cooperation from Giancarla, she managed to launch an advertising campaign in the local newspaper, *La Nazione*. The results were impressive. By the end of October, three new afternoon classes had been formed, populated entirely by senior citizens.

The downside to this success was that she ended up doing the teaching herself as all the other teachers were fully occupied. Before long she realised that they could do with another teacher and, with Steven's blessing, she placed an advertisement on the same website she had consulted back in Cambridge. Steven flew over to London in early November to conduct the interviews – and no doubt eat another curry or two – and a new teacher was duly appointed. This meant that the hunt for accommodation had to start – not easy in this crowded city.

While Steven was in the UK, Debbie invited all the staff out for a pizza after work on Friday night. Everybody came except two. One was Bella, who thanked her profusely for the invitation, but declined because she had to be up at six o'clock the next morning. The other person who didn't come along was Giancarla. This didn't come as a surprise to Debbie. On the one hand, she was relieved that they would be spared her prickly company, but at the same time she rather regretted not being able to have the opportunity of trying to bond with the hostile secretary outside the work environment.

Lessons finished at ten o'clock, so the meal was a late-night affair but, by now, Debbie was getting used to the long hours. Virginia and Claire appeared to be of vampire stock as they quite evidently came alive as the night progressed. When things broke up at around one o'clock, the girls informed her they were going on to a party elsewhere. Claire even asked Debbie if she felt like coming with them and Debbie definitely sensed that she had scored a little victory – even though she declined the invitation and walked home with Rory.

She liked Rory and she often chatted to him around the flat as well as at work. It turned out he had only arrived a couple of weeks before her and he was still feeling his way. Although Debbie had never felt threatened at any time here in Florence, it was reassuring to have his big muscular presence alongside her as they walked through the dark streets.

'Rugby tomorrow?'

'Yes, it'll be my first game in the first fifteen. I hope I don't screw up.'

'You won't screw up, I'm sure. And that tendon trouble you were having? Has that all cleared up?'

'Yes, thanks, I'm fine.'

'So is the big game the reason why you didn't go partying with Claire and Virginia?'

She sensed a moment's hesitation from him.

'That, and a few other things.' He definitely sounded more tentative than normal.

'Such as?'

There was another, longer, pause before he answered.

'Such as the fact that I'm gay, principally.'

'Well, surely there would have been men at the party as well as women?' Debbie had a number of gay friends and most of them were the life and soul of any party. Rory, on the other hand, was obviously made of shyer stuff.

'To be totally honest, Debbie, you're just about the first person I've told.'

'What, the first person over here in Florence?' She glanced across at him and saw him shake his head in the orange glow of the streetlights.

'The first person anywhere.'

This was a surprise. 'Why's that? Surely the days of closets and coming out have well and truly passed, haven't they?'

'Not where I come from. I'm from a little Scottish fishing village, right up north, above Aberdeen. Everybody knows everybody and homosexuality isn't a thing there. I haven't even told my mum. She'd be devastated.'

'Surely not? She'll love you for what you are, I'm sure. You should say something. And your dad?'

'My dad's dead. He was a fisherman and his boat went down one stormy night when I was just ten.'

Debbie could hear the grief still present in his voice and reached across and took hold of his arm.

'I'm so sorry.'

'Thanks, Debbie. There's only ever been me and my mum since then. I sort of knew for years, but I only really admitted my sexuality to myself a few years ago when I got to university. This is part of the reason I thought I'd get right away and find a job abroad.'

Debbie gave his brawny arm an encouraging squeeze. 'Times have changed, Rory. I think you should tell your mum. And I'm sure a big handsome chap like you will be able to find himself a special someone over here very easily. There are some very good-looking Italian men around, you know.' As she spoke, she remembered what Alice had said about good-looking men being the least trustworthy, not to mention her own experience so far. 'Just make sure you pick a good one.'

Rory nodded. 'I'll try. And what about you, Debbie? You just seem to work all the time. You mustn't overdo it, you know. Surely you must have a man stashed away somewhere. You're terribly attractive... well, beautiful, really.'

'Thanks, Rory. You do wonders for my self-confidence. But no, I'm footloose and fancy free these days and loving it. I've had it with men for the foreseeable future.'

—

In Debbie's advanced class on Tuesdays and Thursdays, there was a very striking and elegant lady called Flora, who was always happy to stay and chat after lessons. Flora was probably in her late fifties, but her skin was as smooth as a baby's, and her hair and clothes were always impeccable. Clearly, there was no shortage of money in her family. However, in spite of her privileged background, she and Debbie got on very well and often went for a coffee together after lessons. After a few weeks, Flora invited Debbie to come to her house for tea one Saturday afternoon. As she lived a little way out of town, she promised to send a car.

The car, when it appeared, turned out to be a very swish chauffeur-driven silver Mercedes with tinted windows and the most comfortable leather seats Debbie had ever experienced. She stepped in, feeling like the impostor she was. This was definitely a car for the rich and famous, not for an ordinary person like herself. She resisted the invitation to take a seat in the back and climbed into the front passenger seat alongside the driver, counting this at least a token attempt to appear unpretentious.

The car was driven by a young man called Giacomo, who described himself as the *autista*, or chauffeur. He even had a chauffeur's peaked cap, but he told her with a smile that he never wore it. He and Debbie chatted as he steered the big car expertly through the traffic away from the centre. As they reached the outskirts, Debbie spotted a sign pointing towards Fiesole, where she and Alice had had the lovely birthday meal back in August.

'Does Flora live in Fiesole?'

'The *Conte* and *Contessa*'s villa is on the hillside just below Fiesole.'

Debbie was stunned. She'd had no idea that Flora was a countess. At the school, everybody used first names and now she had to struggle to remember Flora's surname. It came to her shortly after the car reached the sign marked Fiesole. As the chauffeur turned off onto a tortuous, narrow lane that led to an imposing gateway, she remembered – Flora Dellatorre. They stopped briefly while electric gates hummed open, then the car swept along a gravelled drive, flanked by centennial cypress trees, leading to one of the most wonderful houses Debbie had ever seen.

It wasn't enormous, but it certainly wasn't small either. It was a real Tuscan villa, complete with a tower in the middle of the roof. The walls were a deep ochre colour, the windows hung with the same green shutters found elsewhere in Florence. It sat on a flat terrace on the hillside, and it was ringed by trees. The garden, filled with roses, oleander and numerous other flowering shrubs, sloped down from there towards Florence. The view as Debbie stepped out of the car was spectacular and she felt immensely privileged to have been invited to such an amazing place. She also felt more than a little nervous. Just how, she wondered, did one address a count? Should she carry on calling Flora by her first name? She felt her palms begin to sweat as they drew up at the bottom of a short flight of marble steps.

'Deborah, thank you so much for coming. No, Byron, don't jump all over her.' Flora was waiting at the front door as, from behind her, a very enthusiastic black Labrador came charging out to greet Debbie, tail wagging furiously. 'Just push him down if he tries to jump up at you. He's still young and he's always delighted to meet new people.'

Debbie knelt down to greet the dog and made a fuss of him as he whined happily, finally slumping down onto his side and then his back, all four legs waving in the air as she scratched his tummy. Debbie looked up at Flora.

'He's a beauty. And your house, Flora, it's unbelievable.'

Flora came down the steps to take Debbie's hand in both of hers. 'It's been in my husband's family for centuries. We're just the most recent custodians of it. Byron, enough, now. *Basta!*'

'*Byron, vieni qui.*' All three of them looked up at the sound of the voice and Byron leapt to his feet and charged obediently back to the front door where a distinguished-looking gentleman had appeared.

'Deborah, come and let me introduce you to my husband.'

Debbie followed Flora up the steps to the front door. By this time the Labrador had taken up position alongside his master, doing his best to sit still, while his tail was still wagging furiously.

'Enzo, this is Deborah. She's the Director of Studies of the English school.'

Flora's husband gave Debbie a smile and a formal nod of the head and held out his hand. He was probably quite a few years older than his wife, still very well preserved, with impeccably styled silver hair.

'Welcome to our home, Deborah.'

Debbie shook hands and did her best to reply appropriately. 'I'm very pleased to meet you, sir.' Should that have been *Your Lordship*?

'And you've already met Byron.' Count Enzo glanced downwards with a little smile. 'I think you can tell from his reaction that he's also pleased to see you. Do come in.'

The inside of the house was as remarkable as the exterior and Debbie's sensation of being a fish out of water only increased. The floor was made of slabs of white and grey marble, the walls hung with venerable old paintings, and stunning glass chandeliers hung from the high ceilings. Everywhere Debbie looked, there seemed to be priceless furniture, objets d'art and an overwhelming sense of history. It was stunning and terrifying at the same time. Her feeling of discomfort grew and she wondered what her dad, a lifelong trade union member, would have to say about somewhere like this and the people who lived in it.

They walked through a vast living room to a smaller lounge with floor-to-ceiling French windows, offering a breathtaking view of Florence below. Flora and Debbie sat down side by side on an immaculate, tapestry-covered sofa while the count, after a few minutes exchanging pleasantries, excused himself and left. The dog hesitated before deciding to stay with the ladies, plonking himself on the floor between the two of them. A few minutes later he stretched out and closed his eyes with a sigh.

Debbie and Flora chatted a little, mainly about the house and its history – its origins went back to the sixteenth century. She learnt that the trademark tower in the middle of the roof was originally a dovecot that would have produced a regular supply of eggs for the household. Now, like so many others, this one had been converted into a room with magnificent views, currently used by the count as his study. As they talked, Debbie began to relax a bit. The fact was that Flora was a very nice lady and Debbie had grown to like her long before learning of her spectacular wealth or her aristocratic background.

There was a tap on the door and a housekeeper appeared with a trolley. To Debbie's amazement, this was loaded with what she recognized as all the ingredients of a traditional English high tea, even if this was something she had never experienced in her life. From the porcelain teapot, cups, saucers and milk jug to the plates of cucumber and smoked salmon sandwiches, the selection of biscuits and the impeccable sponge cake, it looked like something the queen might order at Buckingham Palace. Debbie wondered idly how this would compare to the cakes Rory made at the weekends when he wasn't playing rugby.

Flora served Debbie with tea and told her to help herself to food. Debbie was very happy to do as instructed and found that it was excellent – the cake every bit as good as Rory's. Gradually her sense of unease diminished as she did her best to ignore the sumptuous surroundings and concentrate on talking to the person behind the façade. By this time, however, she had firmly resolved not to recount this episode to her dad. Some things were best left unsaid. The conversation continued and flowed.

'And are you married, Deborah?'

Debbie shook her head, maybe a touch too vehemently, as Flora caught her eye and raised an eyebrow. Debbie decided to make no mention of Pierluigi. Since sending him her terse text message from Piazza Signoria, there had been no further contact between them and that suited her just fine. She did, however, provide a brief summary of her abortive relationship with Paul, and Flora was very sympathetic.

'How terrible for you. So, now you're here on your own?'

'Yes, sort of. I share a flat with three of the teachers. In fact, I'm looking for somewhere for our new teacher, arriving next week, but it's not easy to find accommodation here in Florence.'

Flora looked reflective. 'Do you enjoy sharing with other people?'

Debbie smiled weakly. 'It's not ideal, to be honest. I had my own flat in Cambridge and I really miss that. Rory's a sweetie, but Virginia and Claire do tend to monopolise the bathroom, and they come and go at all hours of the day and night. I suppose it's because they don't need to get up in the mornings, but I do. Anyway, I'll manage.'

'I don't think I'd enjoy that very much.' Flora played with the piece of cake on her plate for a few moments, before appearing to come to a decision. 'I might have a solution, if you're interested, Deborah. We've got an apartment in the centre of Florence that we don't use. Why don't you give your room to the new teacher and move into our apartment? It's empty.'

Debbie's hopes soared for a moment before she gave herself a reality check. A flat in the centre of Florence would be bound to be out of her financial league. She was about to refuse the offer as politely as possible, when Flora carried on.

'The flat's been used by my daughter until recently, but she and her fiancé have just moved in together. They're getting married next spring, but young people don't wait for things like that any longer – and we were wondering what to do with it. I do think property needs to be lived in, don't you? Could I ask – how much are you paying for your room at present?'

Debbie gave her the figure and saw Flora nod her head a few times. 'Deborah, would you excuse me a moment while I go and have a word with Enzo?'

Flora was out of the room for about five minutes, but the Labrador remained to keep Debbie company. Clearly, with his head on her foot, he was far too comfortable to move. She reached down and scratched his ears while she waited and she heard him sigh happily.

When Flora returned, it was to give Debbie the astounding news that she and her husband would be delighted to rent her their flat for the same amount she was paying at the moment.

'It's not a big apartment. There's a little kitchen, a lounge, and only one bedroom, plus a bathroom, but it should do you, I would think.'

Debbie was flabbergasted and protested that she couldn't possibly accept such a generous offer. Flora tapped her on the arm and shushed her.

'Really, Deborah, you'd be doing us a favour by using it. Enzo wouldn't dream of selling it and it seems such a shame to keep it closed up – like a lot of places in Florence, I'm afraid. It's fully furnished because Claudia, my daughter, wanted all new stuff in her new place. She and her fiancé are on holiday at the moment and I'm sure she'll come back with even more new things.' She lowered her voice and grinned at Debbie. 'To be honest, I'd quite like some new furniture here myself, but Enzo won't hear of it. If it isn't at least two hundred years old, he doesn't want to know.'

Debbie still couldn't really believe her ears and continued to protest, but Flora was having none of it. At the end of a very pleasant afternoon, she gave instructions to Giacomo, the *autista,* to take Debbie round there on the way home, to see if she liked the look of the place.

Debbie *loved* the look of the place.

The flat was in an amazing position, only a stone's throw from the Duomo in the pedestrian area, and barely three or four minutes on foot from the school. It was on the top floor of a Renaissance palazzo that could almost have been a carbon copy of the school building, complete with massive gates opening onto the street and a shady courtyard on the ground floor with a centuries-old fig tree in one corner. The flat was on the top floor and there wasn't a lift, but Debbie didn't mind that one bit. As Giacomo accompanied her up the stairs, she breathed in the sense of history the old building inspired.

The apartment was delightful. There was a decent-sized modern kitchen with granite worktops, a luxurious bathroom, a lovely big bedroom with a lovely big bed, and a sizeable living room with French windows, through which she could see over the roofs of Florence all the way to Fiesole. Even better, the ornate glass doors opened onto a spectacular terrace running the length of the building and connecting with the other flat on the top floor. That apartment, Giacomo informed her, was where the *contessa's* son lived, when he was home. Not a bad place to live at all. She reflected upon the fact that Flora had described the flat as small when, in fact, it was almost as big as the house where she had been born and brought up. Clearly, Flora's standards were very different from hers.

She asked Giacomo to tell Flora and her husband that she would be delighted to take the flat and when he had left, she walked the short distance from there to the school, and let herself in. As it was a Saturday evening it was empty and it felt rather good to be able to walk around wherever she liked without fear of being told off by the grouchy secretary. She turned on her computer, located the file for Flora Dellatorre, found her email address and sent her an email, repeating her thanks for the lovely afternoon and confirming what she had told Giacomo, if they were really sure they wanted her to take it. The offer of the apartment was the best news she could have hoped to receive and she was delighted to accept.

She was humming to herself as she switched the computer off again and left her office. Things were definitely on the up. She was just crossing the main reception area on her way to the front door when she heard a strange noise and stopped in alarm.

It was coming from the principal's office and, for a moment, she wondered if there were thieves in the building. Then the noise came again and it sounded more like somebody in pain. She went over and cautiously pushed the office door open. There, sprawled on his side on the floor, was Steven, doubled up in agony. His right hand was clenching his left arm and he was gasping for breath, his eyes almost popping out of his head.

Debbie had done several first aid courses and she immediately recognized the symptoms. Her boss was having a heart attack. She ran for the phone and dialled 112, the number for the emergency services. After telling the operator what was happening and then giving the address, she dropped the phone and crouched down beside Steven, cradling his head in her arms. As she did so, he gave a choked cough and, to her horror, stopped breathing. Remembering her training, she reached for the big artery at the side of his throat and was appalled to feel that his heart had stopped along with his breathing.

She ripped off her jacket and threw it away while she desperately set about performing CPR on him. She counted to herself as she repeatedly thumped his chest, just as they had taught her, and it was very hard work. Five or six minutes later, she was mightily relieved to hear footsteps outside and pounding on the door. Abandoning Steven, she ran to open it and the paramedics took over. She left them to it and went out into the reception area, breathing deeply. She was bathed in sweat after her exertions and badly needed a sit down. As she gradually regained her breath, she reflected how lucky it had been that she, by sheer chance, had happened to be here on a Saturday evening. If she hadn't been there, she had no doubt as to what Steven's fate would have been.

Five minutes later, one of the paramedics came out with the good news that they had managed to restart his heart and would be taking him to hospital. As he went off to fetch a stretcher, Debbie wondered whom to call. Giancarla was the obvious choice, but she didn't have a home number for her. She suddenly had an idea and went back into Steven's office. He was laid out on the floor, his chest bare, a drip in his arm. His eyes were closed and he looked as if he was still unconscious, but even from the door, Debbie could see the rise and fall of his chest as he breathed once more. The female paramedic glanced up as she came in and Debbie explained.

'I need his phone. I need to tell people what's happened.'

The mobile phone was lying on the desk and she picked it up, hoping it wouldn't be password protected. She breathed a sigh of relief as she saw the screen light up. No password. She hunted for *Contacts* and then scrolled through, realising as she did so that, even after more than a month in post, she didn't know Giancarla's surname. Fortunately, the phone number was in there just under her first name.

Debbie pressed the call button and heard it start to ring. As she waited for a reply, she had a thought and looked down at the paramedic.

'Where are you going to take him?'

'Careggi.'

'Can I come too?'

'Yes, if you want to. You can ride in the back of the ambulance with the patient and my colleague.'

Just then Giancarla answered. Debbie was totally taken aback to hear her voice quite literally screaming down the phone.

'I told you never, ever to use this number again! What on earth do you think you're doing?'

'Giancarla, listen. It's me, Debbie. Steven's had a heart attack.'

There was sudden silence at the other end and Debbie was just beginning to wonder if Giancarla had rung off when she heard her voice again, this time little more than a whisper.

'*Santo cielo*! He's had a heart attack? Is he all right?'

Debbie told her what had happened and said she would ride with him to the hospital in the ambulance. When Giancarla replied, her voice was very different from her usual frosty tone.

'Thank you, Deborah. I'll meet you at Careggi. Thank you again.'

Chapter 9

The next week was strange. So much had changed at the school in the blink of an eye. Debbie was now interim principal, finding herself working even harder then before, but the strangest thing of all was the change in Giancarla.

When the ambulance arrived at Careggi Hospital, Debbie had found Giancarla already there, hovering around the *Pronto Soccorso* entrance, biting her lips apprehensively. As Steven was wheeled out of the ambulance and in through the automatic doors, Giancarla took up station alongside the trolley and took hold of his hand. As she spotted Debbie, she gave her a little smile and Debbie was stunned. She had never, ever, seen a smile of any kind on the secretary's face. It was strangely unsettling.

Back at work on the Monday, the smile reappeared more than once. When Giancarla arrived at school and saw Debbie already there, going through the pile of documents on Steven's desk, she came rushing towards her. Debbie jumped to her feet, frightened she was going to be assaulted, at least verbally, for having the temerity to invade the principal's office. She was then even more startled to be on the receiving end of a big hug and a kiss on both cheeks.

'Debbie, you saved his life. Thank you so much.' Debbie was stunned by two things: first the hug, and second, the fact that Giancarla had called her Debbie. Clearly, Steven's cardiac arrest had brought about some sort of sea change in Giancarla.

The sea change continued to manifest itself throughout the week. As the news from the hospital improved, Giancarla became almost cheerful and everybody commented on it. It was Martha, the teacher who had been there the longest, who supplied the likely explanation.

'Steven and Giancarla were an item when I first started working here. They lived together just round the corner from here.'

Debbie's eyes widened in surprise as Martha went on.

'He did the academic stuff and she looked after the admin, and it all worked really well. Then, maybe five or six years ago, something happened.'

'What sort of something?'

'Nobody knows for sure or, if they do know, they aren't saying. Whatever it was, it split them up and they've been at daggers drawn ever since.' She glanced round to make sure they weren't being overheard. 'For my money, he had an affair with Jodie. She was one of the teachers at the time and you could see that she fancied him. I reckon that's what happened.'

Debbie was very surprised. She had never really thought of Steven, with his drink problem and his pot belly, as an object of desire for anybody – apart from, possibly, a wine salesman.

Martha read her mind. 'He was a pretty good-looking guy back then. I think the drinking started as a result of the break-up.'

Debbie shivered, trying to imagine how it must have been for both of them, working together after an acrimonious break-up. For a moment, she wondered if she could have faced walking into work with Paul after the way he had behaved towards her. She was pretty sure she knew the answer to that one.

'Why didn't one of them go off and get a new job?'

'Jobs are scarce, Debbie. Since the financial crisis, unemployment in Italy's gone through the roof. I'm sure either or both of them would have leapt at the chance to get away, but there was nothing on the horizon.'

So, Debbie thought to herself, presumably the change in Giancarla's attitude towards Steven showed that she still had feelings for him after all. Whether Steven reciprocated those feelings or not remained to be seen. Anyway, whatever the reason, the thawing of Giancarla's manner was greatly appreciated by everybody, and by Debbie in particular.

Back at the flat, she told Rory and the girls that she would be moving out at the weekend and that her room would be taken by Sam, the newly-engaged teacher who would be arriving from England. She thought she saw regret in Rory's eyes and maybe even on the faces of Virginia and Claire as well. She had been getting on increasingly well with all three of them, particularly Rory. However, in spite of that, she was having a hard time keeping a broad, silly smile off her face as she broke the news. It would be so good to regain her independence – and her own bathroom.

On Tuesday, Giancarla arrived at work unusually early. She was quick to explain to Debbie.

'I got a phone call this morning just after seven thirty. It was Steven. He's well enough to use the phone.' She sounded, and looked, delighted. 'His voice was a bit weak at first, but it was him all right. Debbie, he asked me to tell you how grateful he is for what you did to save him and I'm really, really grateful too. Without you, he'd be dead.'

'It's lucky I did those first aid courses. When I felt his heart had stopped, I very nearly panicked.'

'But you didn't panic. You knew what to do and you did it.'

'So, how are you holding up, Giancarla?' It was strange to think that, just a few days earlier, she would never have dared ask the grumpy secretary anything of a personal nature. Now, she saw Giancarla muster a smile.

'I'm fine, thank you, Debbie. I'm so glad you're here. I know I told you I ran the school, but it's always been with Steven. Now that he's out of action, I'd have been lost without you.'

'You're very welcome. Any idea when Steven will be coming out of hospital? And what'll he do then? Will he be able to look after himself?'

'I don't know when he'll be coming out, but I'll look after him.'

Debbie remembered what Martha had told her. Maybe this stroke of bad luck for Steven might turn out to have a silver lining if it brought him back together with Giancarla once more.

She went in to see Steven a couple of times during the week and learnt that he was being released from hospital at the weekend. He looked better each time she saw him, and he continued to be terribly grateful for her part in saving his life. She shrugged off the thanks and asked him how long it might be before he came back to work. He shook his head and said the doctors had told him to take it very slow for a while, so he might not be back for the foreseeable future. He asked her if she was managing and she answered, honestly, that with Giancarla's help, she was. He appeared relieved and thanked her again.

Flora invited her for tea again on Saturday, and said she would instruct Giacomo to give her a hand to move her things to the new flat afterwards. Debbie was delighted to take her up on the offer, but she protested that she could, at least, make her own way up to the villa on the bus. Flora wouldn't hear of it.

'Giacomo's only too happy to pick you up. Besides, the car's just sitting there. Really, it's no trouble.'

Debbie not only received a warm welcome from Giacomo, but she was almost knocked on her back by the boisterous Labrador when she reached the house. Clearly, Byron was very pleased to see her indeed. She wondered to herself if he realised just how enormously lucky he was to be living in such luxury. Some dogs had all the luck.

This time, instead of cucumber sandwiches, Flora's housekeeper produced a selection of Italian pastries along with the tea. These included profiteroles; some with dark or white chocolate topping, some with coloured icing. Along with them came miniature pastry cornucopias filled with whipped cream, delicious biscuits and more. Throughout the afternoon, the Labrador sat between the two of them, his eyes glued to the tabletop, a look of longing in his brown eyes. Flora told her he didn't get food from the table.

'Like all Labradors, he's very greedy, so we keep him on a strict diet so he doesn't get fat.'

Debbie smiled down at him. Maybe he wasn't as lucky as she had thought.

She and Flora talked for a while in English, then swapped into Italian. Debbie learnt more about Flora's background and the fashion business she had created. It soon became pretty clear to Debbie that her initial assumption that Flora had married into money wasn't quite so straightforward. Apparently she had offices and a shop in Florence and, according to Flora, the company also had shops in all the main Italian cities, as well as Paris, New York and in a few other countries. She had built the business up from scratch by herself and clearly was a very talented businesswoman. Maybe, Debbie thought to herself, the fact that Flora had worked for her wealth would make her more acceptable to her dad if they ever met.

At five o'clock, Giacomo appeared with the car and drove Debbie round to her old flat to collect her stuff and, from there, to the new apartment. Presumably he had some special kind of permit that allowed him to enter the pedestrian zone and Debbie felt very self-conscious as they crept through the crowds at walking pace in the luxury limousine. He squeezed the big vehicle in through the gates and parked in the courtyard, insisting upon carrying Debbie's big suitcase all the way up the stairs. All she was left to carry was a small cardboard box with the food she had been keeping in the fridge.

When they got up to the flat, she tried to give him something, but all he would accept was a cup of tea without milk. Together, they sat on the terrace with their drinks and enjoyed the sight of the sun going down over the rooftops. The heat of August was now a distant memory, but with a jacket, it was still pleasant to sit outside. She asked him a little about himself and learnt that he had worked for the count's family for almost ten years, ever since leaving school and, as well as driving the car, he also looked after the garden and did all the odd jobs that a huge property demanded from time to time. He sounded very happy with his life and his work.

His two passions in life were Fiorentina football team and his fiancée, Anna. She and he were going to be married the following year and Debbie almost told him that this had been her plan as well until it had all fallen apart, but she decided against it. She had barely spared a thought for Paul for a good long while now and she saw no need to rake up old memories. And she certainly didn't talk about Pierluigi. He, too, crossed her mind less and less these days, and she had gradually begun to get over the whole sorry episode.

As she unpacked her things, she found herself humming a little tune.

—

On Monday, she received a visitor at work. To her surprise, she recognized the businessman she had met in the Giubbe Rosse restaurant with Steven, back at the beginning of October. As he walked in, she racked her brains for his name, but could just remember his first name, Fausto. Luckily, he appeared to be well known to Giancarla, who greeted him with one of her ever more frequent smiles.

'*Buongiorno, Dottor Montevarchi.*'

'*Buongiorno, Giancarla.*'

Debbie was sitting at Steven's desk, as she had been most of the previous week. With Bella's help she had moved it a few feet so that it was now strategically positioned so that she could see through the door into Reception. She rose to her feet and was about to go out to say hello when Doctor Montevarchi strolled into the office and closed the door behind him, indicating that Debbie should sit back down again. She did so, wondering what was happening. He began to explain.

'*Professoressa* Waterson... Deborah, how good to see you again. I have come to give you my thanks and to show my gratitude.'

'Your gratitude?' She took his outstretched hand and shook it, feeling distinctly puzzled.

He nodded, pulling out a chair and sitting down opposite her. 'Yes, for stepping in and taking over after Stefano's heart attack.'

'I had no choice. Somebody had to take over, after all.' But, she was asking herself, what business was it of his what she did here?

'Well, I'm very grateful, as, indeed, I am for your first-aid skills that saved Stefano's life.' Finally he cut to the chase. 'As you may know, I'm the owner of the school.'

'The owner?' This really was news to Debbie. 'You own the school? But I thought Steven...'

'No, Deborah. Steven works for me. I leave all the running of the school to him, but the school is actually mine. I set it up almost exactly thirty years ago. And a very good investment it's been.' He extended his arms out in front of him, interlocked his fingers and stretched his palms towards her until his knuckles cracked. Debbie did her best not to recoil. 'Anyway, apart from my thanks, I wanted to let you know that I've put five hundred euros into your bank account today and I will do the same every week until Stefano comes back to work. Think of it as a bonus – and a thank you.'

'*Signor... Dottor* Montevarchi, that's very kind, but I wasn't expecting anything. Like I said, somebody had to do it, so I did. Anyway, thank you very much.'

He was smiling broadly as he looked around. 'You've even managed to tidy Stefano's office. He won't recognize it when he comes back – if he comes back.'

'You think he might not?'

'I don't know. The doctors told him his valves and his arteries are a mess and, although they've put in some stents, he really has to avoid any kind of stress.' His concerned expression softened for a moment. 'And also avoid alcohol, I believe, which will be a challenge. Anyway, Stefano was sixty this year and so he may decide to take this opportunity to retire. I don't know. We'll see.' He caught her eye. 'Anyway, are you sure you're happy to keep doing what you're doing in the meantime, until we know what's going to happen?'

'Yes, of course.'

Later on, after Doctor Montevarchi had left, Debbie worked out that this represented a pay rise, at least for the moment, of two thousand euros a month – a fortune. She resolved to use some of it to pay down a bit more of her student loan and some of it to take Alice out for a really good meal when she came across at the weekend.

–

Alice and Debbie had a great time together. Debbie had booked tickets for the Uffizi gallery on Saturday afternoon and they emerged from three hours in there quite shell-shocked from exposure to some of the finest works of art ever created by the hand of man. Debbie had been blown away by Botticelli's *Birth of Venus* and had stood, entranced, in front of it until she was elbowed out of the way by a group of French tourists. Even now, in November, the place was absolutely packed.

Debbie had thought about booking a table at the same lovely restaurant in Fiesole, but then she changed her mind. Alice was only here for such a short time, she deserved to experience somewhere different. It was Steven, with a wistful expression on his face, who came up with a recommendation, as Debbie was sitting at his bedside on his last day in hospital. He told her about a restaurant that was typically Florentine and an absolute must for anybody who wanted really fine Tuscan cuisine. She took his word for it and booked a table. When she and Alice got there on Saturday evening, she instinctively knew that it was going to be something special.

The restaurant was tucked into a narrow street, roughly halfway between the Uffizi and Santa Croce. The entrance was quite narrow and led into a fairly unprepossessing bar, beyond which the restaurant was accessed along a narrow passage. As they emerged from the corridor, they both stopped in silent appreciation. The place was huge. The high-ceilinged room stretched away before them and on their right, windows looked out onto a charming court-yard with an ancient well in the middle, surrounded by box hedging.

As this was a special occasion, Debbie insisted that they should go for a full Italian menu with antipasti, followed by fresh pasta, and then a *bistecca alla fiorentina* between the two of them. It was a good choice. The meal was every bit as delicious as Debbie had hoped.

'So, Al, what about you and men? Anything exciting going on?' She set her knife and fork down, deciding that she just couldn't eat another thing.

There was a slight pause before Alice replied and when she did, she sounded uncharacteristically hesitant. 'I don't want to jinx things, but I've been going out with the same man now for almost a month.'

Debbie sat up and took notice. A month with the same man was almost unheard of for Alice.

'I met him, Guy, a couple of weeks after you left and he's rather nice.'

Debbie listened with satisfaction to the details of this tall, athletic, experimental chemist, delighted that her friend might finally have found her Mr Right. As she listened and watched the happy expression on Alice's face, however, she was impressed to find that she really didn't feel envious.

'I'm so very pleased for you, Al. You deserve to find somebody.' She gave her a grin. 'You've certainly done enough research.'

'And you, Debs, are you all right? Not feeling too lonely?'

Debbie shook her head. 'Not in the slightest.' She met and held Alice's eye. 'Really. I've got lots to do at work and I often don't get home until ten thirty or even later. I spend my whole day with people, talking to people. And when I have got a bit of free time, this city's so jam-packed with places to go and things to see, it's impossible to get bored. No, no question of loneliness.'

'And you don't need a man in your life?'

'Nope. After what's happened to me this year on the man front, I'm well out of it. Besides, I'm in love with Byron.' She went on to describe the Labrador and his master and mistress's house. Then Debbie decided to pull her friend's leg a bit.

'And, of course, there's Rory. He's six foot six, built like a barn door and sweet and helpful to boot.'

Alice looked up from her steak, a smile spreading across her face.

'Rory, eh? I knew it wouldn't take you long. So, do I get to meet him?'

Debbie shook her head, a smile on her own lips now. 'He's away playing rugby in Treviso, so you'll miss him. But he's a real hunk.'

'Tall and strong and a rugby player, eh? What colour's his hair?'

'Fairish. A bit like yours.'

'Eyes?'

'Erm, blue, I think.'

'Anything else you want to tell me about him? Anything more intimate, maybe?'

'Not really, apart from the fact that he's gay.'

She enjoyed the momentary expression of surprise, followed by disappointment, on Alice's face.

'Gay?'

'Yes, and he's a bit lonely, I think. I'd really like to help him out if I can.'

Alice swallowed her disappointment. 'Well, isn't there some hunky man you can fix him up with?'

'There are quite a number of handsome men at the school, but they don't really have labels on them, you know.'

'Surely there must be a gay bar around here. Check the internet. You're bound to find somewhere for him.'

When they left the restaurant, it was just starting to rain, so they made their way home to the flat and sat chatting until well past midnight.

Just as they were folding out the sofa bed in the lounge for Alice, they were disturbed by raucous laughter from outside. Debbie went across to the door and peered through the little spyhole. The lights were on and she saw the door of the flat across the landing from her open for the first time since she had moved in. A tall man was standing at the entrance, fully engrossed in kissing and fondling a girl in a very short dress. As Debbie looked on, he tugged the dress up over the girl's bottom and his hands reached for her. At that point Debbie stepped back, deciding that she had no desire to get to know her neighbour, or his girlfriend, any more intimately. A moment later she heard the door slam shut as the happy couple decided to move inside.

She looked back at Alice.

'My new neighbour's arrived.'

'What was all the giggling about?'

'From what I could see, they were thinking about having sex on the stairs.'

'Classy...'

Debbie and Alice were both woken again at around four o'clock by the sound of the door to the other flat as it slammed shut. There was more giggling and then heels clip-clopped down the stone steps, echoing up and down the stairwell. Clearly, Flora's son was a lot less considerate than his mother.

Debbie sighed and drifted back to sleep, vaguely aware that she hadn't dreamt of her special place for quite some time. Of course, now that she could just walk there any time she wanted, she no longer needed to dream.

Chapter 10

Debbie and Flora went out for tea on Wednesday afternoon as usual. This had become a regular event and they were experimenting with different cafés to see which appealed to them most. It was a cold autumn day, but it was dry, although the sky was grey and rain was forecast for later that evening. Today it was Debbie's turn to choose the café and she had decided to take Flora to the Giubbe Rosse, where she and Steven had had dinner on her first night in Florence. She also chose the route to get there.

'The café I've chosen is in Piazza della Repubblica, but if you don't mind, we'll do a little detour by Via de' Tornabuoni on the way there. There's a fabulous clothes shop that I'd like you to see. It's quite unusual, as they only ever put one or two outfits on display at any one time and there's never a price anywhere. And they're always jaw-droppingly gorgeous. As you know all about fashion, I'd like you to tell me how much you think they might cost. If they're as pricey as I imagine, that'll save me wasting my time going inside and being turfed out again.'

'The shops in Via de' Tornabuoni are among the most expensive in Florence, but we'll see.' Flora's eyes were sparkling, as if something amused her.

When they reached the shop, Debbie saw that, this time, there was just one dress in the window– a stunning light grey evening gown, pretty obviously made of silk. She studied it in awe for a few moments before turning towards Flora.

'Isn't that just the most amazing dress? I told you they had fabulous stuff here.' She noticed that same amused expression on her friend's face once more. 'What is it? Is it going to cost the absolute earth? Am I wasting my time even dreaming of buying something like this?'

'As far as I recall, this gown retails for around six thousand euros.' Debbie couldn't restrain a gasp of astonishment, but Flora went on. 'You've got very good taste, Deborah. Come in and have a look around. I'll show you some of the items from our spring collection.'

'*Your* spring collection? You mean…?'

Flora was grinning more broadly now. She pointed to the oval glass panel above the door. On it was a simple logo consisting of just two letters entwined: *FG*. 'My maiden name was Galli, Flora Galli, so when I set up the business I just used my initials.'

'Your company is FG?' Debbie had never been particularly fashion-conscious but even she knew that name. 'Wow, I didn't realise you're FG. You're a household name.'

The glass door was locked, but as the immaculate doorman spotted Flora, he sprang into action, opening the door and holding it as they went inside.

'*Buongiorno, Cristoforo.*'

'*Buongiorno, Contessa.*' He bowed formally towards Debbie. '*Signorina.*'

Flora led Debbie in through the entrance hallway and up three marble steps into a large bright room, decorated in a combination of the palest greys, pinks and greens, no doubt as an homage to the Duomo just a few hundred metres along the road from here. It looked less like a shop than anything Debbie had ever seen. She could have been in a film star's bedroom.

'Now then, come and take a look at these.' Flora led Debbie across to the far side and started picking dresses from a rail. Debbie's eyes widened. It was like being inside the pages of a fashion magazine.

'Flora, good afternoon. I'm so glad you've come.'

Debbie and Flora turned as one to find a tall, slim, dark-haired lady at the door. She was probably the same age as Flora, maybe in her late fifties, and, like Flora, she was a very good-looking woman. Debbie wondered if she might even have been a model in the past.

'Barbara, ciao. Deborah, I'd like you to meet Barbara. She's our marketing manager, based here in Florence. Barbara, this is my good friend, Deborah.'

They shook hands, but Debbie could see that Barbara had something on her mind.

'Flora, we have a problem.' Barbara glanced at her watch. 'In ten minutes' time we've got that group of American buyers arriving on the train from Milan and Miren's just let us down.' She quickly corrected herself. 'Sorry, that's not fair. Miren's mother's been knocked off her scooter and she's been rushed to hospital and Miren's had to jump on a plane back to Madrid to be with her. Anyway, the net result is that we haven't got anybody to model the clothes for them.'

'Poor thing. I do hope she's all right.' For once, Flora looked bothered. 'What a pity. We really needed her.' She glanced across at Debbie. 'These people from New York are really big. They've got stores all the way up and down the eastern seaboard. They've been at a fashion show in Milan and they're making a special stop here in Florence just to see us, en route to Rome. Miren's a fabulously beautiful Spanish model we engaged specially for this event, and now she's out of it.'

As Flora was explaining, Debbie began to get the impression that she was being watched. She turned towards the door and saw Barbara's eyes on her, giving her a close and clinical examination.

'Flora, your friend here... Deborah, she looks like a pretty perfect 40 to me.'

Flora nodded. 'And to me. Deborah, what size are you in the UK?'

'Um, 8, I think. I haven't bought new clothes for so long, I'm not sure.'

'Well, don't worry. We'll measure you up.'

Debbie swallowed hard. She was beginning to realise where Barbara might be going with this.

Flora already had. 'Tell me, Deborah, have you ever done any modelling?'

Debbie blinked and then found herself giggling. The idea was so preposterous.

'No, never. Somehow I don't think that's for me.'

'Why not? You're very beautiful, you're tall, and I love your long hair.' Debbie saw Barbara and Flora exchange glances. 'Anyway, look, are you busy for the next hour or so?'

Debbie shook her head, still refusing to believe what appeared to be happening. 'No, but...'

'Would you be prepared to help us out by hanging around here for a bit? It could be they won't want to see any of the items on a model, but just in case.' Flora caught Debbie's eye. 'You'd be doing us a great favour.'

'I really don't know...' Debbie was in a quandary. On the one hand, she knew she owed Flora a lot and wanted to help her but, on the other, the idea of standing around, posing, while people stared at her was very, very scary.

'They may be quite happy just seeing the dresses on hangers.' Barbara was doing her best to sound encouraging. 'You may not need to do anything.'

Taking a deep breath, Debbie nodded, blessing the instinct that had made her put on the new underwear she had bought only last week.

'Of course I'll help out, and I'll do my best. I just hope your lovely clothes look good on me.'

The next hour was without doubt one of the most stressful of Debbie's life. In comparison, being observed by a British Council inspector as she did her best to make an assorted group of septuagenarians understand the difference between the present perfect and the present perfect continuous tenses was as nothing.

The American contingent was composed of three stern-faced ladies and they definitely wanted to see a number of items modelled by Debbie. Fortunately, it turned out that she was, as Barbara had predicted, a pretty perfect size 40, and even she herself had to admit that some of the stuff looked really good on her. In all, she had to leap behind the screens and change into eleven separate dresses in the space of less than half an hour. By the end of the session, she was flushed and perspiring.

As Barbara led the ladies out of the room and downstairs to Giacomo and the Mercedes to take them back to the station, Flora came round to give Debbie the good news.

'They loved the new collection and they loved you, Debbie. You were marvellous. Thank you so very much. You really did us a huge favour.'

'Thank goodness for that. I've never been so terrified in all my life.'

'It didn't show.'

'Tell that to my antiperspirant.'

Flora laughed. 'So did you like the dresses? Which did you like best?'

Although the garments she had worn had included the spectacular evening gown in the shop window, Debbie knew which one she had liked best, by far. It was a very simple, slightly formal dark blue dress with a demure V-neck and she had loved it. It had felt as if it had been made for her. She explained to Flora and saw her nod.

'This one, you mean?' Flora took it off the rack and slipped it off the hanger, letting it hang over her forearm, smoothing it with her other hand. 'I couldn't agree more. We're selling a lot of these. It suited you down to the ground. You looked delightful in it.' As she spoke, she located a very swish-looking carrier bag and slipped the dress inside. 'Here, take it with our thanks. You got us out of a hole and we're very grateful.'

Debbie was almost speechless. 'There's no need for that, Flora, honestly. I was glad to help.' She did her best to refuse the gift, but Flora's powers of persuasion were too good.

'Take it, please, Deborah. I'd really like you to have it. You've definitely earned it.'

—

The following Saturday, Debbie went to Flora's for tea once more. This time, as well as Byron the dog, she found somebody else there. It was Barbara from the FG shop.

Debbie fought off the amorous attentions of the Labrador as she shook hands with Barbara, and saw her smile.

'Deborah, hello again and thanks again for helping us out. Flora's been telling me all about you. I gather you're the principal of the English school.'

'Temporary principal.' Debbie went on to recount what had happened to Steven. 'So there's lots to do, but I have to say that I'm enjoying it.' She glanced across at Flora. 'Don't get me wrong – I love teaching. But I find I also enjoy the admin side of things: you know, dreaming up new courses, thinking of advertising slogans and so on.'

'Deborah's a very good teacher.' Flora was quick to add her endorsement and Debbie gave her a smile.

'Thanks, Flora.' Debbie transferred her attention back to Barbara. 'Did the Americans place a decent order?'

'They placed a terrific order. They were really impressed with the clothes and with you. You know what one of them said? She said it was so refreshing to see clothes being modelled by somebody real.'

'Real?'

'Professional models can suffer from dead eyes some-times. You know – it's just a job and they're just a clothes horse. You, on the other hand, were a living, breathing real person and they loved that.'

'You've left out trembling and sweating.'

Barbara laughed and carried on. 'The shop you came to is also our head office. That's where all the design and marketing gets done and where we sell to trade customers.' Barbara exchanged glances with Flora. 'Flora and I were wondering if you might like to help us out again from time to time.'

Debbie looked up from the dog who, by this time, was lying on the floor at her feet, grunting happily as she scratched his tummy with the toe of her shoe. 'Me? Dressing up again?' She wasn't too sure how she felt about that. Her baptism of fire had been pretty terrifying although, deep down, she had rather enjoyed herself, in a strange kind of way. 'You'd seriously like me to model clothes for you again? But I don't know a thing about fashion.'

Flora joined in on the side of her marketing manager. 'Think of what the Americans said. You bring a freshness to the industry. You'd definitely be wonderful. You've got a very elegant way about you, you know.'

This was an adjective that Debbie would never ever have dreamt of using to describe herself. For a moment she wondered what Alice would say if she heard this.

Flora carried on. 'What we need is a tall, slim model who can come in to our head office in Via de' Tornabuoni from time to time to model clothes for special clients.'

'Special clients?' For a moment, Debbie had an image of dirty old men sitting staring at her as she paraded round in flimsy underwear.

'Mainly trade buyers, like the Americans.' Barbara maybe noticed her hesitation as Debbie heard her try to sound encouraging. 'Like I said, Deborah, we sell most of our clothes to the trade, including some of the best-known department stores around the world, including London. From time to time, just like last Wednesday, when we have a new line, we like to be able to show important buyers what the clothes look like on a real person, not just on a hanger.'

'But surely you have real models who can do that...? Like, what was her name? Mireille?' Debbie couldn't understand why they should consider her, a total novice, for this kind of thing.

'Miren. Of course. We have a string of professional models like Miren we can call on when we have fashion shows, but that's not the same. We need somebody close by who can just pop in for half an hour every now and then. The best professional models live in Milan or Rome, or even further away like Miren. By the way, her mum broke her pelvis, but she's going to be all right. The thing is, it's just not feasible to bring them down here just for an hour or less. You see – your apartment and your workplace are barely five minutes' walk away from Via de' Tornabuoni. You'd be perfect.'

Flora echoed the sentiment. 'You'd be just what we want.'

'I'm sure you aren't interested in money, but the pay would be quite good.' Barbara then went on to name an hourly rate that almost made Debbie's knees go weak. 'And, of course, if there's anything you see that you like, you could have trade rates for any clothes you want to buy.'

'Erm… how often do you think you'd need me? I'm really very busy at the moment.'

'It wouldn't be very often. Say, half an hour once or, maximum, twice a week. Some weeks, nothing at all. As I say, it would only be for very special clients.'

Debbie stared down at the dog, desperately trying to think of a valid excuse, but nothing came to mind. There was no doubt – she owed Flora a big favour. So there wasn't really any way she could say no. Besides, the extra money would come in very handy. She took a deep breath.

'All right, I'll try it. But please keep a close eye on me, and don't be afraid to tell me if I'm doing it wrong.'

'That's wonderful, Deborah, and you'll be excellent, I'm sure. Thank you so much.' Flora gave her a big smile.

'Super, Deborah! You couldn't stand up for a moment, could you?'

Debbie did as asked and felt Barbara's eyes on her body again. It was an uncomfortable feeling, but she knew she would have to try to get used to it. 'Could you drop in some time on Monday and I'll get one of our girls to measure you up properly? We need to be sure of your exact size and shape.' She glanced across at Flora. 'And she looks pretty well perfect to me. Now, your lovely long hair is delightful, but could we maybe send you to a salon just to tidy it up? At our expense, of course.'

'Yes, I suppose so.' Debbie suppressed a smile. Alice would be glad to hear this after so long.

'Excellent. We'll get it sorted out for next week. Thank you so much.'

Flora reached over and patted Debbie's wrist. 'And don't worry. You'll enjoy it, I'm sure.'

The following week, Debbie found herself in the hands of a very pricey hairstylist, followed by a manicurist and, scariest of all, Britta, the ex-model. Britta was Danish, even taller than Debbie and, although she was probably well into her forties, she was stunningly beautiful, in a rather forbidding way, with platinum blonde hair, a quarter of which had been shaved off, leaving just blonde stubble above her right ear.

It was Britta's job to teach Debbie the basics of how to stand, turn and walk. Although on the face of it this all sounded pretty simple, it was complicated a hundredfold by questions of posture, even breathing, and the addition of often frighteningly high heels. By the end of half an hour with Britta, Debbie was a nervous wreck.

It came as a great relief to find that her next session as a model turned out to be much less intimidating than the preparation. She was called in to model a selection of the following year's summer fashions for two smiley Japanese ladies who didn't say a word. Half a dozen times Debbie paraded in front of them and then disappeared behind the screens to change clothes as fast as possible. All the while, the Japanese ladies sat immobile, occasionally scribbling on clipboards or sipping tea, smiles firmly in place. Afterwards, Barbara told her these two were responsible for fashion buying for the best-known chain of department stores in Japan – and they had liked what they had seen. Debbie went off feeling relieved and even beginning to think she might quite enjoy this very profitable sideline.

Her main job, meanwhile, continued to occupy her fully, often for twelve hours a day. Although Steven had been released from hospital, he didn't come in to work, and Giancarla told her she was taking him food and generally looking after him. Of course his absence meant that Debbie had to do all his work as well as her own, but she found she enjoyed it a lot. Student numbers continued to rise as new classes were formed and soon the new teacher, Sam, had a full timetable.

Sam was a tall, gangly boy from Southampton who had been teaching in South Korea for the past three years. His decision to return to Europe, partly prompted by Korea's belligerent northern neighbour, had coincided with Debbie's advert for a teacher, and he was proving to be very good at his job. He was also proving to be very popular with the students and staff – in particular, Debbie noticed, with Rory. Pretty soon the two of them were inseparable and Debbie found herself wondering whether this friendship might lead to something more significant. Certainly, Rory was looking happier these days and Debbie was delighted for him.

Over the next few weeks, she was called in twice to model clothes for trade clients and, the more often she did it, the more relaxed she began to feel about being a human clothes horse. The people, Americans and Canadians, were far more interested in the clothes than they were in her, and she soon managed to feel quite detached from the comments she was hearing. Whether compliments or criticism, she very quickly learnt not to take them personally. She did her best, however, to avoid falling into the syndrome Barbara had described as *dead eyes* and made a point of doing her best to look animated. According to Barbara and Flora, her work was greatly appreciated and the orders continued to flood in.

The end of November approached and the days grew ever shorter. The weather finally turned, and a wave of cold, damp air descended upon Florence. She invested some of her spare money in a wonderful warm duck down jacket and some lovely new boots. Walking past the Duomo, huddled into her coat and scarf, it was hard to believe that only a few months earlier the temperature had been in the mid thirties.

Debbie loved her new flat more and more, although she saw very little of it. She was up early most days and often didn't get in until eleven or later. The only downside was that, annoyingly, from time to time, she was woken by noise on the stairs as Flora's son brought yet another of his conquests back to the flat opposite for a tryst. On one particularly noisy occasion she very nearly went out to remonstrate with them, after being woken at three o'clock in the morning by squeals and giggles from the landing directly outside her door. But out of respect for Flora, she bit her tongue and said nothing. The following Saturday, on one of her regular weekly visits to the villa for tea and cakes, she toyed with the idea of bringing up the subject of her son, but decided against it. Either Flora already knew he was an inconsiderate so-and-so, or she would be appalled, and even maybe offended, at criticism of a member of her family.

However, noises in the night aside, Debbie really did love her flat and she was immensely grateful to Flora. The fact that she could walk out of her door and straight into streets and squares that had been frequented by Michelangelo himself was enchanting. Apart from the obvious must-see places like the Duomo, she never ceased to be amazed by little discoveries she made almost every day. She learnt early on that it was always a good idea to look upwards. She soon discovered statues, frescoes and curious architectural features on so many buildings she had previously dismissed as run-of-the-mill. Every day she spent in Florence increased her love for the city and its illustrious past.

From time to time she walked up to the rose garden if she felt she needed a bit of peace and quiet and, every time, she came away feeling more relaxed. As she put it to her mother during one of her regular weekly phone calls, she was starting to feel as if she belonged.

Then, one Saturday night, around mid-December, all hell broke loose. From about ten o'clock onwards, Debbie started hearing footsteps and voices on the stairs. A few glances out of the little spy hole confirmed her worst fears – her neighbour was having a party. She deliberately stayed up, watching an old black and white movie on TV until one o'clock, before heading for bed. Although she finally managed to get off to sleep, she was woken a couple of hours later by a cacophony of noise and the sound of breaking glass. Pulling on a jumper over her pyjamas, she went to the door and opened it.

She was greeted by a scene of Bacchanalian confusion. A girl wearing a sparkly silver dress and just one shoe was slumped on the top step, shards of broken glass from a smashed champagne bottle spread around her. The door to the neighbour's flat was wide open and somebody had turned the music up to its maximum. Some sort of unidentifiable Europop song was belting out so loud that the glass pendants of the chandelier were dancing. Three people of indeterminate sex were locked in an erotic huddle against the far wall and she could see a familiar tall figure leaning against the doorframe, smoking a cigarette. Debbie had had enough.

Slipping on her shoes, she gripped her jumper tight about her and stormed across to confront him. As she came up to him, he blew a cloud of smoke in her face and gave her a welcoming smile, accompanied by a blast of alcoholic breath that almost stripped the skin from her face.

'*Ciao bella*. Where've you been hiding?'

Flora's son was a reasonably good-looking man, around her age, but he was clearly very drunk, or worse. Her rage boiled over and she gave him an earful.

'I live over there on the other side of the landing and I'm sick and tired of the way you think you can just do whatever you want, at whatever time of night you want, and you couldn't care less about anybody else.' If she had been speaking English she might well have used considerably stronger language, but her teacher hadn't taught her much in the way of Italian invective. Even so, she thought she caught sight of something on his face – guilt, maybe?

'Oh, did we wake you?' He took another long drag on his cigarette, but at least this time turned his head away before exhaling. 'I'm very sorry about that.' He didn't look it.

'Listen. I'm very, very tired. Either you take this party into your flat and turn that music right down or I'm going to call the *Carabinieri*. They might be very interested to know where the smell of marijuana's coming from.'

His expression turned to one of concern.

'There's no need for that. We're just having fun. Don't you ever have fun? Why don't you come and join us?'

'You've got one minute and then I'm making the call. And I'm very tempted to call your mother as well.'

'My mother?' He looked bemused, maybe worried.

'You heard me. Just grow up and try to behave like a decent human being, will you? Try showing a bit of consideration to others. Don't just think of yourself. Right: one minute, starting now.'

She marched back across the landing and closed the door securely behind her. As she stood there waiting, wondering whether she should in fact carry out her threat to call the police, she could feel her pulse racing. She was beginning to realise what could have happened to her, dressed in her pyjamas, in the midst of a bunch of strange people – most of them drunk or stoned, or both.

As it was, she didn't have to make the call – at least not this time. To her relief, the music was suddenly cut off and she heard mutterings and movement on the landing. Seconds later, the door opposite closed remarkably quietly, and peace returned to the building.

The next morning when she got up, it was to find that somebody had cleared up the broken glass and a semblance of normality had been restored. Considering that a minor victory, she decided not to say anything to Flora on this occasion, hoping her son would have learnt his lesson.

Certainly, for the next few weeks, peace and quiet returned to the building and Debbie heaved a sigh of relief.

–

The school closed for a two-week break over the holiday period, and Debbie flew home to spend Christmas with her parents in Bristol, followed by New Year with Alice in Cambridge. Everybody commented on her newly-acquired elegance – her auntie actually used that very word – and Debbie was secretly rather pleased. The stylist in Florence had hardly touched her hair, just cut it a bit, but it looked so much better as a result. And, of course, with some of the new clothes she had bought, and the amazing dark blue dress Flora had given her, she felt really rather stylish.

One evening, while her dad had gone down to the pub for a pint, she and her mum were having a chat. The subject of her appearance came up and Debbie sought her mother's opinion.

'Mum, do you think I'm pretty?'

'Of course you are, dear. You've always been a good-looking girl.'

'The thing is, since going to Florence and, in particular, since starting doing the modelling work, people keep telling me I'm beautiful. Of course, in that world, everything's over the top and they bandy words like beautiful about all the time. You know me – I've never really been interested in what I look like before, but I'm beginning to find I really rather like dressing a bit better and looking after myself. Does that make me superficial?'

Her mother smiled at her. 'If your appearance is the only thing in your head, dear, then yes. But that's not the case, and you know it. You've got a very responsible job – and I know you're good at it or you wouldn't have been able to step in when the principal was taken ill. You're a sensible, intelligent girl and if you happen to look good as well, then that's just a bonus. Of course you're not superficial.'

'I mean, it's not as if I went looking for a modelling job. *They* asked *me*, after all.'

Her mother gave her a reassuring pat on the arm. 'Of course they did and you don't need to worry about looking good. Just watch out for the men. When they see a pretty girl, they're only after one thing, you know.'

After her experience in August, Debbie didn't need to be reminded of this.

The next day, hesitantly, she told her mum and dad about her blossoming friendship with Flora and her husband, the count. To her surprise, her father didn't go off on one of his famous rants against the aristocracy. He normally ended up accusing all those who had inherited wealth of being chinless wonders, or having been born with silver spoons in their mouths. Instead, he sounded impressed by the fact that Flora had worked hard to build up her own business and clearly tolerated the fact that her husband had a title as just being one of many strange things done by foreigners. Debbie heaved a sigh of relief.

Her mum was fascinated to hear all about the villa and its furnishings and both she and Debbie's dad had to agree that Flora had been very decent in offering such a lovely centrally-positioned flat to their daughter at preferential rates. And both of them liked the sound of the Labrador.

On New Year's Eve, Debbie went up to Cambridge and met Alice and her new man, Guy. To her relief, she found him pleasant, friendly and, although he was pretty good-looking, definitely unlike Alice's normal choice of paramours. She was really pleased that her friend appeared to have chosen wisely – for once.

In return, Alice was clearly impressed by Debbie's new, more stylish, persona and very complimentary about her clothes and her appearance.

'Blimey, Debs, you've finally done it. So, who's the lucky man?'

'No lucky man, Al.' She went on to relate her experiences as a fashion model and Alice nodded sagely.

'I told you you'd got the bum for it. And your hair – just look at it now.'

Guy tactfully went up to the bar to buy some more drinks, giving Debbie the chance to quiz her friend about the progress of the relationship.

'So, how's it going with Guy? I definitely approve, by the way.'

They spoke every week and Debbie felt pretty sure that Alice was still firmly cemented into the new monogamous relationship. To her surprise, Alice looked decidedly shifty.

'Erm, rather good, actually.'

'What does that mean?'

Alice cleared her throat, now looking really embarrassed. 'Erm, I know it's crazy, because we've only known each other for a couple of months, but he's asked me to marry him.'

'Wow!' Debbie didn't know what to say. 'Wow.' She studied her friend closely. 'And you said...?'

She saw Alice take a big breath. 'Like I say, I know it's crazy, but, well, I said yes.'

'Well, that's fantastic.' Debbie gave her a big hug. 'Have you decided when?'

'He's got the offer of a full-time position from the autumn, so we thought we'd get married this summer and have a good long honeymoon before he gets tied down. I've already spoken to people at work and they're happy for me to take a month off, if I like.' Alice stepped back and looked at Debbie. 'We were thinking about maybe spending some of it in Italy.'

'Terrific idea! Well, you'll definitely have to come and see me.' Debbie was delighted for her. Just for a second, a vague sensation of regret passed through her as she thought for the first time in ages about Paul and her own abortive wedding. But she shook the image from her head, just as Alice read her mind.

'And what about you, Debs? You really still off men?'

'Definitely. Besides, Al, I'm so busy these days, I wouldn't have time for a man even if there were one on the horizon.'

'What about your neighbour? Have you met him yet? After all, if his dad's a count, that makes him a countlet or something, doesn't it?'

'I can think of something a damn sight ruder to call him.' She recounted her showdown with him and his friends a few weeks back. 'If that's the way aristocrats behave, I'm glad I'm working class.'

Chapter 11

There was thick snow on the ground when Debbie got back to Bologna airport on the first Saturday of the new year. Florence itself, when she got there, was free from snow, but freezing cold. Fortunately the heating in her flat worked well and she was soon snug and warm. She had thoroughly enjoyed her few days back in the UK, but she genuinely felt a sense of homecoming now that she had returned to Florence.

The next morning, when she surfaced, she went for a walk and, inevitably, ended up in the rose garden. This time the wooden bench was covered with ice and the plants and lawns were shiny with frost. Nevertheless, she rubbed the seat dry with her gloved hand and sat down, tucking her lovely warm jacket underneath her. Her eyes half-closed as she let her mind roam.

She was very happy for Alice and hoped, desperately, that it would all work out for her. Just because she herself had had a bad experience at the hands of Paul didn't mean that the same would happen to her friend. She crossed the fingers on her free hand just in case.

She thought of her mum and dad who had sacrificed so much so that she could go to university. It had been good to see them again and she could feel how pleased they had been to find her looking and sounding happier once more. It would be their thirtieth wedding anniversary this summer and she had decided to bring them out to Florence for a few days to celebrate the event. Apart from a few package tours, they had never really done much travelling, and had never visited Italy. This, she felt, was the least she could do for them.

She even allowed herself a brief thought of Paul and then Pierluigi. These two disastrous relationships had seriously tarnished the previous year but, now, at the start of a new year, she felt a real fresh sense of optimism for the future. She was doing a job she loved – well, two jobs really if she included the modelling thing – in a city she loved and, with a few exceptions, she had met some lovely people. She opened her eyes and looked down across the rooftops. Yes, she was definitely doing something right for a change.

Two days later, as she was locking her door before setting off to school, she heard a noise behind her and saw the door to her neighbour's flat swing open. She glimpsed the broad shoulders and dark hair of the occupant and hurried off down the stairs before she could get roped into a conversation with him. As she neared the bottom of the first flight of steps, she heard a voice from behind her, calling out.

'*Buongiorno e buon anno.*'

She didn't bother to respond, just turned the corner and made her exit. The less she had to do with him, the better.

At the school, she was pleased to find that all was well. Giancarla arrived dead on nine o'clock as always, and the smile was still on her face. Debbie heaved a surreptitious sigh of relief.

'*Buon anno*. Happy New Year, Debbie.'

'And to you, Giancarla. Here…' She dug out the present she had bought in Bristol and gave it to her. 'It's a tea cosy, to keep your teapot warm. It's only a little token, but a very happy New Year to you as well.'

She had bought presents for all the staff, including Bella, as well as Nando the porter downstairs. She had wondered what to get for a while – Virginia and Claire would probably have benefited from some make-up remover – before settling on teacloths. They were easy to carry and everybody used them. Indeed, they could probably even be used for make-up removal if it came to it.

After waving away Giancarla's thanks, she enquired after her boss.

'How's Steven? Will he be in today?'

Giancarla shook her head. 'No, I'm afraid not.' She managed a little smile. 'He hasn't touched a drop of alcohol since his heart attack, so as you can imagine, it's been a pretty miserable Christmas for him.' Her expression grew more serious again. 'But he's really not very well. The specialist wants to see him in a week's time, and I wouldn't be surprised if he tells him he needs another operation.'

Debbie took a good look at her. Although her attitude was much friendlier than before, she was looking strained, and Debbie had a shrewd idea why.

'How're you holding up, Giancarla?'

'I'm OK. It's been a bit stressful, that's all.'

'Did you spend Christmas with him?'

Giancarla nodded. 'Neither of us have got anybody particularly close any more. My parents, like his, are both dead, and my sister moved to Argentina ten years ago. It seemed to make sense to spend the time together, rather than each of us on our own.'

'He's a nice man. I liked him from the first time I saw him, though I can't say I'm sorry he's had to cut down on his alcohol intake. It looked a bit self-destructive.' Debbie wondered if she really should be saying these things – after all, she was talking about their boss – but Giancarla didn't seem to notice.

'Self-destructive… you're right. He pretty much went to pieces over the past few years.'

Debbie remembered what Martha had told her, but said nothing. If Giancarla decided she wanted to talk about her relationship with Steven, she would be glad to listen and help if she could, but she knew it had to come from her.

'And now, do you think he's getting himself sorted out? I mean mentally, not just physically.'

'Maybe, I don't know. We did a lot of talking at Christmas and I think it was good for him – for both of us.' For a second Giancarla glanced up and Debbie had the feeling she was about to say something, but then her head dropped again. 'But, first things first, he needs to get this heart thing sorted out.'

'Of course. Is there anything I can do to help?'

'Just carry on looking after things here, if you don't mind.'

'Of course I don't mind.' In fact, Debbie felt positively cheered by the prospect, although she felt very sorry for Steven. And for Giancarla.

Lessons restarted and Debbie was delighted to see Flora again. As she had expected, she found herself invited for tea the following Saturday afternoon and she accepted willingly. On the Thursday morning, she got a text message from Barbara in Via de' Tornabuoni, asking her if she could come in and model for half an hour at eleven o'clock. Debbie wasn't teaching until the evening, so she said yes.

This time was a bit different from the previous occasions on which she had been there before. As she stepped out from behind her screen, wearing a lightweight summer dress and sandals, she found that today's clients were a woman and, for the first time, a man. As she walked up and down in front of them, she heard them speaking to each other in Italian and she wondered where they were from. She sensed the man's eyes on her body, rather than the clothes, and, for the first time, she began to feel a bit uncomfortable. He was probably ten years older than her, maybe more; a good-looking man, with immaculately styled, suspiciously jet black hair, but with a hint of grey at the temples. His clothes screamed good taste and expense, as did those of his partner. His eyes followed her every move and she repressed a shudder.

Her discomfort increased when she was asked to pose in one of the new range of swimsuits. This costume had a plunging neckline and virtually no back and Debbie wouldn't have been seen dead in anything like it on a public beach. Business was business, however, so gritting her teeth, she slipped into it, checked that it covered everything, and stepped out. This time she could almost feel the lust dripping from the man as she walked past and turned, trying her hardest to be professional, disinterested, aloof. Even so, she could feel her cheeks colour as she sensed his eyes on her body.

Mercifully, this was the only swimming costume she was called upon to wear and it was with a sigh of relief when she heard Britta tell her the end of the session had come. As she dressed once more, Barbara came in to thank her and to apologise.

'These two have a chain of luxury boutiques all around the coast and they buy a lot of our summer clothes. They're among our best customers here in Italy, so we try to look after them. You've probably noticed that Signor Rossi has a bit of an eye for the ladies. If he makes any advances, I'd advise you to say no.'

'Damn right, I'll say no.' Debbie could still feel his eyes on her.

'But if you can do it without insulting him, I'd be grateful. They do a lot of business with us.'

Barbara's warning was timely. As she walked out of the main door, she found none other than Signor Rossi waiting on the pavement for her.

'Deborah. How good to see you. I was very impressed by your skills as a model, considering that Barbara tells me you're really a teacher.'

Debbie did her best to produce, and hold, a smile. 'That's right. In fact I'm on my way back to the school now.'

'Can I give you a lift? I've got a car coming for me any moment now.'

'Thank you, but there's no need. The school's just round the corner from here.'

'I was wondering, Deborah, if you might like to come out for dinner with me one of these days. I'd love to hear more about your life as a teacher of English.'

Debbie had absolutely no intention of going out anywhere with him, so she shook her head. 'That's very kind, but I'm afraid it's a very busy time for me. I appreciate the offer, but no thank you.'

Signor Rossi looked disappointed, and surprised. Presumably he wasn't used to girls turning him down. Debbie capitalised upon his momentary discomfiture to toss him a quick "*buongiorno*" and hurry across the road, away from his clutches. As she walked back to the school, she reflected that there was no doubt a certain type of girl in this business who wouldn't have hesitated to accept an invitation from such an obviously well heeled patron. For the second time that morning, she repressed a shudder.

–

On Saturday afternoon, Giacomo arrived in the Mercedes and Debbie gave him his Christmas present – an Aston Martin T-shirt she had seen in a shop in Bristol. He was surprised and clearly very pleased at the gift and the two of them chatted as they drove up to Fiesole. He told her that Flora's daughter's wedding was now scheduled for April. Apparently this was assuming the proportions of a major event and loads of people would be invited.

Flora repeated this to Debbie when they sat down for afternoon tea. It was the first time Debbie had seen her friend looking stressed.

'What I can't understand, Debbie, is why Claudia wants to invite so many guests. The number's up to about three hundred already. She seems to be inviting anybody and everybody. The last thing I heard was that she wants to invite some random Greek couple that they met on holiday. They hardly know them. I ask you...'

Debbie did her best to be supportive. At her feet, the adoring Labrador was stretched out, paws in the air, desperate for attention. She scratched his tummy as she tried to find some words of encouragement for Flora.

'Surely not all three hundred will come. After all, April's only a few months away now and many of them will have already made plans.' She looked up from the dog. 'Where's the wedding taking place?'

'That's the problem. We thought it could be here. Well, the service would be at the church just up the road in Fiesole first, and then back here for the reception. This is a big house, but there's no way we can fit three hundred in.'

'What about her fiancé, what does he say about it?'

Flora caught Debbie's eye and smiled. 'You haven't met my daughter yet, have you? I'll have to invite you for dinner one of these days so you can meet her. You'll see. When she makes her mind up about something, Claudia's more stubborn than a mule.' She dropped her voice and grinned. 'Takes after her father, you know.'

'So her husband-to-be doesn't get a say in it?'

Flora shook her head. 'He gets to invite his family and a few friends, but be in no doubt, this is Claudia's wedding, nobody else's.' She gave a helpless shrug of the shoulders. 'And her father just agrees with whatever she wants.'

Debbie wondered for a moment what her dad's reaction would be if she told him she expected him to shell out for a three-hundred-guest wedding. She dropped her eyes to the dog and grinned at the thought.

Before she left, she handed Flora her Christmas present, ignoring her protests. She had spent a morning scouring the antique shops around Bristol before she found what she was looking for. Remembering what Flora had said about her husband turning his nose up at anything less than two hundred years old, she had managed to find something she hoped would be suitable. It was a Royal Doulton hand-painted plate, depicting two apples and an orange, with the date stamp of 1793 on the back. It hadn't been cheap, but she felt she owed Flora and her husband so much for their kindness. She left Flora to open it after she had left.

That evening, as she climbed back up the stairs to her flat, she heard footsteps running down towards her. She glanced up and saw the shadowy outline of a tall man with dark hair, dressed in running gear. Recognizing his silhouette, she hastily stopped and fiddled with her boot, eyes down, as he came past. Once again, she heard him greet her and, once again, she ignored him. As the noise of his feet retreated into the distance, she felt a sense of satisfaction. Her opinion of him and his lifestyle was very low and she had no desire to get involved in any conversation with a spoilt, selfish brat like him.

Alas, on Monday morning, she discovered she had an even bigger problem with a man. The previous Friday, Giancarla had informed her with considerable satisfaction that she had signed up a private student for an intensive course of fifteen lessons – three lessons each morning for the whole of the week. In an attempt to put the student off, as they were so busy, she had quoted him an extortionate amount but, to her surprise, he had agreed and paid up there and then.

Debbie had been equally pleased to see over a thousand euros appear on the balance sheet, even though this would mean teaching most of the lessons herself. What she wasn't expecting was to discover that she knew the student.

'Deborah, how good to see you again.'

Her heart sank to her boots and beyond as she looked up from her desk to find Signor Rossi standing over her. She took a deep breath.

'Signor Rossi, what are you doing here?'

He gave her a broad smile. 'I'm off to an international trade fair in New York in ten days' time and I badly need a bit of a refresher for my English. So, are you going to be my teacher? That's wonderful.'

Debbie didn't know what to say. His course of lessons had been booked, full fees paid, and she was the only available teacher. It looked like she was caught between a rock and a hard place. Taking a deep breath, she smiled sweetly.

'That's right. Well, if you'd like to take a seat at the table by the window, we'll make a start.'

She had been intending to take the lessons in one of the empty classrooms, but something made her think that she would prefer to be within calling distance of Giancarla – just in case. Although he was pretty obviously on his best behaviour now, she couldn't forget the lustful way he had looked at her last week, especially when she had appeared in the swimsuit. She got up and went over to the door.

'Giancarla, I'll be doing the lessons with Signor Rossi in here. Please could you hold my calls.' She hesitated. 'I'll call you if I need you.' She was pleased to see Giancarla nod in silent comprehension.

'Of course, Debbie.'

She turned back into the room, but left the door just slightly open so her voice would carry if need be.

In fact, Signor Rossi, or Tommaso, as he preferred to be called, behaved with perfect decorum that day, and every day that week. His English was already pretty fluent and he turned out to be a serious student who did the homework assignments she set him without fail. By the time the last lesson finished at lunchtime on Friday, his spoken English was definitely stronger and her opinion of him definitely higher. It just showed that first impressions weren't always to be trusted.

'Thank you so much, Deborah. You've been a great help. I don't suppose you might feel like reconsidering my offer to take you out for dinner, say tomorrow night?'

Debbie took her time over formulating her reply. Flora had taken her to one side on Tuesday before her lesson and, after thanking her profusely for the antique plate that had, apparently, met with the count's seal of approval, had passed on a snippet of good news. Apparently Signor Rossi's company had placed their biggest order yet for summer clothes. Both Flora and Barbara felt sure this was due in no small part to Debbie's efforts. She had repeated Barbara's warning that he had a reputation as a womaniser, but had also put in a plea for her to be nice to him, if possible.

Debbie looked at him for a few moments. He was shorter than her and, as far as she could see, he wasn't particularly muscular. If it came to a fight for her honour, she reckoned she could take him on and win. He had behaved himself impeccably, after all, and he was an important client for Flora's firm, so, against her better judgement, she said yes, but hastily added a proviso.

'That's very kind, I'd love to, but could we make it an early evening dinner, and somewhere close by, so I can get home early? It's been a very busy week and I'm exhausted.'

'Of course. Would seven o'clock be all right for you? Now, where do I collect you from?'

'It's probably easier if we meet here at seven. I'll be waiting downstairs by the main gate to the street.' She had absolutely no intention of giving him her home address. A meal in a public place was one thing, but she didn't want him anywhere near her flat. Although his behaviour this week had been exemplary, there was something about him that she still didn't totally trust.

He was clearly unhappy with that, but in the end, he agreed, shook her hand and left. Debbie walked out and told Giancarla what had transpired. Interestingly, she, too, was suspicious of him.

'Just make sure you don't let him take you out in the country. Stay in the street lights.'

–

For dinner with Tommaso Rossi on Saturday evening, Debbie deliberately dressed down. Or rather, she covered up. She wore a knee-length skirt and the most conservative top she had. She could see from the light reflecting in the puddles on the roof terrace that it was raining, so she put on her old raincoat and grabbed an umbrella before going out. All she needed was a plastic rain hood over her hair and she could have been her granny. *Fine*, she thought to herself, as she walked briskly around the back of the Duomo to meet him, *this way he can be under no illusions*.

In spite of the weather, there were still the inevitable tourists everywhere, and she found herself in danger of coming round to thinking of them as pests who slowed the city down and got in the way all the time. Of course, she told herself, only a few months ago, she had been one of them herself – and whether the Florentines liked them or not, the prosperity of the city was largely due to the influx of people from all over the country, and the world. Tourism in so many places like Florence was definitely a mixed blessing.

When she got to the school, she found a black BMW parked half on the pavement. As she approached, the driver's door opened and Tommaso Rossi climbed out.

'Deborah, good evening. In view of the rain, I brought the car. The restaurant's not far away, but I didn't want us to get too wet.' He came round and shook her hand before opening the passenger door for her. 'Here, do get in, please.'

Debbie hesitated. Getting into a car with him had definitely not been part of the plan as far as she was concerned. However, the rain was starting to come down harder now and she could see the logic of his decision. Also, the fact that he had only shaken her hand and had not tried to greet her in any more intimate manner had been encouraging. Making up her mind, she did as he said and climbed in.

As they drove off, he explained about a second change of plan. 'I've changed the reservation. The original restaurant's in the pedestrian precinct, so I've booked somewhere a little further out, where there's parking.'

'It's not too far away, is it? I really need to get home early.'

'Not at all. It's at Piazzale Michelangelo, if you know the area. It really isn't far, I promise.'

Piazzale Michelangelo sounded reassuringly familiar, so she did her best to relax as he drove, surprisingly slowly, out of the old part of town, across the river and onto the sinuous, tree-lined avenue that wound its way up the hillside. Somehow, with this sporty-looking car, she had been bracing herself for some crazy macho driving. The fact that he was driving like a normal person helped her relax even more. Maybe she had misjudged him after all.

Dinner was very pleasant and he turned out to be quite good company. He was attentive, interested, and keen to hear about her. Nevertheless, she drank very little and kept a keen eye on her wine and water glasses just in case. She had heard enough stories of date rape and Rohypnol to be very wary. However, as the evening progressed and his behaviour remained exemplary, she gradually allowed herself to relax.

Everything went well until the return journey.

As they were driving slowly back down the hill towards town, he suddenly turned off into a dark side road leading into what looked like a park. Immediately worried, she sat upright.

'What's happening, Tommaso? Why have you turned off?'

'There's something I want to show you, Deborah.' His voice had changed. Now it was strained, full of raw passion, and she felt a sudden stab of fear. The road, by this time, had deteriorated into a rough track and the trees were closing in around them.

'What do you want to show me? Please go back to the road.' She could feel the fear rising as her blood ran cold. This wasn't good. Wasn't good at all.

'Here, see for yourself.' He pulled hard on the wheel and the car slipped off the track into a dense group of trees and bushes and came to an abrupt halt. As the engine stopped, he turned towards her and she caught a flash of his eyes reflected in the orange lights of the dashboard. Without warning, he lunged across and his left hand grabbed hold of her knee and thrust intrusively upwards.

'Stop it, Tommaso! I said stop it! What the hell do you think you're doing?' She could hear the fear in her voice and, presumably, so could he. His eyes glinted once more as he caught hold of her hair with his other hand and pulled her roughly towards him, his left hand now reaching way up under her skirt. She felt a rising wave of panic and then, to her amazement, this was immediately replaced by a surge of anger. First Paul, then Pierluigi and now this bastard – who did they think they were, to treat her so badly?

With her free right hand, she picked up her bag and swung it as hard as she could at his face. She heard an ear-splitting shriek as she did so and vaguely registered that it came from her own lips. As the bag smashed into his face, she drew her arm back again and this time punched downwards into his groin so hard, she felt the bag split open and heard its contents scatter on the floor. This time he was the one doing the shrieking and she felt his hand let go of her hair as he clutched at himself in anguish.

Taking advantage of his temporary incapacity, she scrabbled for the handle and kicked the door open.

Unclipping her seatbelt, she pulled herself out and ran for her life.

She ran blindly at first, slipping and sliding in the wet grass, until she was well away. Finally, she tripped on a steep slope and landed on her bottom. As she lay there, catching her breath, she listened intently, but heard no sounds of anybody behind her. Presumably he hadn't been in a fit state to give chase. What she did hear, however, were cars in the near distance so, pulling herself to her feet, she hurried clumsily through the bushes toward the road. To her delight, she came out of the trees and saw streetlights, cars and, even better, a bus, just starting to pull away from a bus stop. She ran towards it, waving her arms and, to her infinite relief, the driver spotted her and stopped again, the door hissing open as she arrived.

She climbed onto the bus gratefully and thanked the driver. He gave her a quizzical look, but she hurried past. There were only two other passengers on board – what looked like a couple of immigrant street traders with huge bags of merchandise on the floor beside them. They, too, subjected her to curious gazes, but she slipped past them and took a seat in the corner of the back seat.

Her heart was beating wildly, her tights were ripped to shreds and her knees and legs scratched and filthy with mud. Her hair was soaked and she had lost her handbag. Her old raincoat had snagged on something and one of the pockets had been torn open but, apart from that, she was unharmed, physically at least. She wiped the water from her eyes, some of it rain, and some of it tears. She found a damp tissue in one of the pockets and did her best to clean herself up as best she could. All the while, the bus twisted and turned its way down the hill until they were down level with the river Arno once more. Five minutes later, they reached the main station and she followed the other passengers off the bus, her legs suddenly feeling like lead. As she reached the pavement, the driver emerged from the front door and gave her a sympathetic look.

'Are you all right?'

'Yes.' She had to clear her throat before trying again. 'Yes, thank you. It's all right. Nothing happened.'

As she turned and made her way up the road towards the Duomo and home, she found herself wondering why she hadn't told him the truth. A man had tried to assault and maybe rape her and she had been running for her life. By the time she reached the cathedral, she still hadn't managed to produce the answer and she was too tired to care. She took an inordinately long time to climb the stairs to the second floor. It was only when she was finally outside the door to her flat that she realised her keys, along with her purse and her phone, were lying on the floor of Tommaso Rossi's car.

A wave of exhaustion overcame her and she sank to her knees, the tears she had been working so hard to repress finally pouring out. She suddenly felt very cold and very tired. Her hands had started to shake uncontrollably and her brain was incapable of logical thought. She didn't even hear his footsteps until he was standing over her. Only when she heard his voice did she manage to find the strength to look up.

'Are you all right?' There was a pause before she heard him again, this time speaking more to himself than to her. 'Of course you're not all right. Just look at you.'

By this time she had registered that this was a stranger. At first she had thought he was Flora's son from the flat across the landing. He was tall and dark-haired, with the same broad shoulders, but this wasn't the same man she had had an altercation with before Christmas. She would have asked him who he was, but, for some reason, her mouth didn't appear to want to work.

She was vaguely conscious of him moving away from her and the door to the other flat opening. She just slumped there as he disappeared inside, only to reappear seconds later with a couple of thick blankets. He crouched down and she heard his voice again, this time from close by.

'I've brought you some blankets. You look cold. Here, let me help you.' She felt his hands touch her shoulders and she flinched, but then the tiredness returned and she didn't resist as he wrapped one blanket round her shoulders and the other round her legs.

'Do you want me to call an ambulance? Are you hurt?' His voice was kind and caring and, for some reason, this made her start crying all over again.

'Are you hurt?'

This time the message got through and she managed to find the strength to raise her face towards him.

'No, I'm not hurt. I'm just cold and tired.' Her brain began to function once more. 'I've lost my keys and I can't get into my flat.'

'Don't worry, I'll get that sorted out. We'll get you into your apartment. Do you want to come into my flat while we wait?'

Something in her eyes must have struck him, as he immediately stood up. 'There's no need for that. If you're comfortable here, just wait where you are. I'll make a phone call and then I'll make you a hot drink while we're waiting.'

She felt herself nod slowly.

'Do you like tea?'

She nodded again and saw him turn away immediately, leaving her with a sense of abandonment so strong she started to cry all over again. He was back again very shortly, with a steaming mug of hot tea. Even through her befuddlement, she noticed that he had put milk in it, rather than just leaving it black.

As she took the mug from him, she managed a few words. 'Thank you. And you've made English tea. Thank you so much.'

'Well, you're English, so I took a chance.' He was smiling. There could have been relief on his face. 'Feeling better?'

She took a sip of tea and straightened her back. As she did so, the blanket slipped off her shoulders and she felt him pick it up and replace it for her.

'Thank you. Thank you for everything.'

'You're welcome. Giacomo's on his way with the spare keys to your flat. He'll be here soon.'

Debbie felt a wave of relief. 'That's great, thanks.' She drank a bit more tea and felt her brain and her body slowly start to function once again. As her mind cleared, she took a closer look at him. He was squatting beside her, an expression of concern still on his face. It was a nice face and a kind face and she felt comfortable with him, whoever he was.

'Erm, excuse me, but who are you?'

For a moment he looked puzzled. 'My name's Dario. You're Deborah, aren't you? You're friends with my mother.'

'Your mother?'

'Flora Dellatorre, my mother. You know her, don't you?' He was looking more worried now.

Debbie was confused and it must have showed on her face.

He tried again.

'Are you sure you're all right? Maybe I really should call that ambulance. Have you had a bang on the head, maybe?'

Debbie shook her head. 'No, thanks, honestly, I'm fine. But how can you be Flora's son? I've met her son. He and I had a shouting match back before Christmas when he and his friends decided to have a party up here in the middle of the night.'

She saw comprehension dawn on his face, followed by an expression of regret.

'I owe you a big apology, Deborah. That was my cousin, Arrigo. I've been away on an extended European tour, researching a book, and I've only just come back. Before I went off in the summer, I made the mistake of giving him a key in case he wanted to use the flat at any time. When I came back last week I found it had been trashed. I suppose I should have guessed that he and his friends would have made a racket as well.' He nodded to himself. 'That would explain why you've been ignoring me.'

Debbie felt a sense of relief, knowing that the cause of all the disturbance had not, after all, been Flora's son. She took a closer look at the man beside her as she drank the last of her tea. He was very good-looking and, now that she knew who he was, she could immediately see the resemblance to his father, the count. His eyes, in particular, were fascinating – a deep bottle green colour – but, above all, they were kind eyes. She found she was smiling at him.

'I'm very sorry for ignoring you. If I'd known who you were, I wouldn't have, I promise. Here.' She handed him back the mug. 'I feel so much better now. Thank you for the tea, the blankets and the help. I'm in your debt.'

'Don't be silly. It's the least I could do. So, do you want to tell me what's just happened?' His expression was supportive, rather than inquisitive. 'It might help to talk about it.'

Debbie sat upright and rested her back against the door. She hesitated, searching for the right words.

'I've been very stupid.'

'Stupid? Why, how?'

So she told him. She told him how, against her better judgement, she had let herself be taken in by a man she had mistrusted from the start. Her trust had been misplaced and the result could have been so much worse. As she recounted the facts, as dispassionately as she could, she saw his face darken. He looked appalled. Finally, as she reached the end of the story of the bus ride, her walk home and her collapse here on the landing, no doubt as a result of delayed shock, his expression was one of anger.

'It's not the ambulance you need. It's the police.'

'I'm not so sure.'

'What do you mean, Deborah? The man's a monster. He tried to rape you. You've got to go to the police.'

'And tell them what? That I went out for dinner with a man in a BMW, had a meal and a few drinks with him – the waiters in the restaurant will confirm I wasn't there against my will – and on the way back I jumped out of the car and ran off?'

'But he tried to rape you...' His voice tailed off helplessly.

'Says who? It's my word against his. He didn't leave a mark on me. There's no witness, no DNA, nothing. It would be his word against mine.' For a moment a happier though occurred to her. 'In fact, the only person to be assaulted seriously enough to leave marks was him.' She caught Dario's eye. 'With any luck I gave him a black eye when I hit him with my bag.'

Just then there was the sound of running feet and Giacomo appeared up the stairs. As soon as he saw Debbie, he skidded to a halt, an expression of concern on his face.

'Deborah, what on earth's happened?'

She summoned a smile. 'It's all right, Giacomo. I got lost in the park and got very cold and wet.'

He looked relieved, if unconvinced. 'Here, I've brought the spare keys. Shall I open the door?'

Debbie nodded and began to get to her feet. She felt strong hands grab her arms and help her up. She turned towards Dario and gave him a grateful smile.

'Thank you Dario, and thank you Giacomo. I'm sorry my stupidity's disturbed your Saturday evening.'

'It's nothing. Is there anything else you need, Deborah?' Giacomo had opened the door to her flat and was hovering at the threshold. 'I've got the car outside. Do you want me to go to the chemist or anything?'

Debbie shook her head wearily. 'Thank you, Giacomo, but I'll be fine now. I just need a good night's sleep. You go off, now. I'm fine, really.'

'Very well, but you've got my number if you need anything.'

'Thanks, Giacomo. You're very sweet.'

He nodded to Dario and then disappeared back down the stairs again.

'The same applies to me, Deborah. Anything you need – I'm just across the hall.' Dario made no attempt to follow her into her flat and she was relieved. She just wanted to lock the door, take a very hot bath and go to bed.

'Thank you, Dario. You've been so very, very kind. I thought knights in shining armour died out centuries ago.'

'You're very welcome, Deborah. Just one thing – did you say this man's name is Rossi and he's one of my mother's clients?'

'Yes, but let it go. What's happened has happened. It could have been worse.'

'It could have been a hell of a lot worse. Sleep well, Deborah and remember, I'm just across the hall.'

Chapter 12

Predictably, Debbie didn't sleep well. In spite of her feeling of tiredness, she found it very hard to get off to sleep as her brain ran back through the events of the past few hours. She did her best to process just exactly what she was feeling and identified anger, along with disgust, as well as that same sensation that she had behaved stupidly. Of course the fault was his, but she should have trusted her initial judgement. Even Giancarla had sensed something about him that wasn't quite right, but, even so, Debbie had gone ahead and accepted the invitation. All right, it had been out of a sense of duty towards the company, for whom he was an important client, but the fault was hers. Barbara and Flora had even warned her about him.

And, of course, underneath all these other sensations was one of fear — fear of what might have happened, and the recollection of that moment in the car, before her sense of outrage had kicked in and given her the strength to fight back. Just for a few seconds, she had been more terrified than at any other time in her life and she knew the memory of these events would be with her forever.

Her mother's words at Christmas came back to her. *They only want the one thing*, was what she had said. Well, in the case of Rossi, that had been quite obvious. Had it somehow been, at least partly, her fault, for agreeing to be a model and starting to look after her appearance? Had she contributed to the events of that night? Were all men foul, sex-crazed bastards and was she just setting herself up as a target? These were uncomfortable thoughts.

Finally she had drifted off to sleep, but woke repeatedly throughout the night. Even the thought of her special spot in the rose garden didn't seem to help. The experience had scarred her and she knew it would be a scar she would carry for the rest of her life.

When she finally surfaced, the first thing she did was to take another long, hot bath, determined to scrub any residual memory of what had happened from her body, if not her mind. She spent the morning pottering round the flat, ironing clothes and making a big dish of lasagne that would last her for a few days – doing her best to lose herself in household tasks.

Just after eleven thirty there was a tap on the door. She went across and peered through the spy hole. It was Dario from across the landing and she felt a welcoming smile on her face as she opened the door to him.

'Ciao, Dario.'

'Ciao, Deborah. Did you sleep well?' Her expression provided her answer and she saw him grimace. 'I thought not. And have you changed your mind about going to the police?'

She shook her head. 'Like I say, let's just forget it. What's done is done.'

'It's your call, but I still think you should. The man's a menace.' His expression softened a little. 'If it helps, you not only gave him a black eye when you clouted him, you actually broke his nose. Remind me not to get into a fight with you.'

This news came as a great satisfaction to her. So there was some justice in the world, after all. But how…?

'How do you know that? Have you seen him?'

'Yes, and I managed to get him to give me this.' He held up a plastic bag. Inside it was her phone, her wallet, her keys, and the rest of the contents of her handbag.

'But how…?'

'I got his address from Barbara at Mum's office. He lives just outside Pisa. I borrowed my sister's car and it only took three quarters of an hour to get over there this morning.' He handed her the bag. 'His wife was at church, so I didn't have a chance to talk to her, but at least I can confirm that he looks like he's had a bad road accident – probably what he told his wife.'

'His wife?' Debbie didn't know what to say. She was doubly appalled now. 'Dario, I wouldn't like you to think I'm the kind of girl who'd go out with somebody else's husband. I had no idea.'

'Of course you didn't. Barbara and Mum both know what sort of rat he is.' He gave her a little grin. 'But at least he's a rat with a broken nose.'

Debbie gazed down at the bag of her belongings. 'I don't know what to say. You shouldn't have done that for me. It could have been dangerous.'

Just for a fraction of a second she spotted a glint in those amazing green eyes. 'Don't give it a thought. With hindsight, it's probably just as well you broke his nose. The way I was feeling, I might just have done it for you.'

Suddenly aware that they were still standing on the landing, she opened the door fully. 'Would you like a coffee? I bought myself a new coffee machine for Christmas and, if I say so myself, it's really rather good.'

'I'd love one, but only if you're sure. You maybe prefer to be on your own? We can do coffee another time.'

She stepped back. 'No, really, it's the least I can do, and I'd like the company.' As she spoke, she realised she meant it.

He came in and sat down, looking around appreciatively. 'I'll tell you this, Deborah, this place is a hell of a lot tidier than it ever was when Claudia was living here.'

'Please, my friends call me Debbie. Now, how do you like your coffee?' This, she knew by now, was an essential question for any Italian. Everybody appeared to like it in subtly different ways: with hot milk or cold, lots or little, sugar or not, double strength or whatever.

'I've just come back from Paris, Berlin, London and a few other places. While I've been away over the past few months, I've drunk so much awful coffee, I can't tell the difference any more. I'll take it as it comes.'

'I normally go for a little espresso with just a tiny splash of cold milk.'

'*Macchiato freddo*. Perfect.'

She busied herself with the coffee machine and soon the wonderful aroma filled the air. She handed him one of her new little coffee cups and sat down across the table from him, looking out of the window. The overnight rain had stopped and the sky was a very pale blue. It looked cold out there.

'So, why have you been going round Europe, if you don't mind me asking – business or pleasure?' As she posed the question she took a closer look at him. He was probably a couple of years older than her, maybe early or mid-thirties. He had the lean appearance of somebody who looked after himself and she remembered she had

188

seen him going off for a run. The sleeves of his jumper were pulled up, exposing a pair of strong forearms. She realised that he most probably could indeed have broken Rossi's nose if he had wanted to.

'I've been doing research for a book I'm writing.' He sipped the coffee and pronounced it excellent. 'Nothing terribly exciting. My subject is history of art. I could bore you with the details, but most of my friends' eyes glaze over as soon as I start trying to explain.'

'I'd like to hear about it. I've always been interested in history of art. That's one of the reasons I've been studying Italian.'

'You speak it very well. *Complimenti.*'

She switched to English. 'So, presumably you speak English as well as Italian?'

He replied immediately and seamlessly.

'Nowadays it's a necessity. Besides, I did my PhD in London.'

Just for a moment, an image of Pierluigi crossed Debbie's mind, but it immediately disappeared again. She concentrated on Dario. His English wasn't just good. It was excellent, near native.

'Wow, I can see why your mum's in my top class. It must run in the family.'

He shook his head. 'I cheated. We had a Scottish nanny for years.' He grinned at her. 'Fiona's been like a second mother to me. I still correspond with her and try to go over and see her when I can. In fact, my English – albeit with a Scottish accent – was apparently better than my Italian when I went to elementary school. They all thought I was a foreigner. In fact, for years, until I was in my teens, my nickname at school was *l'Inglese* – ironic really, when you think that Fiona was Scottish.'

Debbie had never met anybody who had had a nanny before and this rather reinforced the vast social divide between them. She wondered what her dad would say if he ever heard about this or about Dario's parents' chauffeur and housekeeper. Surreptitiously, she glanced at Dario's chin. It was strong, with just a hint of a Kirk Douglas dimple in it. Certainly her dad would be on thin ice if he tried to describe Dario as a chinless wonder. The thought cheered her.

'So, what about you, Debbie? What brought you to Florence?'

She hesitated. 'You really want to know?' Seeing him nod, she found herself revealing the secret of her special place. As she did so, she found herself questioning just why she was telling this man she barely knew such an intimate thing. Maybe last night's events had created some kind of bond between them. It was strange because, apart from her mum and Alice, she had hardly told anybody about it. As she described what it had come to mean to her, and how she had decided to come over to Florence to seek it out, she checked his face for scepticism or ridicule. Far from it. He looked deadly serious. When she finished, he caught her eye.

'I must go up to your rose garden myself one of these days. I'd like to see if it has the same effect on me. I'll tell you a secret: when I was a little boy, I had my own special place, just like you. In my case it was… is… a strange little grotto in the garden. I've never been able to work out if it's a natural rock formation or some kind of manmade shelter of some kind, but it was a special place to me. I used to go off and hide there when the boys at school had been bullying me for being "English". I think we all need a place like that every now and then.'

Debbie gave him a big smile. He smiled back, drained the last of his coffee, and stood up.

'I'd better let you get on. Thanks for the coffee. I gather from my mother that you're very busy at the moment, so I won't encroach on your free day. And remember, I'm just across the landing if you need anything.'

'Thanks, Dario, I've enjoyed talking to you. Really. And next time I'll expect to hear about your book. I promise my eyes won't glaze over.'

Chapter 13

The next week was chaotic. Both Virginia and Claire were off with flu and Debbie found herself teaching a double timetable. Fortunately, Rory stepped in and increased his hours and, between them and the other teachers, they just about managed to cope.

To make matters worse, Debbie got a text on Monday afternoon, asking her to come in the next morning to model the summer range for a group of buyers from China. She wasn't teaching that morning, now that her private lessons with Tommaso had finished, so she went along at half past ten as requested, although the idea of exhibiting herself in public again filled her with very mixed feelings. When she got there, she found Barbara waiting for her, an anguished expression on her face.

'Deborah, Dario told me what happened. I'm absolutely appalled. I knew Rossi was a *donnaiolo*, a womaniser, but I never thought for a moment he'd resort to physical violence.'

Britta appeared at her shoulder and, to Debbie's surprise, proceeded to wrap her long arms around her and give her a warm hug, followed by kisses on the cheeks.

'All men are scum, Deborah. Remember that.' Britta squeezed her again before releasing her. 'Scum.'

Debbie caught Barbara's eye. 'Well, maybe not all men, but to be honest, I haven't met too many good ones recently.'

Barbara smiled. 'There are still some good ones out there, you know. They're just few and far between.'

Britta snorted and strode away.

All went well with the Chinese contingent and, although the group was composed of men as well as women, Debbie sensed no repeat of the lascivious gaze of Tommaso Rossi, to her great relief.

It took her until the end of the week to find the time to pop out and buy a bottle of good malt Scotch as a thank you present for Dario. She had seen his mother at school that week and Flora had given Debbie a big hug, whispering in her ear how sorry she was for what had happened with Signor Rossi. She invited Debbie for tea on Saturday afternoon to talk about it.

When Debbie got home on Friday evening, feeling pretty worn out, she dumped her jacket, picked up the bottle of whisky, and walked across to Dario's door. She rang the bell and waited, but there was no response. A few seconds later, just as she was turning to go back to her flat, she heard footsteps and saw Dario running up the stairs towards her. His face broke into a smile as he saw her.

'Hi, Debbie. I gather from my mother that you've had a busy week.'

'I'll say. But at least it's over now and I've got the weekend to rest and recuperate.'

'She tells me you're going to her place for tea tomorrow.'

'That's right. Are you going to be there, too?'

He shook his head and she felt a sense of what could have been disappointment.

'No, I'm going skiing with a bunch of mates, so I'll be away all day.'

'That's a pity, although I'm sure you'll enjoy the skiing. Listen, I'm sorry it's taken me so long, but here's just a tiny little present to say thank you for your knight in shining armour act last weekend. I don't know what I'd have done without you.'

'I didn't do anything special, and you're very welcome. There was absolutely no need for a present. Like I told you before: I'm just across the landing from you. If you need anything, just shout.' He glanced at his watch. 'I'd invite you in for a glass of this or something else, but I'm just on my way back out again. We're going skiing in the Valle d'Aosta and it's a five hour drive to get there.'

'You're doing a five hour drive now, tonight?'

He nodded and grinned. 'Yes, I know it sounds pretty crazy. But this way, we get a full day's skiing tomorrow and we miss the worst of the morning traffic.'

'And sleep?'

'I'll make up for it on Sunday morning. By the way, if you're still interested in hearing about my book, and if you're free on Sunday afternoon, there's something I'd like to show you.'

Debbie froze. His use of the exact same words that her would-be rapist had used in the black BMW came as a shock so powerful, it felt for a moment as if she had been slapped across the face. For a split second, she could distinctly feel Tommaso Rossi's hand gripping her hair and she took an inadvertent step backwards, swaying unsteadily. She felt Dario's hand reach for her arm, but she shook it off angrily, turning away.

'Debbie, are you all right?' He sounded puzzled and concerned. Maybe it was his tone – so different from the gruff menace of the other man back there in the car – but it cut through her rising sense of panic and dragged her back to the present. She stopped, turning her head towards him, an apologetic expression on her face.

'I'm sorry.' She had to cough to clear her throat before she could carry on. 'I'm sorry, Dario. Just for a moment there... I...' She hesitated for a few seconds. 'I think maybe I'm not quite as over what happened last weekend as I thought. Give me a shout tomorrow afternoon if you aren't too exhausted. I'd like to hear about your book.'

He still looked worried.

'Listen, Debbie. I could call the guys and tell them I'm giving the skiing a miss if you like.' She shook her head violently, but he continued. 'Are you sure you're going to be all right on your own? I really could stay here if you want. I can go skiing any time. That way, you'd know there was somebody close by if you get spooked.'

'Thanks Dario, that's awfully sweet, but I'll be fine.' She ran her hands through her hair and managed a smile. 'Really, I'm fine. I just had a momentary flashback to last Saturday night. I daresay I'll have more of them before I truly manage to put what happened behind me, but I *will* get over it. And, no, of course you shouldn't cancel your skiing trip. You go off. I'll be OK and you can give me a shout on Sunday afternoon if you aren't still fast asleep. Drive safely.'

'Well, if you're sure...'

'Of course. Anyway, thanks for the offer. That was very kind, but it isn't necessary. Now, make sure you all drive safely.'

She waved goodbye as he went into his flat. Once inside hers, she rested her back against the door for a minute or two while she collected herself. Finally, shaking herself out of her reverie, she glanced at the time. It was almost nine o'clock. She reached into the fridge, pulled out a bottle of Prosecco and drew the cork with a hiss. She filled a glass and took a big mouthful before refilling it, returning the bottle to the fridge, and picking up her phone. She called Alice.

'Hi, Debs, how're you holding up?' She had spoken to her friend several times already this week, grateful to be able to talk through the events of last weekend. As ever, Alice had been a rock, providing support and comfort.

'Not too bad, Al. What about you? How's your Guy?'

'My Guy's great, thanks, but what about you… really? Are you over the shock of what that bastard tried to do to you?'

Debbie recounted her reaction to Dario's invitation and Alice was quick to offer reassurance.

'You're bound to be shaken up for a while, Debs. But don't worry, you'll get your head sorted out before too long. So, tell me more about Dishy Dario.'

'How do you know he's dishy? I never told you that.'

'I just knew. I could tell from your tone when you talk about him.' There was a momentary pause. 'Well, tell me I'm wrong then.'

'You're not wrong.' Now it was Debbie's turn to pause for thought. 'He's really good-looking, he's intelligent, he's caring and he's got a lovely body.' She hesitated, before clarifying. 'Not that I've seen it in any detail, you understand.'

'So, what are you waiting for?'

'Who says I'm waiting?'

'Deborah Waterson, I know you well enough by now. Of course you're waiting. What could it be this time that's holding you back? How about: he's too handsome, hunky and perfect, and you feel inferior, even though you're currently employed as a model?' Hearing no response from Debbie, she tried again. 'I know – he's a nob and you're a prole, and never the twain shall meet. He's out of your league. Am I getting warm?'

'No… well, yes, sort of… maybe.'

'I knew it. You're digging up all that class business your father's been feeding you. When will you get it into your head that that stuff no longer counts? You're just two people. It doesn't matter these days whether you're big or small, black or white, rich or poor, a prince or a pauper. He'll accept you for what you are and you should do the same for him.'

'It's much more complicated than that, Al. Besides, it isn't as if he's tried to ask me out or lay a hand on me.' She remembered how she had reacted when he touched her arm to steady her. 'The fact is that, after last weekend, I'm only looking for a friend. I'm sick and fed up of being some sort of sex object in the eyes of men.'

'They're not all like that, Debs.'

'That's what they've been telling me here, too, but for now, I'd really like Dario to become a good friend – nothing more. It would be nice to be able to be in the company of a man who isn't just thinking of trying to get me into bed.'

'Well, there is always the gay option. Surely you can find yourself one of them?'

'I've already got Rory for that, thanks.' A thought occurred to her. 'Maybe Sam, the new teacher, as well.'

'No chance your Dario's just a tiny bit gay, is there?'

Debbie had no hesitation. 'Not even a bit, Al. That much I'm sure of.'

'So what are you going to say if he asks you out?'

'I suppose it would depend. Maybe a visit to an art gallery or a museum...'

'That's a start. Remind me to tell you some time what I did in the dinosaur section of the Natural History Museum with Craig, that big Canadian chap, a few years back.' Debbie heard a chuckle. 'I called him Tyrannosaurus Sex from then on.'

'Al, can we just get off the subject of sex, please?'

So, she thought to herself, how did she feel about maybe going to a museum or gallery with Dario? The more she thought about it, the more the idea appealed. She liked him, she enjoyed being in his company, and she knew she would like to keep him as a friend, just like his mother. Well, maybe not *exactly* like his mother.

After the phone call, her mind turned to food. She cut herself a slice of the wonderful unsalted Florentine bread that had fast become one of her favourites. She broke a chunk of Parmesan from a wedge in the fridge, sliced a big tomato and sprinkled it with the thick, green, extra virgin olive oil that she got from Nando, the porter at the school. This, he assured her, was produced by his brother who farmed in the hills around Montespertoli and the result was amazing – it was tangy and fiery, and caught the back of the throat as you swallowed. She sipped her wine as she ate, reflecting on her conversation with Alice.

Alice hadn't been too far off the mark when she had talked about a class divide. Somehow, Debbie felt sure that her kind and Dario's kind were just too different. Quite probably, when his father died, Dario would become Count Dario. The idea of her father ever coming to visit their family villa at Fiesole and seeing their opulence was unimaginable. And just what elegant, immaculate, stylish Flora would think of her mum, with her silver curls and her clothes bought at Cribbs Causeway, was equally unpredictable. But there was more to it than that.

Although she didn't quite share Britta's damning opinion of the whole male population, the fact remained that her luck – if that was the right word – with men had been pretty dire. After the way she had been treated by Paul, then Pierluigi, and now Rossi, she knew it would take an awful lot before she even began to contemplate forming any kind of new relationship any time soon.

And finally, the touch of Dario's hand on her arm earlier on tonight had caused a seismic shock to run through her body – and not one of pleasure. Somehow, the idea of getting physical with a man filled her with revulsion, whether round the back of a dinosaur in the Natural History Museum, or even in a five-star hotel room, overlooking the snow-covered Alps, with an open fire blazing and champagne in a silver ice bucket at the bedside.

She really had had it with men.

–

On Saturday afternoon, Giacomo came to pick her up at three. By this time he had heard the true story of what had happened and his reaction was similar to Dario's. Once Debbie had managed to convince him that there was no point in going to the police, his next reaction had been to suggest collecting his friends and going round to Rossi's house to duff him up. It took the whole journey and a lot of persuasion by Debbie before she talked him out of it. Still, she thought to herself, it was rather nice to be surrounded by supportive men for a change.

When they got to the villa she gave him a kiss on the cheek.

'You're very sweet, Giacomo, but I'm fine. Nothing happened.' If she kept on repeating that mantra, hopefully she would start to believe it.

Another friendly male then greeted her effusively. As Flora opened the door, Byron came charging out to meet her, his tail wagging so much his whole body was weaving from side to side. He skidded to a halt at the top of the steps and rolled onto his back, legs kicking furiously in the air. She stopped to give him a cuddle before straightening up again and making her way over to Flora who, unusually today, was accompanied by her husband.

'We were very sorry to hear of your bad experience last weekend, Deborah.' The count extended a welcoming hand towards her. 'Quite unforgivable.'

She shook it and then hugged Flora. Both Flora and her husband looked appalled. Debbie did her best to make light of it.

'Never mind, nothing happened. I'm just furious with myself for trusting a man like him. And luckily your son was on hand when I got home, to offer moral and practical support.'

'Yes, Dario said you were badly shaken up.' Flora took Debbie by the hand and led her indoors. The Labrador came barging in past them and earned himself a telling-off from his master in the process.

They went into the sun lounge as usual and Debbie had to retell her tale. On the one hand she was beginning to get a bit fed up with repeating the events of last Saturday but, on the other, she was finding that it became a little bit easier each time. Maybe talking was part of the healing process. Finally, she managed to drag them onto a different topic. It was not, however, an uncontroversial topic: their daughter's forthcoming wedding.

'The list of invited guests is now three hundred and thirty.' Flora sounded incredulous and distinctly peeved.

'Three hundred and thirty-two to be precise.' The count didn't sound any happier.

Debbie repeated what she had said before. 'But surely not all of them will be able to come. We're January now, and April's just round the corner.'

'Claudia's convinced they'll all come.' Flora was looking as stressed as Debbie had ever seen her. 'And if they do, I really don't know where we're going to put them all.'

Debbie glanced out of the window. Although they were on the hillside, there was a flat area of lawn directly in front of the house. 'Back home, lots of people hire marquees. You could have one out there on the lawn, surely.'

The count's expression made clear what he thought of that as an idea.

Tea arrived and the conversation changed to less contentious matters. Debbie noticed the plate she had brought from England standing on an old bureau, and the count waxed lyrical about her choice. It turned out that he was something of an expert on English china in general, and Royal Doulton in particular. Apparently, more by luck than by design, the plate she had found had turned out to be quite a collector's item. She heaved a silent sigh of relief that he seemed genuinely pleased at her choice.

It was as she was about to leave that Flora mentioned something that set bells pealing in Debbie's head. They were talking about holiday destinations and Flora happened to mention that Claudia and her husband-to-be had had a wonderful holiday in Greece. When Debbie asked where they had been, Flora told her it had been a rented villa, with a swimming pool, on the island of Santorini.

'Greece in the autumn is delightful. I think I might look into it for us for next autumn. What do you think, Enzo?'

The count was still mulling it over as the Mercedes arrived and Debbie took her leave of them, her brain also churning – *Santorini!*

As they drove out through the gates, she tried checking with Giacomo.

'Um, Giacomo, do you know Claudia's fiancé?'

He shook his head. 'Not really, to be honest. I never drive them anywhere. They always drive themselves. I've seen him a couple of times. He's a tall guy with dark hair.'

'Do you know his name?'

Giacomo racked his brains for a minute before admitting defeat. 'I should do, but I've forgotten. To be honest, back home we just refer to him as Claudia's fiancé.'

Debbie did her best to hide her frustration.

'Do you know what he does for a living?'

Giacomo answered immediately.

'Yes, he's a doctor.'

Chapter 14

Debbie spent the rest of that evening thinking about what she had heard. She kept telling herself that it was probably just a coincidence that Claudia's husband was a doctor and that they had been on holiday in Santorini. Surely lots of doctors went to Greece for their holidays. She even checked on the internet, which confirmed that there were a good number of villas to rent on the island, complete with their own private swimming pools. But all the while an annoying little voice in the back of her head kept repeating the name: Pierluigi.

The following morning, as she did most Sundays, Debbie started by doing the ironing, tidying the flat and thinking about preparing food for the week. Today she deliberately chose something complicated, so as to occupy her mind with something other than the prospect of receiving confirmation that she had, in fact, spent most of one week last August in bed with Flora's future son-in-law.

It didn't bear thinking about. If this turned out to be the case, what should she do? Should she seek Claudia out and break the news that her fiancé had been cheating on her, or should she say nothing and have to live with her conscience for the rest of her life? And what if she

204

ever met the happy couple? It was an appalling choice to have to make.

For now, as a displacement activity, she chose to prepare something she had never tried before – something she really felt anybody living in Italy should be capable of doing. In one of the kitchen cupboards she had found a box, and inside it was a shiny, little-used pasta maker. Daunted, but not deterred, she set out to make her own fresh pasta.

After spending a long time on the internet, checking and comparing advice on how to do it, and an even longer time trying to read and attempt to digest the instructions in the 24-page booklet that accompanied the hand-cranked machine, she set about the task.

Making the initial mix was ridiculously easy and, before long, she had two impressive-looking rolls of pasta ready to go. That was when hubris struck and it all suddenly started to fall apart. Either her mix was too dry and hard, so that she couldn't turn the handle, or it was too wet, and rapidly assumed the proportions of a highly effective glue, or possibly mortar. Either way, the machine was soon bunged up good and proper.

She had to make a complete fresh start on two separate occasions, after spending ages cleaning out the machine that she was rapidly coming to hate, loathe and detest, before she finally managed to get it more or less right.

This took her most of the morning and definitely fulfilled her objective of stopping her from agonising over the identity of Claudia's husband-to-be. Midday was just sounding on the church bells outside her window as she finally finished, and she had two nests of soft pasta, now sliced into imperfect ribbons, on the table before her.

It was at that moment that she heard the doorbell. She glanced down. It looked as if a flour bomb had gone off in the kitchen. Her hands were sticky with dough and she was covered in flour and bits, all the way up to her elbows. The floor at her feet was little better and she could feel things attached to her face where she had scratched or rubbed herself without thinking. Grabbing a cloth from the sink, she wiped her fingers sufficiently so she could turn the door handle, but had no illusions as to the impression she would present to any visitor.

'Wow, you look as though you've been busy.'

It was a very suntanned Dario. He looked clean, tidy and very handsome. She flicked her eyes downwards and noticed a spot of dough on the end of her nose. However, as soon as she wiped it off with the back of her hand, she saw that she now had a white nose. She nodded weakly.

'Oh, yes, I've been busy all right. I thought I'd try something new.'

'You've been trying your hand with the pasta machine, at a guess.' His face split into a grin. 'Not easy, is it?'

'It's bloody near impossible.' She glanced back over her shoulder. 'Two hours to make the pasta, and it'll need another two hours to clean up the mess.'

Still smiling, he glanced at his watch. 'So, if I call at, say, four o'clock, would you feel like coming with me for a short walk?'

Debbie looked out of the window. It was dry outside, but it looked chilly. The wind was blowing and she could see little vortices of dust dancing in the corners of the roof terrace like tiny tornadoes. Still, it would be good to get out, even though she felt pretty sure they would end up in a museum. Relegating any thoughts of Alice and dinosaurs to the back of her mind, she nodded.

'I'd like that. Do you have anywhere special in mind?'

'See if you can guess.'

'Seeing as it's your speciality, I presume it's got something to do with history of art?'

He nodded.

'Is it a gallery?'

He shook his head.

'A museum?'

He shook his head again. 'Not really, but you're on the right track. I'll put you out of your misery. It's just a couple of blocks away in Via Cavour, not far from the Duomo. It's a fabulous Renaissance palazzo, built fifty years before Columbus set off for America. There's a fresco in there I'd like you to see.'

'Terrific. I promise I'll be a bit cleaner next time you see me. And you can tell me all about your ski trip. Now, if you don't mind, there's a train wreck behind me to be sorted out.'

–

At bang on four o'clock, she heard the doorbell. Picking up her winter jacket and her gloves, she went over to open the door.

'Hi, all clean again?' He was wearing a thick anorak.

'Yes, but that's the last time I try my hand at making pasta for a good long while. Talk about tricky.'

Dario led her out into the street and from there into the Piazza del Duomo. The huge bulk of the cathedral loomed over them as they walked round the back of it. The tables and chairs outside the restaurants were stacked up and the people they met were all huddled into their warmest clothes as a bitter wind cut into them. Debbie was very glad of her wonderful cosy jacket and her gloves.

As they walked, Dario told her about the previous day's skiing in Cervinia. Although the weather down on the plain of the river Po had been grey and misty, they had risen above the clouds and had a perfect day, skiing in the shadow of the Matterhorn. He glanced across at her.

'Ever been skiing?'

Debbie shook her head. 'Only once, on a dry ski slope. It frightened the life out of me. It was when I was still at school and we went as a group. One of the boys almost ripped his thumb off and I vowed I'd never go near a pair of skis again.'

'That's a shame. With the new skis these days, or snowboards, it's got a lot easier. Any time you feel like trying it, just say the word. I'd be happy to give you some lessons.'

Just then they turned off the square and found themselves heading straight into the full force of the wind. Debbie screwed up her eyes and hunched her shoulders, pulling the collar of the jacket up to cover her ears, rather regretting having left her woolly hat behind. Fortunately, it was only a matter of minutes until they reached their destination: a massive fortress of a building, situated on a corner, the bottom part of the walls made up of imposing blocks of rough stone.

'Welcome to the Medici Palace. Or as it's called now – the Medici Riccardi Palace.' Dario led her through the huge entranceway into a dark courtyard and through it to another, this time open to the sky high above. It was freezing cold there, but at least they were now sheltered from the wind. She was relieved when he carried on across the open courtyard and through doors to a stone stairway leading upwards. He flashed a pass of some kind to the lady on duty who waved them through. Here, at last, it was warm again and Debbie unzipped her jacket and pulled off her gloves.

'So, Dario, this was where the famous Medici family lived?' She knew the name well. 'They were one of the most powerful families in Italy in the, what, fifteenth century?'

'That's right, the Medici were very definitely among the movers and the shakers in the 1400s.'

They were walking along a corridor and Debbie looked around. It was nice, but not stunning. 'So why have you brought me here?'

'I thought you might enjoy looking at a bit of historical propaganda. The Medici were really good at self-promotion and they were just about the first people to invent "fake news" to hide their dirtier deeds.'

Just then they reached an unimportant-looking door and he pointed. 'This way, please, *signorina*.'

'*Grazie, signore.*' She smiled at his mock formality.

Debbie found herself in an unexpectedly small room. The ceilings were high, but the room itself was no bigger than the living room in her apartment. What was striking, however, was the fact that the walls of this room had been completely covered by frescoes. By the look of them, they had been restored fairly recently, as the colours were rich and vibrant.

'What you're looking at is the fifteenth-century equivalent of having a big photo on your wall of yourself, standing alongside the Queen. Or Elvis. Or both.'

Debbie studied the huge, brightly coloured frescoes with interest. A large group of men, some on horses, most on foot, were walking along a rocky path, with a backdrop of hills and fields. The men on horseback, and the horses themselves, were dressed in the finest silks and satins, and gold sparkled everywhere. Clearly these were men of substance.

'So which one's Elvis?'

She looked across at Dario and couldn't miss the expression of awe on his face as he stared up at the images. He turned his face towards her and smiled.

'Take your pick. The fresco's called *The Procession of the Magi*, but it actually depicts the Emperor and the Patriarch of Constantinople on their way to Florence, invited by the Medici. If you know what to look for, you'll see that the painter, Gozzoli, has included the faces of most of the major players of the day, including, naturally, the Medici themselves.'

'Sort of like a huge medieval selfie.'

'Exactly. And everybody who visited the Medici was brought here to this little chapel to "pray" – but in reality, it was so that they could see just how powerful their hosts were.'

'And this is important for you and your book?'

'Very much so. And, by the way, it wasn't just the Medici who were good at self-promotion. Just in case you were in any doubt as to who painted it, Gozzoli's written his own name on his hat. That's him over there.'

As her eyes strayed across the fresco, Debbie noticed something strange. So strange, in fact, that she leant across the rope cordon so as to get as close as possible to it. There was no doubt about it. One of the men looked exactly like Dario. The likeness was quite uncanny. She turned back towards him.

'Am I seeing things?'

He stepped forward, his shoulder brushing against hers as he did so.

'What're you looking at?'

She pointed with her finger. 'There, just to the right of the guy on the white horse, the man with the red plant-pot hat on. He's you.'

'Me?' Dario stretched towards the fresco to see for himself. 'I see the guy you mean. I suppose there is a bit of a resemblance. Who knows?'

'A *bit* of a resemblance? He's your spitting image.'

Dario turned back towards her. 'I'll take your word for it. You might be right, you know. I've read that one of my distant ancestors, Lodovico Dellatorre, was a close associate of the Medici. Maybe that's him there.'

Debbie shook her head in wonder. Here she was, Debbie Waterson from Schooner Street, Bristol, in the company of a Florentine aristocrat, whose relatives had kept the same company as the Medici. She glanced across at him while his attention was once more on the fresco. She didn't need her father to tell her there was an abyss between the two of them. Just like each time she stepped into the big Mercedes, she felt like the fraud she was. Who did she think she was to be rubbing shoulders with people so far out of her league?

They spent half an hour in the palace, admiring these and other paintings, including some amazing frescoed ceilings, before heading back out into the cold again.

'Fancy a drink?' Dario stopped as they came out of the main gate into the full force of the wind. It was quite dark now and, if anything, even colder than earlier.

The sensation of being a fish out of water that the fresco had aroused in her was still strong, but she couldn't deny the fact that she was enjoying his company. And she was freezing cold.

'I'd kill for a hot chocolate.'

He nodded approvingly. Crossing the road, he led her into a narrow side street where the bulk of the surrounding buildings provided a degree of shelter from the wind, but Debbie wasn't sorry when they reached a café and went inside. It was an old-fashioned café on two levels, with smart waiters and waitresses dressed in black and white, and it had a cosy feel to it. In here it was very warm, crowded, and quite stuffy. They found a table and she stripped off her jacket. Her hot chocolate, when it arrived, was exactly what she needed – thick, syrupy and so hot it nearly burned the roof of her mouth. As she cradled the hot cup in her hands and sipped at it, she listened as he told her more about his book.

'The book's about power in the late medieval period, especially here in Italy. In particular the way the big players managed to massage the truth to make it mean whatever suited them. And whatever helped them to stay in power.'

'*Plus ça change, plus c'est la même chose.*'

'Absolutely. Of course, the Catholic Church has to take most of the credit. They were the original experts in faking it.'

Debbie listened with interest to what he had to say. Clearly, he knew his stuff and enjoyed talking about it.

She was still having trouble with the idea that she was in the company of a descendent of one of the noble families he described as "big players", but she did her best to repress that same sensation of being a phoney. Above all, it was just nice to spend time with a handsome man with whom she felt completely safe. He talked at length about his subject and in the end she had to remind him to drink his cappuccino before it went completely cold. As he did so, she responded.

'Fascinating, Dario, and look – my eyes haven't glazed over even a tiny bit.' She gave him a grin. 'So, how come you know so much about that period?'

'That's my job. I work in the history of art department at the University of Florence. My speciality is the late Middle Ages and the Renaissance.'

'No shortage of raw material here in Florence for you to study.'

They spent the best part of an hour in the café and she felt a pang of what could have been regret when the time came for them to leave.

'I was thinking – I don't know what your plans for tonight are, but I've got a load of fresh pasta that needs eating. If you feel brave, would you like to help me eat it?'

'That would be brilliant, but only if it's no trouble. You've had a hard week and I daresay next week'll be tough as well.'

'I've got to eat, and cooking for two's no harder than cooking for one.'

'Well, yes, thank you then. I've got some ham I can bring if you like.'

'I never say no to some good Tuscan ham.'

They decided to eat at seven o'clock so she would be able to get to bed early for a good night's sleep. When he arrived at her door, he was carrying a plate of ham and olives as well as two bottles of red wine. As he came in, he sniffed the air.

'Pesto? Is that what I can smell?'

Debbie nodded. 'I've got a basil plant I bought back before Christmas and somehow it's managed to survive, so I've just made the pesto now. I've been meaning to do it for ages and I'd already got a packet of pine nuts. I hope you like it. At least it'll be fresh.'

'Well it certainly smells great. Shall I open one of these bottles or would you like something else? I'm afraid I've only got a few bottles of fairly ordinary white left in my flat, because all the good stuff got drunk by my beloved cousin and his noisy friends. I bought these a couple of days ago as a stop-gap until I can persuade my dad to let me have the keys to the cellar up at the villa. He's got some amazing stuff in there.'

'Some red'll be great, thanks. There's a corkscrew in the top drawer.' She busied herself with the pasta. 'Your parents' villa's the most amazing house I've ever been in. Don't you miss it, living here in a flat? I know it's a lovely historic flat in a gorgeous location, but it's not quite in the same league, is it?'

'This place is just so convenient for work. I'm actually in the process of renovating an old farmhouse in the hills outside Florence, but it's a real labour of love and it's taking forever – especially with me having just been away for three months.'

'You're doing it yourself?' Debbie was impressed. She would have imagined that with all his family wealth, he would have had a team of architects and builders on the case.

He nodded as he opened the wine. 'As much as possible by myself, yes. I love doing it, to tell the truth.' His eyes caught hers for a moment. 'I suppose I'm a bit of a hermit, really. There's nothing I enjoy more than a quiet day in the country knocking down walls or whatever.'

'Knocking down walls doesn't sound very quiet. But what about the technical stuff? Do you do all that yourself, as well?'

'I don't touch electrics or plumbing, but most of the rest of it's been down to me.' He gave her a grin. 'Not that I'm showing off or anything, but I'm a pretty good plasterer now.'

'*Complimenti*.'

To Debbie's considerable relief, the pasta and the pesto turned out to be really rather good. She wasn't too sure how long it would take to cook, so she kept on checking it every few seconds and realised it was ready after just a couple of minutes. As a result, they ate the pasta first and his wonderful ham afterwards, with some pecorino cheese. The wine – a Chianti Classico with the *gallo nero*, the black cockerel, on the neck of the bottle – was excellent, although Debbie limited herself to just one glass as she knew, as he had predicted, that she would probably have a busy week coming up and she wanted to start it with a clear head.

At the end of the meal, she found a packet of cantuccini and a bottle of Vin Santo that one of her students had given her for Christmas and they sat dipping the biscuits in the sweet wine and nibbling them as they continued to chat. She toyed with the idea of asking him about his sister and the identity of her fiancé, but the opportunity never really arose, and she didn't want to appear too nosey. Besides, she felt sure she would be able to get the information the following weekend when she would meet up with Flora again. Claudia and her forthcoming wedding were topics that were bound to come up and she would find a way of wheedling his name out of her.

What she would then do with the information remained to be seen.

What she did discover about Dario was that he was four years older then her, recently turned thirty-three, that his hobbies were squash and skiing and, apart from his old farmhouse renovation project, his main passion in life was art history. At no stage did he mention a girlfriend, fiancée or wife and Debbie told herself firmly that she wasn't interested.

What she did find, however, was that she got on very well with him, aristocrat or not, and she had already added him to her list of friends – very high up the list as well.

Chapter 15

Debbie was early into work on Monday, hoping to clear her desk of all the things she hadn't had time to sort out the previous week. Virginia and Claire phoned to say they were feeling better and would be back that afternoon, and Debbie heaved a sigh of relief. As a result, life would become a bit less hectic for everybody, and for her in particular.

When Giancarla arrived, she told Debbie the result of Steven's latest visit to the specialist and confirmed that another operation would be necessary – this time some pretty complex heart surgery. Debbie was quick to offer support.

'I'm sure he'll be fine, Giancarla. Try not to worry. They can do amazing things these days.'

Giancarla smiled gratefully. 'Thank you, Debbie. I know he's in good hands, but it doesn't stop me worrying.'

'You like him a lot, don't you?'

There was a little pause before Giancarla replied, her voice little more than a whisper.

'I've loved him for half my life.' Debbie saw her wipe the back of her hand across her eyes. 'I thought I was over all that, but I'm not.' She looked up into Debbie's eyes for a few seconds, her own glistening with emotion. 'I really thought I hated him, but I was wrong.'

'And how does *he* feel?' Debbie kept her voice low, desperately hoping she wasn't intruding into matters that were too personal.

'He told me he never stopped loving me.' Giancarla looked up again. 'We did a lot of talking over the Christmas period. He asked me to give him another chance.'

Debbie would dearly have liked to ask her what she intended to do, but she thought it best to let Giancarla work that one out for herself. Instead, she asked for more detail of the upcoming operation and discovered it would be in the next few days, but nobody knew when, or if, Steven would be fit to return to work. Debbie told Giancarla she was happy to carry on as she was at present, and she really was, in spite of the long hours. Besides, the extra pay was going a long way towards starting to make real inroads into her student loan debt.

By the end of their conversation she felt closer to Giancarla and, more importantly, she got the impression Giancarla was closer to making some big decisions. Debbie hoped for the sake of both Giancarla and Steven that things would work out well for them.

On Tuesday night, when she got home, she found a note slipped under her door from Dario.

Thanks again for the pasta on Sunday. I seem to remember you saying that you finished early on Wednesdays. If you're free tomorrow, I've got to go to a champagne reception at the Palazzo Vecchio for a delegation from the European Union Fine Arts Commission. It's at eight and it will be crushingly boring, but your company would make it a lot more tolerable for me. In return, afterwards maybe I could take you out for dinner and bore you some more with tales of the Renaissance.

Dario

Now that things had calmed down after the flu outbreak the previous week, Debbie was only working late on Tuesdays and Thursdays. Those nights she was at school until ten, but on the other three nights, her lessons finished at seven thirty. She had no other commitments this Wednesday, but she slipped off her jacket and sat down at the kitchen table to consider her response all the same.

She liked Dario. In fact, she liked him a lot and she was very grateful to him for all the help he had given her. She enjoyed his company and she felt sure she would have a good time with him if she said yes to his dinner invitation. The question occupying her mind was whether she should accept. Dinner together on Sunday and then dinner together again three days later was maybe a bit too cosy. She didn't want him to get the wrong idea about their relationship, which for all sorts of reasons couldn't go anywhere. She liked him but, at least for now, she really didn't want to get too close to him, or any man. Her scars were still too fresh. Besides, as she had told Alice, she and he were from two totally different backgrounds, and she felt sure it just wouldn't work.

After a cup of tea and a lot of thought, she took her courage in both hands and headed across the landing to his door, wondering if he would be in. He was.

'Hi, Debbie, want to come in?'

'I'd better not, thanks, Dario. It's late and there's stuff I've got to do.' She didn't tell him she had yet to eat, in case he insisted on returning the favour after Sunday. 'I just wanted to say thanks for the invitation for tomorrow night. Of course I'll be happy to keep you company at the reception thing, but I'd better say no to dinner.' Crossing her fingers, she added her invented excuse. 'I'll have a load of homework to mark before Thursday, so I'll need to get back straight afterwards, or else I'll be up until all hours.'

For a second, a flash of disappointment crossed his face, and then he was smiling at her again.

'Well, maybe some other time. That's great about the reception though. Thanks, I owe you.'

'Not at all.' A thought occurred to her. 'Is it going to be a dressy affair? Presumably not just jeans and a jumper?'

'I've been told to wear a suit, so I suppose you'd better glam up a bit. Not that you don't look absolutely lovely just as you are.' His gallantry would have been more convincing if he hadn't winked at her as he said it.

'Straight from school with whiteboard marker pen ink all over my fingers? It's the latest fashion on the catwalks. All right, I'll put on a dress tomorrow. Where and when do we meet?'

'Shall we go from here at eight fifteen? I'll come and knock on your door?'

'Great. See you then.' She left him and returned to her flat, the expression of disappointment she had noticed on his face still worrying her. She really didn't want him to get the wrong idea about this relationship. They were friends, hopefully good friends, but she did so hope it wouldn't become complicated by feelings. She really couldn't cope with any more feelings for a while.

She had a modelling session the next morning at ten for two rather haughty-looking ladies from Paris. It was almost impossible to read their expressions and it was with relief that Barbara told her afterwards that they had been very pleased and were placing a big order. Debbie took advantage of Barbara's presence to quiz her on what she should wear for the reception that evening. As it turned out, Barbara was also going to be there with her husband.

'It'll be very showy. There'll be quite a turnout of the great and the good of Florentine society there, so you'd better make sure you look the part.'

'I was thinking of wearing that gorgeous dark blue dress you and Flora gave me.'

Barbara stepped back and studied Debbie for a few moments, her thumb stroking her chin.

'Yes, that would look good, but I've got another idea. How do you feel about strong colours?'

'Depends on the colour, I suppose.'

'I was thinking about blue again, but lighter than the other one. In last year's winter collection we had a fabulous peacock blue dress, classic fit, square neck, long sleeves. We sold out in the space of a couple of days as I remember, but we should have the original still here. Just give me a moment.'

Barbara was back within a minute, carrying the dress. Debbie took one look at it and immediately fell in love. It was amazing. It was quite obviously made of silk and the colour was the most perfect rich blue. Peacock blue, Barbara had called it, and it did, indeed, remind Debbie of peacocks she had seen.

'Here, it's a 40. Your size. Try it on.'

Debbie slipped out of her clothes and into the dress, feeling it adhere to her body as she pulled it up her legs.

'*Squisita*.' Debbie heard Barbara's voice from behind her back. 'You look exquisite. Take a look at yourself in the mirror. It fits you like a glove.'

Debbie walked over to the mirror and surveyed her image. There was no getting away from it; she looked really good.

'I love it, Barbara, but it's got to be way out of my price range. It's silk, isn't it?'

'It's the very best silk as well. These retail at just under four thousand euros.' Debbie almost fell over. 'It's last year's stock, though,' Barbara continued, 'so you can have it for a thousand or, if you prefer, you can wear it, bring it back and just pay for the cleaning.'

'Barbara, that's terrific. I can't possibly afford to buy it, but if I can just borrow it for tonight, that'll be wonderful.'

–

Before going out that night, Debbie couldn't resist taking a couple of photos of herself in the amazing dress and her highest heels. She sent one to Alice and one to her mum, wondering what she and her dad would think of it. She had curled her hair up onto her head in the quick and casual way Britta had taught her, with just a few fronds hanging down one side of her face, and had resisted adding any jewellery. She reckoned she looked pretty good, but if she had had any doubts, they were instantly dispelled when she opened the door to Dario and saw his reaction.

'Wow.'

'That's all? Just "wow"?' She grinned at him. 'How about, "Good evening, Debbie"?'

'Good evening, Debbie.' His voice sounded as if somebody had been grabbing him by the windpipe.

'So, will I do?'

'*Porca miseria*, you look amazing.' He still sounded half-choked.

By the time she had picked up her coat and put it on, he appeared to have regained the power of speech, even though his vocabulary was still very limited.

'Debbie, you look absolutely wonderful. Wow.'

Together, they went down the stairs and into the street. She was relieved to find that her recent experience as a part-time fashion model had made her a lot less uncertain on her feet when wearing heels and she managed to negotiate the stone slabs of Via del Proconsolo without too much difficulty. Beside her, Dario finally regained control of his vocal chords and explained what would take place this evening.

'There'll be half an hour or so of standing around, drinking warm champagne and talking to people whose names I've forgotten. It's all right for you. You probably won't know anybody, so you won't have to worry about names. Then some random Eurocrat will make a speech about something, and then a random Italian politician will make another speech and, when that's all over, there'll be a mad rush to join the queue for the cloakroom to collect coats before the great and the good disappear into the priciest eating houses in Florence.'

'Do I detect a slightly cynical note in your voice, Dario?'

'Not at all. It's a *totally* cynical note, not a slight one. These things are all the same, even down to the canapés that are just too big to eat in one bite and end up dripping all down your front.'

'I'd better not drip anything down my front. I've just borrowed this dress. It's got to go back tomorrow.'

'Really? It suits you so well, you should keep it.'

'Even with an immensely generous discount, it's out of my league, Dario. Besides, when am I ever going to need a dress like this again?'

'You never know. You're director of a well-known school. Has it occurred to you that your presence here tonight elevates you to the ranks of the chosen few of Florentine society?'

She could see the smile on his face, but she wasn't smiling inside. She was under no illusions that she was only here because she was at his side. There was absolutely no way she was part of these upper echelons of Florentine society. She was a fraud; even if he wasn't prepared to admit it, she knew that's what she was.

The reception went pretty much as Dario had predicted, but with a couple of differences. First, he was wrong in thinking she would know nobody. Standing behind the counter at the cloakroom as they arrived to deposit their coats was none other than Bella, the cleaner from the school. She gave Debbie a big smile when she saw her.

'Debbie, you look wonderful. Absolutely wonderful.' She took their coats and then leant over the counter towards them as she handed them the ticket. 'There'll be a big queue afterwards. You come to that door over there.' She pointed to their right. 'Knock three times and somebody will give you your coats.'

'Three times?' Debbie was grinning.

'Yes, it's a sort of code.'

'That's very kind, Bella. Thanks so much.'

Dario added his thanks. 'Thank you very much indeed, Bella.' Out of the corner of her eye, Debbie saw him slip a banknote into Bella's hand. As they walked off, he lowered his mouth towards her ear. 'Debbie one, Dario nil.'

'The game's only just started.'

He was wearing a dark grey suit and looked very smart indeed. You didn't need to be Christian Dior to recognize that it had been hand-stitched. Debbie suddenly felt glad she was wearing the amazingly expensive dress. She reflected that she and he went together rather well. As friends.

They followed the other guests into the massive Salone dei Cinquecento, helped themselves to glasses of not too warm champagne, and Dario began pointing out some of the many items of artistic interest, starting with the amazing paintings that covered the compartments of the ceiling, crisscrossed by sculpted beams, highlighted in gold. He had just started talking about the paintings by Vasari on the walls, when they were approached by a middle-aged man wearing a dinner jacket.

'Dario, good evening.'

'Good evening, sir. Can I introduce you to my friend and neighbour, Professoressa Deborah Waterson. She's the director of the Florence Institute of English Studies, the best school of English in Florence.' He turned to Debbie. 'This is Professor Archangelo, dean of my faculty.'

Debbie and the dean shook hands and she felt his eyes linger on her body. She did her best to ignore the sensation of repugnance this provoked in her and managed to produce a smile for him.

'I'm pleased to meet you, Professor Archangelo.'

'And I you, Professoressa. And I you.'

He eventually dragged his eyes off her and launched into a conversation with Dario about internal university matters and Debbie's attention soon began to wander. She caught Dario's eye and indicated with her fingers that she would go for a little walk around the room. Leaving them to it, she made her way through the crowd and got her second surprise of the night.

'Deborah, isn't it?'

Debbie turned towards the voice and saw a face she recognized, but it took her a few moments to place the woman. She was very elegant, wearing a dress that certainly hadn't come out of a supermarket, and she was dripping with gold: huge pendant earrings, heavy bracelets and enough rings on her fingers for her hands to be classified as offensive weapons. Debbie got a shock as she suddenly realised who this was. She was none other than the woman who had been alongside Tommaso Rossi when Debbie had modelled the summer collection back at the beginning of the month. Could this be his wife, maybe? She instinctively glanced round for any sign of him and was relieved to see the woman on her own.

'Good evening. You are Signora Rossi?' The woman nodded and Debbie realised she had guessed right.

The woman smiled. 'Yes, and I must say that dress looks absolutely amazing on you.'

'Thank you, and yours is gorgeous, too.' Although in truth, to Debbie's increasingly trained eye, it looked a bit vulgar, not just because of the plunging neckline, but because of the shiny, ostentatious, silver and gold cloth. She risked a question.

'And your husband, he's not here?'

'No, he's still recovering. I'm afraid he was attacked by a gang of youths the other night. He fought them off bravely, but sustained some cuts and bruises, along with a broken nose, in the process.'

'Oh dear.' Debbie kept her face straight. 'And have the police managed to find the culprits?'

Signora Rossi shook her head. 'He's in regular contact with the police, but I believe they're still looking. It could take some time.'

Damn right it could. Debbie didn't know whether to laugh or explode. What a rotten, lying bastard he was. "He fought them off bravely" indeed! It occurred to her that now would be the perfect opportunity to open the woman's eyes to just what a bastard her husband was. Unfaithful and a liar – maybe it was her duty to tell his wife what he was really like, even though she knew this might not be good for Flora's business. She was still debating the right course of action when a man appeared.

He came complete with a deep blue dinner jacket, an expensive suntan, and an even more expensive set of teeth. Debbie felt his eyes flick over her, check her out, and then move on, leaving her feeling almost defiled by the intimacy of his gaze. She was just about to turn away when she saw him slip his arm around Signora Rossi's shoulders, his eyes now drawn magnetically to her cleavage. She looked up and beamed.

'Davide! Here you are at last.'

Signora Rossi looked and sounded very pleased to see him. She wrapped her free arm around him and kissed him on the cheeks – not the usual perfunctory fleeting touch of cheek to cheek, but hard enough to leave the impression of her lips clearly visible on his face as she drew back again.

'Antonia, *carissima*. You look stunning, irresistible.'

There was something about the way he said it that convinced Debbie that he certainly wasn't going to resist whatever came his way. Signora Rossi was staring into his eyes, her fingers now resting against his cheek, and looked ready to ravage him right there, right now.

This, Debbie decided, was the moment to return to Dario – pronto. And as for opening the woman's eyes to her husband's foibles, it looked very much as though the pot calling the kettle black. She gave them both a nod of the head, unseen by the man in the blue suit, whose eyes were once more lost deep in the Signora's audacious décolleté, and went back across the room, shaking her head in disbelief. It would seem, after all, that Signora Rossi and her husband were made for each other.

'If you would excuse me, Professor Archangelo.' Dario gave her a surreptitious wink as he shook hands with his boss and made good his escape, taking Debbie by the arm and leading her a safe distance away. This time, Debbie didn't recoil from his touch and she felt pleased. When he released his hold, she was surprised to find she had rather enjoyed the contact.

'I make that Debbie two, Dario still nil. That's a good system you've developed. If you see me get locked into conversation with somebody again, would you repeat the process? Just wander off for a few minutes and then come back again to call me. If you're feeling creative, you could throw in a line or two like "I simply must introduce you to…" or "you'll never guess who's been asking for you…"' Dario laughed, shaking his head. 'That was great. I thought I was going to be stuck for the whole evening with the dean. Without you, I would have been.'

Debbie gave him a smile as he drained the last of his wine and took her now empty glass from her.

'I think we both deserve a drink.' A passing waiter provided replacements and Dario took a big mouthful of his. 'Getting warmer, but still just about cool enough to be drinkable. So, did you see anybody you know?'

'Well, actually, I did.' Debbie told him about her encounter with Signora Rossi and she saw him roll his eyes heavenwards.

'*Per l'amor del cielo*! I never cease to be amazed and appalled by my fellow man… and woman.' He caught her eye and smiled. 'Well, nobody can accuse you of not being multi-talented. I see you've graduated from school director to fashion model – and now you've become a whole gang of teenage hoodlums.'

'You'd better be nice to me, or I'll get my gang on you.'

'I promise I'll be nice to you.'

They were interrupted by a howl of electronic feedback, followed by the unmistakable sound of a finger tapping a microphone. All eyes turned to the stage. Debbie felt Dario's breath against her ear.

'At least we've got full glasses. Try not to fall asleep.'

In fact, the speeches were over remarkably quickly. From what Debbie could hear and understand, the European delegate thanked the Italian government for doing something, although she couldn't work out what, and the Italian politician then thanked the European Commission for thanking them. At the end, after polite applause – always difficult when holding a glass in one hand – they followed the crowd out towards the cloakroom and Debbie slipped along to the secret door, knocked three times and was impressed to receive their coats immediately. Ignoring the indignant looks of the people in the long queue, she and Dario headed for the exit.

Outside, it was still dry, and though the sky had clouded over and the temperature was maybe a degree or two higher, it was still bitterly cold in the increasingly gusty wind. Dario paused on the top step and turned towards her.

'Home? Or can I tempt you to a bite to eat after all? I notice you didn't risk the canapés.'

Debbie hesitated. Maybe a quick meal with him wouldn't be too compromising. After all, they were neighbours and it was quite normal for neighbours to see each other regularly. Wasn't it? She was still deeply involved in internal debate when he tried again.

'Come on. You must be hungry, surely.'

She made up her mind.

'Yes, I am hungry and stop calling me Shirley.' She saw him smile. 'Go on then, you've twisted my arm, but I really mustn't be late.'

An expression of relief and satisfaction crossed his face and she hoped she had done the right thing. He would know they were just two friends hanging out together, wouldn't he?

'If you want something really, really quick, we can always go and have a burger.' He didn't look enthusiastic. 'Alternatively, I've still got the reservation I made at a place halfway between here and home. The food's good and we can tell them we're in a hurry.'

'That does sound lovely.'

The restaurant chosen by Dario was the sort of place Debbie would never have dreamt of entering. There was just a fairly anonymous door, sandwiched between a shop selling T-shirts and another selling lingerie. The only indication of its identity was a small brass plate bearing two words, *Numero 12* – no menu, not even the word restaurant. She followed him in and up the stairs to a glass door. Inside was the restaurant.

It was a large room with a handsome beamed ceiling and an ancient wooden floor made up of wide oak boards. There were probably around twenty tables in there and almost all were full. She couldn't see a single tourist anywhere. An immaculately dressed man, probably no older than they were, advanced towards them. As he recognized Dario in the subdued lighting, his face broke into a broad smile.

'Ciao, Dario. I haven't seen you for ages.'

He and Dario shook hands warmly.

'Michelangelo, this is my friend and neighbour, Deborah.'

Michelangelo shook hands politely.

'*Piacere.*'

At that moment, another waiter appeared and relieved them of their coats. Then Michelangelo escorted the two of them to a table in the far corner. As they got there, Dario explained the situation.

'We're in a bit of a hurry. What can you do that's going to be quick?'

Michelangelo held Debbie's chair for her as she sat down and then pushed it gently in.

'How about a few slices of ham along with a salad of fennel and parmesan as a starter? Then, maybe *pappardelle alla lepre*? That's quick and won't take much time to prepare. If you're still hungry after that, we can easily do you something on the grill. How does that sound?'

'Debbie?' Dario looked across the table at her.

She had no hesitation.

'That sounds perfect, although I doubt if I'll get past the pasta.'

Michelangelo nodded. 'Water? Still or sparkling?'

Debbie shrugged, so Dario opted for still water.

'Wine?'

Dario glanced at Debbie again. 'Red or white?'

'Whichever you prefer. Red, maybe?'

'Red it is. Michelangelo, could we have a bottle of Villa Antinori?'

As Michelangelo retreated, Debbie breathed in the atmosphere of the place. This was what she loved about Florence. A verbal menu, unusual dishes like raw fennel, and her favourite pasta – the wide ribbons called *pappardelle,* along with the iconic Tuscan sauce made with roast hare.

'Let's see if these *pappardelle* are as good as yours.' Dario was grinning.

She grinned back. 'My *pappardelle*, for your information, were meant to be *tagliatelle*, but I gave up trying to cut the strips any thinner.' She shuddered at the memory. 'That bloody machine! I've been having nightmares about it.'

He looked a bit more serious. 'If those are the only nightmares you've been having, then you're doing well. Are you sleeping OK?'

'Yes, thanks.' She nodded. 'For the first couple of nights sleep was a bit broken, but I'm fine now. Besides, I'm so busy at school at the moment, I'm absolutely worn out by the time I get back home and that helps.' She smiled at him. 'Thanks for asking.'

'That's what friends are for.'

The meal was perfect, exactly what Debbie wanted. The fennel, finely sliced and drizzled with the unmistakable Tuscan olive oil was minty, crunchy and excellent, and went very well with slices of freshly carved ham. The pasta was as good as she had hoped and neither of them needed anything else afterwards, apart from a little espresso to wash it all down.

As the coffees arrived, Dario caught her eye from the other side of the table.

'Have I told you how amazing you look?'

'I assumed from the incoherent noises you made when you first saw me in this dress that you thought I looked all right.'

She was torn. She rather liked the fact that he evidently approved of her appearance, but her intention had been for him to think of her as nothing more than a friend.

'You definitely look more than all right.'

There was something in his eyes and in his voice that made her sit up. Maybe this dinner had been a mistake after all, as she had feared. She did her best to steer the conversation back to the everyday.

'Well, you scrub up pretty well yourself, Dario. The main thing is that I didn't spill any of the lovely pasta sauce on this gorgeous dress.'

Maybe he picked up the lightness in her tone, but she saw him smile.

'Pasta sauce wouldn't dare. Don't forget, you're a gang leader. Anyway, I'm glad you liked it.'

'It was a super meal – simple, tasty and perfect. I rather think that evens the scores – Dario two, Debbie two.'

'Mm, still two-one, I think. I know when I'm beaten.'

'Not at all. A meal like this deserves two points. And it's good to eat with friends. You're a good friend, Dario. I really like having you as a friend.'

He nodded, no doubt noting her repetition of the word, and she saw what could have been comprehension on his face. 'I'll try to be as good a friend as possible. That's a promise.'

He held out his hand across the table to her. She took it and shook it, but held onto it for a moment.

'Thanks, Dario. That means a lot.'

Chapter 16

Next morning the wind had abated and the sky was clear once more. When Debbie got to school, she saw Bella with her vacuum cleaner and stopped to thank her again for her help with the coats at the Palazzo Vecchio. Bella waved away her thanks.

'You're very welcome. I work at the Palazzo Vecchio every now and then when they've got a big function and they need more staff. It's useful extra money.'

'Well, you certainly did us a favour.'

'Debbie, you looked wonderful.' Bella's eyes looked as if they were going to water. 'You looked like a princess.'

Debbie smiled at Bella. 'That's very sweet of you, but it was all down to a dress I borrowed.'

Bella shook her head. 'You were beautiful. You are beautiful.'

As starts to the day went, this was just about as good as it got. Her self-confidence bolstered, Debbie went through to her office and found herself humming as she worked her way through the papers on her desk.

The air outside was cold but drier and, instead of coming home for a cup of tea and a sandwich at lunchtime, Debbie decided to go for a walk. It had been a busy morning. Giancarla had taken the day off to be with Steven who was having his big operation. Giulia, the other secretary who normally worked in the evenings, came in to cover for her, but Debbie had spent most of the morning in reception, helping out. A stroll in the sunshine to clear her head was just what she wanted.

She walked out of the school and instead of going round the back of the cathedral, she headed round the front, past the Baptistery, to Via de' Tornabuoni. She was greeted by Cristoforo on the door as an old friend and she went upstairs to the offices and returned the peacock blue dress for cleaning, thanking Barbara most warmly once more. Barbara gave her a broad smile.

'Two people have already told me you were the belle of the ball.'

'Really?' Debbie was stunned.

'Yes, I'm sorry I didn't get a chance to talk to you last night, but I caught a few glimpses of you and you looked perfect. And I've had two calls this morning already asking me who the outstandingly beautiful girl on Dario's arm was.'

'I wasn't on his arm, just by his side.' Debbie felt it was important to make the distinction. Barbara didn't reply, but her raised eyebrows made Debbie blush.

Outside once more, Debbie set off walking through the narrow backstreets, as ever in search of new things to see, new little details she had missed up to now. It was cold, but in her cosy jacket, she was very comfortable, and the feel of the crisp January air on her face was just what she needed after a busy morning inside. Scooters and cycles weaved around the crowds of tourists who even now flocked to the city. As she walked, she was constantly having to step aside or move into the road, keeping a watchful eye for bikes and the silent electric taxis as she did so, to let groups of Brazilians, Poles, Chinese – in fact, visitors from all over the world – go by. Like anybody living and working in such a busy tourist hub, Debbie had got used to the crowds by now and, although they could be annoying on the days when she was in a hurry, she quite liked being surrounded by happy people.

Her meandering walk finally led her into the Piazza di Santa Croce. At the end of the square was the impressive white marble façade of Santa Croce church, the greatest church of the Franciscan order. She had visited it a few months back with Alice and it had been awe-inspiring to walk among the tombs of such giants as Galileo, Machiavelli and Michelangelo.

The thought of Alice had her reaching for her phone. Now warm as toast after her walk, she took a seat at a table outside a café at the side of the square as she called her friend.

'Hi Al, am I disturbing you?'

'Not at all. I'm on my way down to London for a meeting and I'm standing at the station, waiting for the next train. How's things?'

As they chatted, a waiter appeared and Debbie mouthed the word "cappuccino" to him. The coffee arrived as she was listening to Alice telling her about the weekend she and Guy were planning in a romantic little hotel in deepest Suffolk. Debbie was delighted to hear that all was still going well with them. Alice then turned the conversation, inevitably, to Debbie and men.

'So, any developments on the hunky neighbour front?'

Debbie told Alice about the drinks reception and dinner the previous night and repeated what she had been telling herself, namely that she and he were developing into really good friends and that was the way she intended it to stay. Also inevitably, Alice wasn't having any of it.

'So is this still because of the whole *Upstairs Downstairs* thing? Humble serving wench and handsome prince forever divided by the class barrier?'

Debbie was reminded for a moment of Bella's comment about her looking like a princess.

'He's not a prince.'

'Poetic license. So is that still it?'

'No, not really. He may be from a very different background, but he's a genuine sort of guy.' Debbie found herself sounding almost grudging as she spoke. 'No, it's more just a self-preservation thing, Al. I'm pretty emotionally battered and bruised at the moment, one way and another. I like him a lot and I want to keep him as a friend, without it becoming weird.'

'Since when has sex been weird?'

Debbie decided not to bring up the dinosaur incident at the Natural History Museum again. 'I mean I just think it would be better to keep feelings out of it for now. Maybe in a year or two, I may feel differently.'

'Debs, in a year or two, if he's as hunky as you say, he'll be married to some princess, with triplets on the way. You've got to strike while the iron is hot.'

'That's the point, Al. This particular iron isn't hot at the moment.'

As she spoke, her eyes opened wide. Coming diagonally across the square towards her was none other than Dario, looking good in a dark brown leather jacket and jeans. Clinging onto his arm with both of her hands was a very pretty dark-haired girl. As they approached, the girl reached up and caught hold of his shoulders, tugging him towards her until she could nuzzle up against his neck. Debbie saw his arm stretch around her waist as he hugged her tightly to him.

Still clutching the phone in one hand, Debbie grabbed the laminated menu off the table and buried her face in it until a full minute had elapsed, before raising her eyes once more. Dario and the girl were just visible in the distance, now holding hands, turning the corner at the end of the square, in front of the cloisters. A moment later, they disappeared from view.

'Debbie, have you been listening to a single word I've been saying?'

She became aware of the phone in her hand and Alice's voice sounding decidedly shirty. She cleared her throat and took refuge in a white lie.

'Sorry, Al, the waiter just brought the cappuccino and I had to pay him. What was it you were saying?'

'I was asking you what your feelings are towards your neighbour. Do you really mean it when you say you see him as just a friend?'

If Alice had asked that question a minute or two earlier, Debbie would have had little or no hesitation in answering yes. Now, the waters had suddenly been muddied. And the cause of the muddy water was an inexplicable, but unmistakable, sensation of jealousy that had sprung into her head as she watched her neighbour and his very pretty girlfriend canoodling in the square, without a care in the world. And where there was jealousy, there were feelings. Could it be she had fallen into the very trap she had been seeking to avoid?

'You still there, Debs?'

'Yes, Al, sorry. I was just thinking.' Debbie gave herself a mental shaking. 'Anyway, he's just a friend. Period.'

Alice must have heard something in Debbie's voice, because she immediately changed the subject. They chatted for another couple of minutes about events and people in Cambridge before ringing off. Debbie dropped the phone on the table and picked up her now lukewarm coffee and sipped it.

He's just a friend. The words still echoed in her head.

She glanced at her watch, knowing where she really wanted to go now. It was half past one, so she should have ample time. Heading for the river once more, she crossed the Ponte alle Grazie and walked back along the riverbank until she reached the turnoff for the steps. She climbed slowly, but steadily, and reached the rose garden not too badly out of breath.

She went in through the wrought iron gates and was momentarily disappointed to see two people sitting on her bench. She needn't have worried. As soon as they saw her, they stood up rather guiltily and Debbie got the distinct impression they had been canoodling, just as Dario and his girlfriend had been, back in the square outside Santa Croce.

She waited until the couple had walked out through the gate before taking her usual seat alongside the bronze statue. She reached out and took hold of the metal fingers, feeling them still warm from the hand of the girl who had been sitting there. She leant back until she could feel the statue's arm cradling her shoulders and let her mind roam.

Debbie felt all at sea. After everything that had happened to her over the past year, and particularly over the past couple of weeks, she really hadn't had any intention of letting herself get caught up with any man, however kind and considerate he might appear. And yet, it was quite clear now that her subconscious had had its own agenda. But what neither she nor her subconscious had known, was that he had been unavailable all along. Or, even worse, he might be out of the same mould as Pierluigi and Rossi, hoping to have his cake, or rather two cakes, and eat both of them.

She didn't start crying, but she felt an overwhelming sense of loss – ironic really, seeing as only half an hour earlier she hadn't been aware of having anything to lose.

Her eyes followed the contours of the ground as the hillside fell away towards the roofs of Florence below. These same roofs had been in exactly that same position for five, six, seven hundred years. Beneath them had lived countless thousands of people, some of whom had lived blameless lives, some who had cheated, some lied, some loved, some lost. She was just one more in this endless chain. This knowledge that she was just an insignificant grain of sand on the beach of humanity should have cheered her.

But it didn't.

She leant back against the bronze arm of the statue and steadfastly refused to let the tears run. For once, her special place was unable to provide the comfort she was seeking.

–

Giacomo arrived in the Mercedes just after three o'clock on Saturday. He gave Debbie a searching look as she climbed into the passenger seat.

'So, are you all right again now, Deborah?'

Debbie gave him a reassuring smile. 'I'm fine, thanks, Giacomo.'

'It's just that you looked a bit bothered, standing there on the pavement. I'm sorry I was a bit late. I got stopped by the police again, and had to produce my documents for them. They think I look too young to be driving a big car like this.'

'You weren't late, and I was just thinking about work. No, it's all good, honest.'

In fact, he had been pretty close to the mark. Ever since seeing Dario and his girlfriend, she had been wrapped in her thoughts, trying to unscramble the confused sensations going through her head. She had been so sure that all she wanted was a simple friendship with him – but if that were the case, why on earth had she felt that stab of jealousy? The only logical explanation was that she had, deep down, been developing feelings towards him. But, if so, where did this now leave her? Could she still be friends with a man who – she was reluctantly coming round to accepting – meant more to her than that? Not to mention that, as the scene in Piazza di Santa Croce had revealed, it would appear that he was already well and truly spoken for.

Just this morning, she had got a text message from him, asking if she felt like coming to a performance of *La Traviata* with him that evening. She had replied fairly tersely.

Thanks, but I'm busy.

She got a text back from him almost immediately.

OK. I'll go skiing with the boys again. Ciao.

Now, as she drove up to Fiesole to have tea with his mother, she had this lingering regret in the back of her mind, as well as the ever-present fear that she was shortly going to discover she had slept with Flora's future son-in-law. Yes, Giacomo had been right when he said she had looked bothered.

This time, as they drove up the gravel drive to the villa, there was a very smart silver Porsche parked by the steps. Giacomo drew up alongside it and Debbie got out. As she did so, the front door opened and a familiar black shadow came charging towards her. She crouched down to say hello to her four-legged friend and did her best to persuade him not to lick her face. Once his initial, albeit affectionate, assault had been repelled, she straightened up again and headed up the steps to the front door.

'Deborah, hello. Come and let me introduce you to my daughter Claudia. She's been dying to meet you.' Flora greeted Debbie with a kiss on each cheek and ushered her into the house and through to the sun lounge. A dark-haired girl got up as she heard Debbie's footsteps and turned to greet her. Flora made the introductions.

'Deborah, this is my daughter, Claudia. Claudia, this is my lovely English friend, Deborah.'

The winter sun was shining brightly through the French windows and it was only as Debbie got close enough to shake Claudia's hand that she realised she had seen her before. This was none other than the same pretty girl who had been clinging onto Dario in the Piazza di Santa Croce.

'Deborah, hi. It's good to finally meet you. Mummy and Dario have told me so much about you.' Claudia's English, like her brother's, was impeccable.

Debbie gave her a big smile as she did her best to process what had just happened. The thought rushing through her head was the fact that she was guilty of misjudging Dario and, to make matters worse, she had just told him to take a hike when she would have loved a night at the opera with him. Nevertheless, she kept the smile on her face and did her best to sound cheerful as she replied.

'Claudia, hello. Wow, you and your brother speak the most amazing English. I'm very impressed and it's very good to meet you. Your mum's been telling me all about you. I gather wedding bells are in the air.' At least, with Claudia here, there should be no difficulty in finding out the name of her fiancé.

Of course, if it turned out to be Pierluigi, as she feared, what then?

The three of them sat down together, the dog as usual lying on his back beside Debbie, and the conversation very rapidly turned to the forthcoming wedding. By the sound of it, Claudia's father must have finally put his foot down about numbers, as Claudia was soon pleading with her mother to be allowed to invite a few more people. 'Three hundred and fifty's not that many, really...'

'Where do we put them, Claudia? We've had a hundred in the house before, with dancing in the ball-room.' Debbie blinked. She hadn't realised there was a ballroom in the villa. 'If we do without dancing, we could fit another fifty to a hundred in there and another hundred or so squeezed in throughout the other rooms, but nobody's going to be able to move as it is. If all the people you've invited so far accept the invitation, we're already going to be camping on the lawn.'

The conversation was interrupted by the arrival of Lina, the housekeeper. Debbie now knew that Lina was Giacomo's aunt and she and Lina were on good terms. They smiled at each other as Lina unloaded tea and cakes, including what looked like homemade scones, from the trolley onto the table. From his position on the floor, Byron looked as if he was smiling too, his nose sniffing with considerable interest as the food was laid out.

As Lina left, Flora pointed to the scones. 'Deborah, these are an experiment. I got an English cookery book for Christmas and I've been trying a few of the recipes. As you're a real English person, I need your opinion of them. Unfortunately, though, I'm afraid I haven't got any clotted cream. You just can't find it here in Italy, but I'm hoping butter and jam will do instead.'

Debbie duly sampled the scones and pronounced them excellent. And she meant it. As they drank their tea, the conversation returned to Claudia's wedding and Debbie risked a direct question.

'So how come your fiancé's not here this afternoon? Dario's gone skiing. Have they maybe gone together?'

Claudia shook her head. 'No, he's working this weekend. He's a doctor, you see.'

'Ah, so is it a pain, him having to work unsociable hours?'

Claudia rolled her eyes, looking for a second just like her brother. 'I should say. He spends more time at Careggi than he does with me.'

Debbie's heart sank as she heard the name of the hospital. It was all beginning to fit together ominously easily.

'It's not because he doesn't love you, darling.' From the speed with which Flora cut in, the weekend working thing was obviously a well-known source of frustration for her daughter. 'Piero's a very caring doctor. It's only right he takes his turn on all the shifts.'

Piero! Debbie's heart, which had already dropped like a stone as she heard of his place of work, now sank through the floor. Piero was a very obvious contraction of Pierluigi. *Oh, God*, she thought to herself miserably, *what have I done?*

'I know, Mamma, but it's no fun being all on my own so much of the time.' Claudia, Debbie noticed, had a tendency to whine.

'It won't be for much longer, darling, and then you'll have him with you all the time.' She smiled at Debbie. 'Then she'll be complaining that Piero's home too much.'

Debbie was running through the various different scenarios ahead of her. If she told Claudia about her brief liaison with Pierluigi back in the summer, this would almost certainly result in the wedding being called off. Apart from maybe cheering Lina and the other caterers, this would seriously piss off Claudia, her mother and father and, by extension, her brother. Debbie knew she didn't want to hurt anybody, most particularly Flora and Dario, so did that mean that her only option was to bite her tongue and say nothing? Certainly, she valued her friendship with Flora and, of course, Dario, and this would almost certainly go by the board if she spoke up. And she would, in all probability, also lose her wonderful apartment. Like it or not, she was the Other Woman and would have to face the consequences. But if she didn't speak out, she would have to live with her conscience.

She was roused from her reverie by Flora's voice.

'You've not met, Piero, have you, Deborah?'

Luckily, Flora didn't wait for a response. She stood up and disappeared back into the sitting room, returning a few moments later with a photograph in a handsome silver frame. She handed it to Debbie.

'This was taken on the day they announced their engagement. Don't they look lovely?' Flora sounded like a very proud mum, and Debbie's heart dropped another few feet. Taking the photo from Flora's hand, she braced herself and looked at it.

She studied it very closely. The happy couple were standing on the front lawn of the villa, with the house in the background, and a slightly younger Byron lying at their feet. Claudia looked stunning in a little red dress that shrieked class and style and, beside her, wearing an equally stylish grey suit was... somebody Debbie had never seen before. She blinked twice and, had she been alone, she probably would have smacked her forehead.

It wasn't him.

Piero was not Pierluigi.

She hadn't gone to bed with the groom-to-be.

She wasn't the Other Woman after all.

She fought hard to suppress a squawk of delight. It was all right. She was in the clear. Finally mastering her elation, she looked up from the photo, directly at Claudia.

'You both look fabulous.'

Claudia nodded and smiled. 'Thank you, Deborah. I think he's rather gorgeous. I know! How would you like to come round to our house for dinner one night? That way you can meet him. And Dario could come too, so he'll show you the way.'

'Or Giacomo can pick both of them up.' Flora clearly approved of the idea. 'When's Piero's next free evening?'

'I'm not sure. I'll check with him and then could I give you a call, or text you, Deborah?'

Debbie agreed happily and they exchanged phone numbers. She was absolutely delighted that everything was all right after all – and, as a bonus, she would be having dinner with Dario in a few days' time.

Chapter 17

The first thing Debbie did once Giacomo had dropped her off outside her flat around five o'clock was to text Dario.

> Hi, Dario, sorry I was a bit abrupt this morning. Woke up with a headache. Would love to go to the opera if you're around. If not, would you come for dinner here tomorrow? Debbie

She very nearly added a little x, but decided against it. She wasn't very happy with the headache excuse either – it was something of a cliché, after all – but it was all she could think of on the spur of the moment.

His reply arrived only a minute later, just as she let herself into her flat. She pulled out her phone and read his message.

> Great. We're at Abetone. Just finished skiing. Should be home by seven, eight latest. Opera starts at nine. I'll call when I get home. Dario

Debbie heaved a sigh of relief. He hadn't taken umbrage at her tone earlier. The relief was immediately followed by a wave of anxiety. She now had a date with him for this evening, but what did that mean to her? She had worked out, after her reaction at the sight of him with someone she had assumed to be his girlfriend, that she had developed feelings for him. But just how deep were these feelings? Should she be plunging into a hot bath and digging out her very best underwear, or was this more of a slow burn thing?

She immediately knew that she was going to need to take it slow. Yes, she liked him – liked him a lot – but only a few days earlier his touch on her arm had made her jump. Apart from anything else, although she felt pretty sure he was keen on her, she had yet to discover the depth of the feelings, if any, he held for her. Slow was definitely the order of the day for both of them.

Practical considerations kicked in. If he was coming back from skiing he would be hungry, probably ravenous. She would prepare something for them both to eat before the opera. It wouldn't do for either of them to spoil the performance with their rumbling stomachs. She headed for the fridge.

At just after seven-thirty, she heard the doorbell. She ran to open it and felt a strangely powerful urge to throw her arms around Dario's neck and kiss him, but of course she didn't. Instead, all she gave him was a smile.

'Welcome back. How was the snow?'

'Terrific, thanks. And Abetone's less than two hours away, even with Saturday traffic. You'll have to come with me some time.'

'I'll come as a spectator. Like I told you, I'm not sure I'm made for skiing.' She checked him out. He was still wearing his ski clothes and he was carrying a heavy-looking bag, probably containing his boots. Presumably he had left his skis downstairs in the little cellar. He leant against the doorframe and told her about the opera.

'I'd better explain about tonight. There are no big names involved, and it's in a church, rather than an opera house, so the scenery's going to be pretty minimal. But it's a touring opera company I've seen before and I promise they're good. Is that all right?'

'Of course it's all right. Do we need to book tickets?'

'To be honest, I booked two tickets last night in the hope that you'd be able to come.'

'Oh dear, so my grumpy text this morning must have been extra annoying.'

'It was fine. I knew I could always bully my sister into coming with me. Her future husband works shifts at the hospital and she and I often go out together.'

'I met her this afternoon and we're both invited to her house some time next week for dinner.' However, she didn't mention that she had seen the two of them together earlier in the week and drawn her own – erroneous – conclusions. That was already filed away in the closed compartment in her brain that handled embarrassing mistakes.

She glanced at her watch. 'Listen, Dario, why don't you go and get changed and then come back over here for a quick something to eat before we go out? I've got some homemade lasagne left over from last week.' She gave him a grin. 'That sounds a bit grim, but it's just because I made a big one and then cut it into portions to freeze it.'

'It doesn't sound grim at all. It sounds great. By the way, thanks a lot for the invitation to dinner tomorrow. Under normal circumstances I'd really have liked that, but I won't be here. I'm on the six thirty train to Milan for a two day symposium on Botticelli and I'll be there until Wednesday.' Debbie immediately felt a twinge of disappointment, but did her best to hide it.

'Are you there as a spectator or a performer?'

He chuckled. 'I'm performing. I'm giving a paper on Monday and chairing a seminar on Tuesday.' He checked his watch. 'Anyway, something to eat now would be great. Can you give me fifteen minutes? I'll come back just before eight?'

'Perfect.'

While he was getting ready, Debbie dug out the lasagne and heated it up. She quickly made a mixed salad and toasted a few bits of bread and goats' cheese to go with it as well. She was just opening the other bottle of red wine he had brought last Sunday when he returned; clean, fresh and very handsome. He also smelt rather good.

The opera took place in a little church not far from where they lived. It had a very bland exterior, in comparison to the majestic beauty of so many Florentine churches, but inside it was what Dario described to her as a Renaissance gem, and she had to agree. The roof soared high above, supported by sculpted columns, and side chapels containing representations of the lives of the saints dotted the walls. The decoration throughout was quite beautiful in its geometric simplicity. Debbie had walked past it quite a few times, but had never been inside.

They got there at just before nine. The place was packed and, unusually for a church, it was lovely and warm. Dario had managed to get really good seats in the middle of the auditorium, near the front, and they had a spectacular view.

Ten minutes later the lights dimmed and the orchestra struck up.

By the end of the opera, Debbie, along with half the audience, was in tears. The tragic death of Violetta had touched her, as it had done countless others over the century and a half since the opera's first performance. But there was something else. Somehow she felt a link with the courtesan, Violetta, being hounded out of the family for bringing down its good name. Although no courtesan herself, here she was, daring to consider getting together with a member of the aristocracy. Would she also be hounded out? Somehow, she feared her own love affair might also end in crying.

As they made their way out of the church into the cold January air, she did her best to banish these negative thoughts and dried her eyes. Beside her, Dario could see her distress, and he gave her arm a little squeeze.

'You've got to hand it to Verdi. *La Traviata's* a real tear-jerker.'

Debbie caught hold of his arm with both her hands and drew strength from him as they walked back home through the streets of Florence.

When they arrived on the top floor of their building, she reluctantly released her hold on his arm and checked the time. It was already midnight. She was about to invite him in for a coffee when he surprised her.

He caught hold of one of her hands, leant towards her, kissed her gently on the cheeks and then turned away. As he reached the door to his flat, he looked back with a little smile.

'Goodnight, my friend.'

And he disappeared from sight.

Debbie let herself into her flat and slipped off her coat. Absently, she put the kettle on and dug out a camomile teabag. As she filled the mug with boiling water, two things were going through her head.

First, he was obviously a man of his word and that was a very good thing. She had told him she just wanted to be good friends with him and that was what he was doing.

Second, and more annoyingly, the opera they had just seen kept intruding into her thoughts. Was she totally crazy even to consider entering into a liaison with Dario, the future Count Dario? Would it all end in tears?

–

Next morning, as Debbie was doing the week's ironing and keeping a watchful eye on the shepherd's pie in the oven, she got a text message.

> I'm going to my place in the hills to do some decorating. If you'd like to come, I'd be very happy to show you round... PS Are you any good at painting and decorating? D

She phoned him straight back.

'So you're looking for some unpaid help, are you?'

'Who says it's going to be unpaid?'

'My rates are pretty high, you know.'

'Let's see how good you are first. Then we can settle on appropriate remuneration.'

'Deal. I'd love to see your place. What time do you want to go there?'

'How about leaving here at noon? The car's in a garage round the corner. I'll bring some bread and cheese and I can do a few sausages on the barbecue for lunch if that appeals.'

'Absolutely. There's salad left over from last night. I'll throw another few leaves in and bring it.'

'Terrific. But please don't wear anything smart. Of course you don't need to help with the painting, but I'd enjoy your company. I just wouldn't want to mess your clothes up, or your gorgeous hair.'

Debbie rather liked his use of the word *gorgeous*.

'I've done a fair bit of painting in my time, and I'd enjoy giving you a hand.' In fact, she and her dad had redecorated their house from top to bottom during one summer vacation from university so she knew what she was doing all right. 'And don't worry – I'll wear my scruffiest clothes. You won't recognize me.'

'I would recognize you in a rubbish sack.'

'I'll see if I can find one that fits. See you.'

The car was in an underground garage a couple of blocks away. As they walked down the ramp and past an array of mostly flashy cars, she remembered that Dario's sister's car was a Porsche. She was just wondering what sort of car he drove when he stopped and pointed.

'Here she is. Let's hope she starts. Polly doesn't like the cold.'

Polly was a very battered old Fiat. Fortunately it was a sort of rust colour, as this masked most of the real rust – and there was a lot of that. It was so small, the roof barely came up to Debbie's chest, and when she glanced inside, she saw that the back seat was missing and the boot was a clutter of buckets, paint pots and tools. She whistled admiringly.

'This is one fancy-looking motor.'

'She and I have been together for twelve years now. That's longer than most marriages – statistically.'

'Nobody can say you only care about looks.'

'Definitely. Although I do appreciate beauty when I find it.'

The drive out to the farmhouse, once Polly the Panda had been persuaded to start, took less than half an hour. It was to the south west of Florence in the hills, and the views, as they bumped along the rutted track leading to the house, were phenomenal. The house itself, sheltered by three massive ancient umbrella pines and half a dozen tall, slim cypress trees, was a delight, and Debbie found herself falling in love with it even quicker than with the peacock blue dress.

It was an ancient stone house with a colonnaded loggia along one side. The roof was made of wonderful old pink terracotta tiles, and the windows, shutters and doors were all oak. All around the house, the ground was strewn with builders' materials and piles of debris, but the view out over the hills towards the river Arno and the Apennines beyond was breathtaking.

Inside the house it was bitterly cold and Dario went round opening all the windows and shutters so that the comparatively warmer air could rush in from outside.

Debbie wrapped her old jacket tightly round herself and followed him on a tour that revealed what an amazing job he had been doing. The floors had all been renewed, but using old reclaimed terracotta tiles. The massive beams supporting the ceilings were original, but had been sand-blasted, as had most of the walls.

'Mind your step as you come in here.' Dario led her into the kitchen and she blinked as he pushed back the shutters on the window and the hefty double doors that opened onto another loggia, and the sunlight came flooding in. From here she could see all the way to Florence itself.

'Although you'd hardly believe it on a freezing cold day like today, this loggia's an amazing place in the heat of the summer sun. There's normally a bit of breeze and it's always cool out there.'

Debbie went across to the doorway and stood in silent appreciation. It was truly wonderful. Just then her phone whistled to indicate the arrival of a text, followed imme-diately by his. She pulled hers out of her jeans pocket and saw that it was a message from Claudia.

Hi Deborah and Dario. Dinner here on Wednesday evening all right with you? Piero's day off. Say, eight o'clock? X Claudia

She heard Dario moving about behind her and turned towards him, to find him looking at his own phone. He glanced up from the screen.

'Wednesday all right for you?'

Debbie nodded. 'Wednesday would be fine. Is it far?'

He shook his head. 'No, we can walk there from home. They've got the top floor of a palazzo on the Lungarno, quite near the American Consulate. If you like, I'll reply for both of us.'

While he replied to his sister, she studied the big kitchen, with its wooden beams, stone fireplace and wonderful old floor, before her eyes were drawn to the view once more, knowing that she loved all of it. After a while, she turned back towards him.

'Now, this is going to sound funny, Dario, seeing as your parents' villa is so magnificent, but I really think this is the nicest house I've seen since I arrived in Tuscany. And I'm not just saying that because it's your labour of love. The thing is, it's not too big, not too small, not in the least bit ostentatious, absolutely dripping with history, and I just love it. And you've worked your heart out.'

'I've certainly put in the hours, but you're right about it being a labour of love. I love the place. You can almost feel the history of it. I reckon the original structure goes right back to the Middle Ages.' He gave her a smile. 'But don't worry. I haven't come across any ghosts yet.'

He dumped the cardboard box he had been carrying and produced a couple of glasses. From a cupboard in the corner of the big kitchen he retrieved one of half a dozen traditional straw-covered Chianti flasks and removed the loose cork with his fingers. As she watched, he grabbed a handful of what looked like straw and dipped it into the neck of the bottle. Intrigued, she went over for a closer look.

'What are you doing?' She could see that the straw-like stuff was soaking up a thin film of transparent liquid lying on the surface of the wine.

'Ever heard of *olio enologico*?' Seeing her shake her head, he explained. 'The country folk round here have been using it for centuries. It's special odourless oil that they use to preserve the wine. Dribble a little on top of the wine once you've bottled it, and it stops the air getting in. I stick a cork in afterwards to keep insects and dust out, but there's no need. Like this, wine keeps for months and months. It works out cheaper than using corks and Tuscan farmers are among the canniest in the world when it comes to saving money. You use this stuff to soak up and remove the oil before pouring. There, that's done!'

Debbie saw that the oil had all been soaked up by what wasn't after all straw, but some sort of sisal-like natural fibre, vaguely like rough, brown cotton wool. He tipped an inch of light red wine into each of the two tumblers and passed one across to her.

'Cheers, Debbie. Thank you for coming.'

She clinked her glass against his.

'Cheers, Dario. I feel privileged.'

He swallowed the wine in one mouthful and smiled back at her. 'You should be. I don't really bring anybody here. If you like, it's turned into sort of my special place – just like your rose garden.'

'Well then I feel even more honoured.' As she spoke, Debbie found herself wondering just what his criteria were for inviting the chosen few who had been here so far.

'Now, before I show you the bedroom I'm hoping to paint, just let me light the fire so we can grill the sausages.'

He made short work of piling and lighting a heap of kindling on top of the ashes of previous fires in the big open kitchen fireplace. Unlike most English fireplaces, the fire itself wasn't at floor level, but around waist height, and there was a terracotta shelf on either side of it, clearly for the cook to use when grilling over the embers. As the flames took hold, he added larger bits of wood and huge pinecones and then led her through to the bedrooms.

There were three bedrooms and three bathrooms and the largest of the three, clearly the master bedroom, was at the back of the house and it had a stunning view up the hillside behind the house, towards a hilltop with twin humps. All along the spine of the crest were pine trees and cypresses standing out in silhouette against the clear blue of the winter sky. It could have come from a "Visit Tuscany" poster. Debbie found herself imagining waking up to a view like that. It would be amazing. Maybe almost as amazing as the man she would have lying beside her.

'So, when do you think it'll be finished?'

He gave her a slightly funny look. 'I bought it years ago and I've been working on it bit by bit ever since. In a way, I never want it to be finished. That way I'll always have a reason to come up here.'

'If it was mine, I'd never need to invent a reason to come up here.' She walked back across to the window and looked out again. 'In fact, if it was closer, and if you didn't mind, I'd adopt it as my new special place.'

'I'd be honoured if you did.' Dario smiled, then turned for the door. 'I'd better get back to the fire in the kitchen. It would be embarrassing if I burnt the house down.'

They sat on a scaffolding plank set on top of two piles of bricks, and ate their sausages and salad along with sips of red wine. The stone wall behind them had been slightly warmed by the sun, even now in January. In front of them were rolling hills, mostly covered in either vineyards or olive groves, and beyond them, in the far distance, the unmistakable shape of the cupola of the Duomo.

Debbie couldn't remember being happier than this at any time since arriving in Italy. It was a perfect, if cold, day and she loved being here with him. An image popped up in her mind of the house, completely finished, and of her living here, cooking over the open fire and drinking wine from old Chianti flasks. In her daydream, she imagined him outside in the sunshine, stripped to the waist, the sweat running down his muscular body as he chopped logs for the fire. The image was so graphic, she felt a shiver of good old-fashioned lust sweep across her and hastily swallowed a big mouthful of wine.

Of course, although it was an idyllic image, she felt sure, it was just a pipedream. He was caring, attentive and generous with her, but had given no sign that he wanted things to develop into more than friendship. Of course, she told herself, it was probably her fault for telling him in no uncertain terms that all she wanted was a friend.

As she set her empty plate down on the dusty tiles at her feet and sipped the last of the wine in her glass, she had no doubt at all that if he were to turn towards her now and kiss her, she would kiss him back with all her heart, and probably never let him go.

But he didn't.

After lunch, he cleared the plates and glasses back into the cardboard box and they went through to one of the smaller bedrooms and set about painting the walls and ceiling. He gallantly opted to do the ceiling, which Debbie knew from experience to be a tougher, more uncomfortable job. As he did that, she ducked around below him, running the roller across the walls, trying to dodge the inevitable splashes from above. To avoid her getting too much paint in her hair, he made her a rather fancy hat out of a sheet of newspaper. Deciding that this made her look like Napoleon, she gave him her phone and got him to take a photo of her wearing it. The hat came in very useful, as it took them an hour and a half to finish the job, and by the time they had finished, she was decidedly speckled.

Time and again, as they moved round the room together, she felt herself bumping into his legs and had to admit that she rather enjoyed the sensation. Whether her clumsiness was in any way intentional was something she wasn't prepared to admit, either to him or to herself. At one point a big drop of white paint splashed from his roller down onto her cheek and he bent towards her and wiped it off with the side of his hand, then licked his fingertips and smoothed them over her skin once more, as he ensured it had all been removed. Given the sensations aroused by his touch, Debbie felt like telling him he could pour paint all over her all day long if he were prepared to wipe her skin clean each time in such a gentle yet sensual way. But, of course, she didn't.

Back in the kitchen, the fire had died down, but there was still some slight residual heat in there along with a lingering aroma of pinecones. Dario retrieved an old orange box from under a pile of rubble, stamped on it and then broke it into pieces with his hands, before throwing the dry wood onto the fire. Within seconds, it was ablaze. He produced a battered kettle, blackened around the sides from the flames, and poured water into it from a plastic bottle before setting it on top of the fire.

'Have you got mains water up here?'

He shook his head. 'No, but there's a well and a pump. It works surprisingly well. I had the water tested and it's remarkably pure, but I still use bottled water for drinking, just in case.'

'So you've got a source of free water if you ever felt like planting a rose garden up here. Or anything else.'

Dario went over to the doors and beckoned.

'Here, come and take a look at this.'

She followed him out into the garden, picking her way through the rubble and detritus until they were maybe twenty or thirty metres from the house. The ground here rose up a fraction and was clear of builder's rubbish. A few wild vines covered the ground, along with clumps of grass and rosemary. A single umbrella pine stood guard over a few tumbled down dry stone walls. In the midst of them was a rose bush. Debbie stopped as she got there and looked on in awe.

It wasn't so much a bush as a tree. The stem was the thickness of her leg and branches ran out from it in all directions, entwining themselves among the rocks, creating the impression of a huge, spindly octopus, clinging jealously to its territory. Now, in winter, there were no flowers, but Debbie could well imagine the display it would create in the summer.

'It's a dog rose. It produces an absolute mass of pink flowers that cover this whole area. I can't even begin to describe the scent. Even if the individual flowers have got just the faintest smell, together they become overwhelming. But I wanted to show you something else. Come over here and look.'

Debbie walked across to where he was standing. There, on this little outcrop of the hillside, in the shade of the pine tree, somebody, a long, long time ago, had built a bench, set on a rough stone base. Two massive strips of weather-beaten oak provided the seat and the backrest, their surfaces now pitted by the ravages of insects and the elements alike, silver with age.

'Why don't you sit down and admire the view?'

Debbie did as she was instructed. The view was indeed magical, down across row after row of olive trees and vines towards Florence in the distance. But it wasn't the view that struck her. As she sat down on the bench, she got the funniest feeling. It was a sensation of belonging, a feeling of familiarity along with a comforting presence, as though somebody, just like her bronze statue, was cradling her back with a warm, outstretched arm. For a second she was almost scared by the intensity of the sensations aroused by this incredible place, but then she found herself settling back happily, just as she had done in the rose garden.

'Are you all right, Debbie?'

He sounded concerned. She felt him sit down beside her and take her hand. She squeezed it warmly and turned her face towards him.

'I'm fine, really fine. This is an amazing place.' She was looking straight into his deep green eyes. 'I could stay here forever.' Without even thinking, she leant towards him and kissed him softly on the lips. 'Thank you for bringing me here, Dario. I love it.'

As she drew back, she saw that his eyes had closed. Unsure what this meant, she remained motionless, waiting for him to react. It was a good while before she heard his voice.

'Debbie, could we do that again?'

Without waiting for her response, he raised his free hand and let his fingers rest against the nape of her neck for a moment before pulling her gently towards him and returning her kiss. As he did so, Debbie felt her head and her heart begin to spin as she kissed him back until they both had to pause for breath and she realised that her own eyes were now closed. She opened them to find him smiling at her.

'So, is this what friends do these days?'

His tone was light, but she sensed an undercurrent of anxiety.

'That's what really, really special friends do.'

'It's just that you told me pretty clearly that you and I were just friends.'

'Well, I was wrong, wasn't I?'

He smiled and kissed her again before, reluctantly, standing up again.

'Kettle. Tea. Remember?'

Tea was pretty low on her list of priorities for now, but she stood up all the same and followed him back into the house.

It was with real regret that she helped Dario close up again after they had drunk their tea. As they left the house and he locked the door, she felt a sense of separation, almost as if she was leaving a person she loved behind.

They drove home to Florence in almost complete silence, but it wasn't in the least bit awkward or strained. She had had a wonderful day. Back home, however, for the first time that day she did begin to feel awkward, standing there on the landing, wondering how to conclude this magical afternoon. She saw him smile as he stretched out his hands towards her.

'*Ciao, amica mia.*'

'*Ciao, amico mio.*'

She caught hold of his hands and pulled him gently towards her, then leant up to kiss him softly on the lips. As she did so, she heard what could have been a sigh from him. She pulled back a few inches and spoke to him.

'I love your house, Dario, and I'm very, very grateful you took me there. Like I said, I feel privileged.' For a few moments she hesitated, still holding his hands, still close enough to his face to feel his breath on her cheek. 'Can I ask you something?'

'Anything.' His voice was little more than a whisper.

'You said you rarely showed your house to anybody. I was just wondering, why me?'

'Because you said you were good at painting and decorating, of course...'

She kissed him again to silence him.

'No, seriously, surely you must have taken other girls there. I mean, look at you.'

There was a puzzled expression on his face, so she explained.

'You're tall, you're handsome, you've got the most amazing eyes, you're kind, you're generous and, of course, you're an aristocrat. Surely you must've had girls climbing all over you since childhood.'

He extracted his hands from hers and enveloped her in a warm hug, holding her tightly to him. His head rested on her shoulder, his cheek against her ear, muffling the sound of his voice as he formulated his reply.

'That's pretty much been the problem. Not the handsome thing – there are loads of better-looking men than me, but my family background.' He paused for a moment.

'There have been girls – a number of girls, to be honest – but there was only one particular one... up to now.'

'What happened?' Debbie did her best to sound only mildly interested, although his "up to now" comment had sounded really good.

'It didn't work out. We were such different people. It was as if we were from different worlds, to be honest.'

Debbie's warm, fuzzy glow suddenly began to dissipate as her fears were reignited. What was it Alice had called it – the *Upstairs, Downstairs* thing again? She risked asking him another question, although she was dreading the answer.

'Why? Was she from a working class background?' She almost added, *like me*.

To her surprise, she heard him laugh. 'Very much the opposite, Debbie. She's from a very important Venetian family – far more important than ours. We'd known each other since childhood, on and off, and after university, she moved to Florence and we started dating, much to the satisfaction of both families.'

He straightened up and caught her chin gently in his fingers, his eyes now right in front of her face. He looked unusually serious.

'Looking back on it now, I suppose it was, in effect, an arranged marriage. I was a suitable match in the eyes of her family and my family felt the same way about her. Anyway, we got on pretty well together, but, like I say, we were such different people.' He lowered his voice, even though there was nobody else in the building.

'To be honest, she was a bit like my sister. You know – she liked the good life, the Porsche, the stupidly expensive clothes and, worst of all as far as I was concerned, she just lived for socialising.'

She gave him a little supportive kiss on the lips, but he hardly noticed.

'I think I maybe once told you I was a bit of a hermit. I'm not really, but the fact is that I've never been into that sort of thing. I've never enjoyed being a member of the chattering classes, and I really couldn't give a hoot who's going out with whom, or getting engaged or married or whatever, but she loved all that kind of stuff.'

'I remember you weren't exactly enthusiastic at the idea of going to that drinks thing at the Palazzo Vecchio.'

'Exactly. But the crunch came when I bought the farmhouse.' He caught Debbie's eye. 'And, by the way, I've really bought it – myself, not my family. I bought it seven years ago, when I got the job here at the university, and I've got another eight years of mortgage repayments to go, but I'll get there.'

'She didn't like it?'

'She hated it. All right, I'll admit she didn't have a very good first impression. A family of snakes were living in what's now the kitchen and she got a bit of a scare.'

Debbie shivered.

'But she hated everything about it. She hated the position – said it was too remote. She hated the house itself – too old, the garden – too overgrown, and she said it was too small.'

'Too small? I'd love to live somewhere like that.'

Dario caught her eye and smiled. 'I know you would. I could feel it when we were there today.'

'I loved everything about it, but especially that rose bush and the bench. If you ever take me out there again, I know where I'm going first.'

Regretfully, Dario looked at his watch and shook his head. 'I'm afraid I've got to dash or I'll miss my train. I'll see you on Wednesday and, Debbie, you know you're welcome at the farmhouse any time.'

'Which reminds me, we never did discuss the appropriate remuneration for my decorating efforts.'

'I think I know how to resolve that.'

He kissed her hard on the lips and then disappeared into his flat.

Chapter 18

Next morning at school, Debbie got two surprises.

The first was a visit from Dottor Montevarchi. He confirmed the news Debbie had received from Giancarla a few days earlier that Steven's operation had been a success, but the surprise was when he went on to tell her that he and Steven had had a long talk the previous afternoon in the hospital. The result of their conversation had been Steven's decision to retire. In consequence, as owner of the school, Dottor Montevarchi had come to offer Debbie the position of principal, if she would like to accept it.

She had no hesitation. She accepted the offer immediately, especially when he went on to outline the pay and conditions. At this rate, with her modelling job as well, she stood a good chance of paying off her student loan within a much shorter space of time than she had ever hoped. And that would feel so, so good.

The second surprise was a parcel. It was wrapped in brown paper and was delivered by hand. There was note in an envelope attached to the outside.

I hope you agree that this is appropriate remuneration. Thank you for everything, Debbie, not just the decorating. With love. Dario.

Inside the package was the amazing peacock blue dress. She stood there stupidly for a few moments, staring down into the box, running her fingers over the smooth surface of the silk. For some reason she found tears in her eyes and she wiped them away. Setting the precious dress down on her desk, she reached for her phone and wrote him a text message.

> Definitely not appropriate remuneration. This now means I will have to work with you every weekend until debt extinguished. You shouldn't have done this, but thank you from the bottom of my heart. With all my love, Debbie.

She didn't get his reply until lunchtime. Presumably he had been tied up with the conference all morning.

> No debt, but would definitely love your company. X.

Seconds later another text arrived from him.

> Suggest you wear it on Wednesday. Claudia's dinner parties tend to be dressy. X

Debbie ran home from school as soon as her class finished on Wednesday evening and changed into the peacock blue dress in record time. As before, she curled her hair up in that quick, casual but classy way and muttered a silent prayer of thanks to Britta. She was just checking herself in the mirror when she heard the doorbell. She ran to open it and this time she didn't hesitate. She threw herself into Dario's arms and kissed him until she almost ran out of breath.

As she fell back, gasping for air, he gave her a warm smile.

'Can I take it you're pleased to see me?'

'You can certainly take it that I'm pleased to see you. I'm so, so pleased to see you.'

He stepped back and studied her. 'I've said it before and I'll say it again – you look absolutely gorgeous.'

They made a false start – or at least, Debbie did. She suddenly remembered the bunch of flowers she had bought for Claudia when she was already halfway down the stairs and had to dash back up again to collect it. Outside it was raining, not hard, but an insistent drizzle. She huddled against Dario underneath his big umbrella, but she knew she would have huddled against him even if the sun had been shining. The happiness she had felt out at his house in the country flooded through her whole body and she came close to purring with contentment.

It took barely a quarter of an hour to get to the Lungarno, the road that runs alongside the river. Claudia and her fiancé lived on the top floor of a fine, four-storey building and, from the marble-clad entrance hall to the state of the art stainless steel and glass elevator, it was the complete antithesis of Dario's house in the hills. Even the mailboxes were gold. Dario's, she had noticed on Sunday, was an old biscuit tin on a stick.

Claudia was out on the landing, waiting for them as the lift doors hissed open.

'Ciao, Deborah.' She came over and air-kissed Debbie theatrically, before turning to her brother and giving him an affectionate hug.

'Ciao, big brother.'

She was wearing a dress that Debbie recognized as belonging to Flora's spring collection, and Debbie was rewarded by a widening of Claudia's eyes as she took Debbie's coat from her and spotted the peacock blue dress.

'Deborah, that dress could have been made for you. You look absolutely charming.'

Claudia accepted the bunch of flowers with a smile and led them into her magnificent apartment. Debbie was duly complimentary. Clearly, no expense had been spared in ensuring that the place looked like something out of the pages of those magazines you find in a dentist's waiting room – the ones with adverts for multi-million-pound mansions in the front pages. Everywhere she looked, she saw contemporary style and opulent luxury.

Beautiful as it was, it only heightened her sensation of being a fish out of water. In Dario's house in the hills, she had felt comfortable, as if she belonged. Here, she felt like a visitor from another planet. She spared a thought for what her father would say if he saw the marble floors, the silk drapes, the impressionistic paintings on the walls, and the ultra-modern furniture. Somehow, she knew it wouldn't be, "Oh, how charming." The thought of her grumpy old dad comforted her and she smiled inwardly.

They were welcomed by Piero, who fitted perfectly into this opulent mould. As she had seen from his photograph, he was a good-looking man, and tonight he was wearing a suit, collar and tie. What else would you wear in your own house when your future brother-in-law's coming over for a meal, after all?

'Deborah, I'm delighted to meet you. What a stunning dress.' For a moment she thought he was actually going to kiss her hand, but he restrained himself and shook it instead. Then he turned to Dario.

'Ciao, Dario, how's the Renaissance?'

'Hasn't changed a lot since the last time you asked, Piero. How's the hospital?'

'Busy.'

Sensing a bit of a lull, Debbie decided to help Dario out with the social chit chat. She gave Piero a big smile.

'So, are you all ready for your wedding?'

Piero managed a weak smile in return, but Debbie could see the effort it cost him.

'You're asking the wrong person. Claudia has all the answers on that subject.'

They went through into a spacious lounge with leather sofas, a gas-powered open fire, a frighteningly vulnerable-looking snow-white rug on the floor and suitably subdued lighting. Carefully avoiding the rug, Debbie walked over to the windows and looked out. From here she could see directly out over the river and across to the massive bulk of Palazzo Pitti on the other side, with the Boboli Gardens just discernible in the shadows of the hillside above it, and the illuminated Ponte Vecchio below it. *This*, she told herself, *is one hell of a view. And no doubt one hell of an expensive view.*

Claudia reappeared from the kitchen and Piero opened a bottle of champagne. Although very inexperienced in the ways of champagne, even Debbie recognized the Bollinger label. After clinking glasses together with the others in a rather formal toast, Debbie took a mouthful and, grudgingly, had to admit to herself that it was pretty damn good. What was that thing about money not buying happiness, but making unhappiness a lot more comfortable?

In fact, Claudia and Piero looked far from unhappy and Debbie reflected that they were living what was no doubt the dream of countless millions of couples. Maybe the fact that it didn't get her going said more about her than it did about them. Fundamentally, she just preferred something old and simple, with a lot less bling.

She glanced across at Dario. Now, she thought to herself, when it comes to things that get me going... Sensing her eyes on him, he looked up and caught her eye for a second and winked. She felt a warm sensation course through her body, which was interrupted by the sound of the doorbell.

Claudia put her champagne down on the glass-topped coffee table and headed for the door.

'That'll be Isabella. They're always late.'

Helpfully, Piero turned to Debbie and explained.

'Isabella and Pierluigi are two of our closest friends. He's another medic and I've known him for years. We shared a villa in Santorini with them back in the autumn, and we've been wondering where to go next year.'

Debbie felt as if somebody had slammed a massive great hammer into the pit of her stomach. She very nearly buckled under the news, as her whole life was turned upside down in the flash of an eye.

She was still desperately trying to subdue a rising sensation of panic when Claudia returned, followed by an attractive redhead and, alongside her, somebody Debbie knew only too well. The only consolation she was able to get from this encounter was the sight of Pierluigi's face turning the colour of the rug on the floor when he clapped eyes on her.

'Isabella, of course you know my brother, Dario. And this is a friend of ours – Deborah. She's the director of a big English language school here in Florence. Deborah, this is Isabella and this is Pierluigi. They're getting married only a few days after us at Easter.'

'Deborah, I'm so pleased to meet you.' Isabella gave her a sparkling smile. She was quite short and the red hair had probably started life a different colour, but she was attractive and ebullient. In fact, she was as bubbly as the champagne. 'Claudia tells me you speak the most amazing Italian. I do so envy people who have a talent for languages. Personally, I'm terrible. Some days it feels like I can't even speak Italian properly.'

Isabella glanced across at her fiancé who still looked as if he had been struck by lightning. Debbie wondered if some sort of response was required, but Isabella had no need of anything like that.

'Pierluigi's so much better than me at languages. He studied in England, of course, which is bound to make a difference. Isn't that what you did as well, Dario?'

Debbie saw Dario open his mouth to say something, but Isabella didn't give him the chance to reply either. Within seconds, she was once more in full flight.

'When we were in Santorini, Pierluigi soon learnt enough Greek to be able to order drinks and food and everything. Didn't you, darling? And that included buying things in the shops. Of course there wasn't much choice in a little place like Santorini, but all the same...'

She continued to prattle on inexhaustibly and, for once, Debbie was grateful to be in the presence of somebody who just wouldn't shut up. Isabella kissed Dario on the cheeks and then shook hands with Debbie, without a break in the flow. As if in a dream, or rather a nightmare, Debbie saw Pierluigi shake hands with Dario and then turn towards her, his arm extended.

'Good evening, I'm Pierluigi. I'm very pleased to meet you.' There was a flash as his eyes met hers for an instant. She read fear in them.

Debbie took his hand like it was a live snake and shook it briefly.

'*Buona sera.*'

'... and the idea I had was maybe to give the south of France a try. I know the Côte d'Azur gets terribly busy in the summer, but if we go in September, especially towards the end of the month, surely we'd be fine. Besides, I suppose one or both of us might be pregnant by then, Claudia, so it might make sense to be somewhere a bit closer to home than Greece and somewhere we could get to without getting on a plane. I don't know what the regulations are for pregnant women on flights, but I'm pretty sure there's something about not being able to fly after so many weeks...'

As Isabella rabbited happily on, Debbie felt Dario's hand on her arm. She looked up from her wineglass at him. He looked worried.

'Are you feeling OK, Debbie? You look a bit pale.'

She made a supreme effort and managed to rustle up a smile from somewhere.

'No, I'm fine, thanks. I must have got a bit cold as we were walking here.'

'We'll take a taxi home afterwards.'

'I'm sure I'll be fine. I just need to warm up.'

The meal was excellent, the wine top class, and the conversation, at least from Isabella's direction, flowed like water, but Debbie didn't taste a thing and, if interrogated afterwards, would have been unable to repeat ninety-nine percent of Pierluigi's fiancée's non-stop chatter. All the while, she was turning over and over in her head just what this encounter had done to her and her whole future.

It was quite clear from Pierluigi's behaviour that he intended to act as if he and she were strangers, meeting here for the very first time. The success of his plan relied upon Debbie likewise keeping her mouth shut about the events of last August. What emerged in the course of the evening was that he and Isabella had got engaged on the very same day as Claudia and Piero – Easter Monday – the previous year. So his protestations to her, back in Cambridge, that his job as a doctor had kept him free from romantic entanglements had been barefaced lies, simply designed to get her into bed.

And his lies had worked.

Debbie was under no illusions that if she were to stand up at this dinner party and announce the truth of what had taken place, all hell would break loose. Isabella would in all likelihood slap Pierluigi across the face and break off the engagement. However, almost certainly, she would then decide to shoot the messenger. Claudia, seeing the damage done to one of her best friends, would most likely fall in alongside her and throw Debbie out after Pierluigi.

As a result, Claudia would no doubt tell her mother that Debbie was a slut and an adulteress and the connection with Flora that Debbie valued so much would also be severed – lost along with her flat in the centre of Florence. But she couldn't help thinking even that was a price worth paying in order to get the truth out there. Isabella might be an air-headed chatterbox, but she looked like a genuinely nice person and it was surely Debbie's duty to make her aware of what sort of cheat she was about to marry. However, Debbie's overriding concern was the effect this bombshell could have on Dario and her relationship with him.

It had been her intention for some days to tell him all about her past, including Paul of course, but also Pierluigi. She wanted there to be no secrets between them as they, hopefully, started a relationship that, deep down, she knew to be something very special. Yes, he was from a different social stratum to her, but, for once, Alice was right. What mattered was the chemistry between the two of them, not their family trees.

The revelation of the connection between Pierluigi and one of his sister's best friends would put Dario in a difficult position. How would he react, knowing, every time he saw Pierluigi in the future, the handsome doctor had slept with her before him? When all was said and done, Dario was an Italian, and Debbie knew enough about Italian opera to know that Italian men generally tended to react badly in such situations. It could be the end of their nascent relationship, scuppering it before it even started.

As the dinner dragged on, Debbie began to develop a screaming headache. In the end, she took advantage of a temporary lull in the noise levels, brought about when Isabella went off to the bathroom, to ask her hostess if she had a paracetamol to spare.

'Of course, Deborah. Don't forget, you're in a doctor's house. We've got enough drugs in the cabinet to treat everything from the common cold to Ebola. Come along with me.'

Debbie followed her through to what was no doubt the master bedroom. This, too, was a symphony of modern chic, steel, glass and natural wood, with a silk canopy hanging over the bed. The medicine cabinet was, indeed, packed, and Claudia produced a sheet of tablets in silver foil and insisted Debbie keep them. She poured her a glass of water and watched as she took one. But she didn't seem in any hurry to return to the dinner table.

'So, Deborah, would you mind if I ask you about Dario?'

'Of course not. What about him?'

'I can see from the way he looks at you that he likes you a lot. I was wondering how you felt about him. I wouldn't want to see him get hurt. I love my big brother, you know.'

Debbie was pleasantly surprised that Dario had been exhibiting such signs, but then, as Alice never ceased to tell her, her track record at reading signs was pretty lamentable. On the one hand, this confirmation that he maybe did have strong feelings towards her was heartening, but on the other, given the present circumstances, it made the potential repercussions of her breaking the news of her affair with Pierluigi even more tragic.

She answered honestly.

'I like him a lot – an awful lot. He's kind, he's funny, we get on so well together and he's so... natural.' She caught Claudia's eye. 'Do you know what I mean?' She could have gone on to say that he was so different from the other guests here tonight, but she didn't. After all, the same applied to her host and hostess.

'I know exactly what you mean. I really do.' Claudia caught Debbie's eye, her expression now more serious. 'He and I come from a very privileged background. You know that. Personally, I've learnt to embrace it, but all his life, he's struggled against it. The thing is, Deborah, we can't choose our parents. We are what we are, but he can't accept that. Tell me, has he told you about his house in the country?'

Debbie nodded. 'He took me out there on Sunday and we painted a bedroom together. It's the most amazing place.'

She saw Claudia's eyes widen.

'He took you out there?' She reached over and caught Debbie by the arm. 'Then that just confirms what I've been thinking. He likes you an awful lot, Deborah. Please don't break his heart.'

Debbie felt a wave of emotion wash over her. 'I'd never, ever, want to do that.'

Claudia smiled and patted Debbie's arm before removing her hand and straightening up.

'That's wonderful to hear. And, Deborah, I think you would be so, so good for him. I can see the two of you together.'

So could Debbie, but things had suddenly become very, very complicated.

They went back into the dining room and Debbie helped collect the cheese plates and take them back into the kitchen, while Claudia prepared the dessert. From the dining room, the sound of Isabella's voice still carried along the corridor and through the door. The kitchen, predictably, boasted every possible modern convenience, from a fridge big enough to sleep in to what looked like no fewer than three ovens, as well as a coffee machine of commercial proportions.

Claudia chatted as she pulled the dessert out of the fridge.

'I borrowed my mother's English cookery book and I've made individual summer puddings. I know we're in the middle of winter, but I just loved the idea. Do they look like they're supposed to look?'

She sounded genuinely concerned and Debbie was quick to reassure her. She was getting to like Dario's sister who, underneath the inescapable bling, was really rather nice. And she was also, undeniably, a very good cook. Together, they took the desserts through and, gradually, Debbie's headache began to fade – not completely, but enough for her to begin functioning normally again.

By this time she had made up her mind. The very first thing she knew she wanted to do once they got out of here was to tell Dario all about last August and hope that he wouldn't judge her too harshly.

The summer pudding received the compliments it deserved and later they all returned to the lounge for coffee. Dario sat on the cream leather sofa beside her and the feel of his thigh against hers was reassuring. During a brief hiatus, while the others crowded round to look at the photos of Greece on Claudia's iPad, Debbie surreptitiously rested her lips against his ear and whispered.

'I really like you an awful lot, you know.'

She wasn't sure why she did that, but his response was immediate. He turned towards her, lowered his head and kissed her hard on the lips, with a passion she hadn't sensed before. Then, just as immediately, he drew back and whispered to her in his turn.

'That's the greatest news I've heard all night... Make that all year.'

As he was speaking, Debbie glanced over his shoulder and saw Pierluigi watching closely from the other side of the room. She took a deep breath and looked away, dreading the conversation she was due to have with Dario later. Unaware of what was going on, he was still whispering.

'And in case you hadn't noticed, I think you're amazing.'

Ignoring Pierluigi, she caught Dario's cheeks between her palms and kissed him tenderly, knowing as she did so, just how badly she was going to miss him if the result of this debacle was their separation.

A bit later on, Debbie went to the bathroom – predictably a marble wonder, *or monstrosity*, she thought, *depending upon your taste*. As she came out again, she found Pierluigi lurking in the hall.

'Hi, Debbie.'

She glanced around. They were alone.

'Debbie's what my *friends* call me, Pierluigi. You're no longer one of them.'

'Look, I'm sorry... Deborah. I know what I did was a bit sneaky, but you must admit we had some good times together.' He looked anything but penitent, and Debbie felt a wave of rising anger.

'*A bit sneaky*? You lying bastard.'

'Well, yes, I suppose so, but a little white lie never hurt anybody.' She felt his eyes roam across her body and her stomach turned. 'Now that we're both living so close, maybe we could find time for some fun together. I'll always remember that thing you do, when you...'

Debbie leapt in before he could utter another word. There was a heavy-looking brass Buddha on a side table and she was very, very close to picking it up and smashing it across his head. She took a step towards him and was rewarded by the appearance of a shifty, fearful expression on his face. She lowered her voice to a threatening growl.

'If I ever see you again – even if I just bump into you at the market – I'm going to scream blue murder and tell everybody you tried to rape me. That's not a warning, that's a promise. Read my lips – I never want to see you or hear from you again after tonight. Is that quite clear?'

She didn't wait for him to reply, but his eyes told her the message had got through.

The evening drew to a halt around midnight and Debbie received kisses from Claudia and Isabella, along with an open invitation to visit Isabella for a chat sometime. *For chat, read monologue,* Debbie thought to herself as she picked up her coat, shook hands with Piero and successfully avoided shaking hands with Pierluigi in the general confusion. The four of them travelled down in the lift together and, once again, Isabella's incessant chatter was a welcome alternative to what would otherwise almost certainly been an uncomfortable silence.

They were just repeating their goodbyes on the pavement, and Debbie was bracing herself for the talk she was going to have with Dario, when the door behind them opened and Piero came running out.

'Dario, wait. Your mother's just phoned. Your father's had a funny turn and they've taken him to hospital. Claudia's getting the car. She'll take us to Careggi.'

Dario stopped dead, a look of shock on his face. 'What does a "funny turn" mean?'

Piero shook his head. 'I don't know. Maybe his heart? We'll find out.'

Just then there was a squeal of tyres and Claudia's silver Porsche came roaring round the corner. Dario shot a quick look at Debbie.

'There's only really room for three in the Porsche, and there's no need for you to have a disturbed night as well. Are you going to be all right going home on your own? Why not call a taxi?'

'I'll be fine. You go.'

Dario blew her a kiss and wasted no time in folding himself onto the microscopic rear seat of the Porsche. Piero jumped into the passenger seat, slammed the door, and they disappeared in a blue cloud of burning tyres.

'Deborah, would you like a lift home with us?' Isabella caught hold of her sleeve. 'Whereabouts do you live?'

Debbie had absolutely no intention of either getting into a car with Pierluigi or revealing her address to him, so she summoned a smile and shook her head.

'Thank you, Isabella. That's very sweet, but I live very close by. You go on, thank you.'

'Well, if you're sure.'

Debbie gave her a little wave and headed for home. The rain had stopped and the moon was just visible behind scattered clouds in the sky. It was colder than before, but Debbie hardly felt it. She was far too wrapped up in her thoughts to have time for mere physical considerations.

She was very concerned for the count and hoped his "funny turn" wouldn't prove to be too serious. She felt for Flora, who must be worried sick and, of course, for her children. She spared a thought for how she herself would feel if news were to arrive that something had happened to her own father or mother, and resolved to phone home the following day to check they were all right.

She walked down the side of the river before turning left into a narrow side street leading in the direction of the cathedral. There weren't many people about and the sound of her heels on the pavement echoed around her. She crossed Via del Purgatorio and entered Via del Inferno and she hoped these names weren't an omen.

Pierluigi's suggestion that she might like to hop back in bed with him and continue where they had left off had threatened to make her physically sick. Was this all that men like him thought of her? Was she just some sort of object? She had dressed up in the peacock blue dress so as to look good for herself, for Dario, and for the people she was going to meet. She hadn't dressed up as some sort of come-on to slimy toads like Pierluigi.

The count's illness hadn't resolved anything yet – only delayed things. She had been building herself up to making her confession to Dario and now she felt slightly deflated, if a bit relieved, albeit temporarily. The sooner she spoke to him, the better. She had to know how he felt – one way or another.

As she walked across the Piazza del Duomo, she paused for reflection between the cathedral and the Baptistery. The whole square was floodlit and the light reflected back from the white marble walls and the golden doors of the Baptistery. A few hardy tourists and a couple of cold-looking armed police were standing around, and it was as quiet as she could ever recall seeing it. It didn't take much effort to imagine horses, carriages and immortals like Michelangelo and Leonardo de Vinci walking round the square.

Once again she reminded herself that she was just one tiny, insignificant part of the eternal tapestry – but, just like last time, it didn't help.

Chapter 19

She didn't sleep very well and when her phone whistled just before dawn, she was awake in a flash. It was a text message from Dario.

> Minor heart attack. Not too serious. Prognosis good. Talk later. Love

She replied immediately.

> Good news. Thinking of you all. All my love.

She got up shortly afterwards and was in work before eight. She found she was able to clear her desk and prepare her lessons for that evening by lunchtime. When Giancarla arrived, she could see she had something – or somebody – on her mind.

'Debbie, can I ask you for your advice?'

Debbie was gradually getting used to the new, softer, Giancarla, but this was the first time she had ever been asked to give advice. She nodded.

'Of course. Come and sit down.'

'It's about Steven.'

'How is he?'

'Better, remarkably better. The operation was a great success and I think now that he's made the decision to retire, he feels reassured. Anyway, I don't know if you were aware that he and I were engaged to be married at one point.'

Debbie managed to avoid answering — not wishing to let Giancarla think that Martha or anybody else had been talking about her behind her back. It didn't matter. Giancarla wasted no time in continuing with her tale.

'Then, six years ago, he had an affair with another woman. After more than twenty years together, I could hardly believe it, but it was true. He came to me and confessed and asked me to forgive him for his aberration, but I couldn't. I threw him out and I would have left Florence if my mother hadn't been so poorly.' She looked up at Debbie, her eyes damp with emotion. 'She died last spring.'

'I'm so sorry for you. It must have been awfully tough over the last few years.'

'It hasn't been easy.'

Debbie reached across the desk and took hold of Giancarla's hand. As she did so, the secretary looked up in surprise, before clasping Debbie's hand tightly with both of hers. Debbie could feel the nervous tension running through Giancarla's whole body and gave her a gentle squeeze of solidarity and support. She heard a muffled reply.

'Thank you, Debbie.' Giancarla sounded genuinely grateful.

There was a long pause before Debbie finally decided she should be the one to interrupt the silence.

'And now, Giancarla? What happens now with you and Steven?'

Giancarla released her grip on Debbie's hands. She ran her hands up to tidy her grey hair and took a deep breath before replying.

'Now Steven's asking me to try to forgive him and move back in with him again and I don't know what to do.'

For a moment, Debbie saw a parallel with her own situation. Of course, in her case, she had had the affair with Pierluigi without any idea that what she was doing was wrong, while Steven had definitely behaved appallingly towards Giancarla. But, just as she hoped for forgiveness from Dario, she urged Giancarla to do the same.

'Giancarla, I saw you that night at Careggi Hospital when the ambulance arrived at the emergency department. I'll never forget the expression on your face. I don't think there's any doubt about it – you still love him, don't you?'

She caught Giancarla's eye and, after a brief delay, she saw her nod her head.

'Then, there's your answer. Forgive him, Giancarla. Take him back, forget the past, and enjoy the rest of your lives together.' She took a deep breath. '*I* would.'

'Thank you, Debbie.' The tears were running down the sides of Giancarla's face now. Then Debbie saw her reach up with her hands and wipe them away with a sudden movement as she struggled to sound businesslike again. 'Thank you, Debbie. Now I'd better go and unlock the doors.'

As she went off to regain her equilibrium, she left Debbie hoping her answer to Steven would be positive and that Dario would react in the same way towards her when he heard the news she had for him.

As noon approached, Debbie decided she needed some fresh air and the chance to clear her head. She told Giancarla she would be back in good time for her evening lessons and, unusually for her, took the afternoon off.

She took the bus to Careggi Hospital, unsure whether she would be allowed in to see Dario's father, but she knew she owed it to him to try. Upon arrival at the hospital she couldn't help but be reminded of the first time she had visited. That had ended badly, or so she had thought at the time. Now, looking back on it in the light of the revelations of last night, she realised that, brutal as it had been, it had saved her from much more heartache, or worse.

The girl on the reception desk directed her up to the Cardiology Department on the first floor. The first person she saw upon arrival in the waiting area was Flora, sitting alone by a window, looking drained. Debbie went over and gave her a hug and a kiss on the cheek. As she did so, Flora looked up and a smile spread across her face.

'Deborah, my dear, how sweet of you to come.'

'Hi, Flora, what's the news?'

'Quite good, I think. Enzo's been moved out of intensive care into a private room and they think he might only be in here for a day or two. Two specialists are in there with him now.'

'That's really good news.'

'Come and sit down beside me, dear. Dario and Claudia were here all night and they've gone home for a rest. I had a sleep earlier on. Claudia tells me you looked stunning in your blue dress last night. She also said how much she liked you.' Flora paused for a moment and shot Debbie a more serious glance. 'She also told me that Dario likes you an awful lot.'

'And I like him an awful lot too, Flora.'

Flora smiled contentedly. 'I'm so, so pleased, Deborah. My son's a good boy and a very bright boy, but he's always been a bit of a loner. He needs the love of a good woman like you.'

Debbie hesitated and then decided to take the plunge.

'I don't know how good a woman I really am, Flora.'

Seeing the expression on Flora's face, she took a deep breath and told her the whole sad story, starting with falling off her bike in Cambridge, right through to meeting up with her nemesis the previous night. As she recounted the events, she glanced across at Flora's face from time to time, but could read very little on it. At last she reached the end of her tale and sat back, surreptitiously wiping the sweat off her palms on a tissue. Finally, she turned to face Flora.

'I know – you must think I'm stupid, I'm gullible, and probably a tramp. I'm not like that, really, honestly, and I'm terrified I've messed everything up as far as Dario's concerned. And the very last thing I ever want to do is to hurt Dario, or to hurt you.' She looked Flora straight in the eye. 'This will probably only confirm how stupid I am, but I think I'm falling in love with him. I know it's crazy as I've only known him for such a short time, but I really believe it. And now I'm afraid my actions last summer could result in my losing him, just at the time I feel the two of us drawing ever closer together.'

She dropped her eyes to the floor and blew her nose on a tissue. After a few seconds, she felt Flora's hand on her arm.

'I don't think any the worse of you, Deborah. What happened before you met Dario, or me for that matter, is your affair and your affair alone. Isabella's fiancé, on the other hand, is a very different kettle of fish. He's as bad in his way as that awful Rossi man who attacked you.'

Debbie felt a rush of relief.

'As for my son, I can't speak for him, but if he feels the same way about you as you do about him, you needn't worry. Like I say, what happened before you met is neither here nor there.'

'And you wouldn't mind if we got together?'

Flora grinned. 'Deborah, I wouldn't mind if you got *married*. All right, I know that's all very premature, but honestly, like I said before, I can't think of anybody better for Dario or, indeed, as a daughter-in-law.'

Debbie really hadn't been expecting this.

'But… you're part of a noble family and I'm just a… nobody. Doesn't that matter to you?'

Flora was still smiling. 'That sort of thing doesn't matter any more. Besides, Deborah, look at me. Do you think I'm of noble birth?'

Debbie had never really considered it.

'I don't know. I just assumed…'

'Deborah, I was born into a very bourgeois family in a very bourgeois part of Turin. I lived there all through my childhood and I only came here to work when I finished university. When I met Enzo, I was selling homemade dresses off a stall in San Lorenzo market. I'm about as noble as Byron the dog.' She stopped and corrected herself. 'No, that's wrong. Byron's got a far more impressive pedigree than mine.'

'So you really wouldn't mind…?' She didn't have the chance to say more as a nurse arrived to inform Flora that she could go back in to see her husband.

'Excellent. You come along with me, Deborah. I know Enzo will be pleased to see you.'

The nurse shook her head.

'I'm sorry, *Contessa*, the specialist said only one visitor and not to stay for too long. Your husband needs as much rest as possible.'

'Well, you go in, Deborah.'

Debbie patted her arm. 'I wouldn't dream of it. Go and be with your husband and please give him my love. As for me, I'm going for a long walk to clear my head.'

She kissed Flora goodbye and went back down the stairs. Outside, the sun had poked through the clouds, and the temperature, while still low, had at least risen a few degrees. She walked slowly back through the streets, attracted as a moth to flame to the Ponte Vecchio and the hillside above it. It was just after two o'clock when she walked in through the iron gate and sat down on her bench, secure against the arm of the bronze statue.

She pulled out her phone, thought about calling Dario, but decided to let him sleep after his broken night. Instead, she called Alice and recounted the events of the last twenty-four hours. Alice let her finish before giving her verdict.

'Well, sounds like you've cracked it as far as the future mother-in-law's concerned. I was having terrible trouble convincing Guy's mum that I was going to make a suitable wife for her son, but then I discovered she likes chocolates. You know those handmade, terribly expensive Belgian ones you can buy in the posh shop down by the bridge? A few quid's worth of those and she's eating out of my hand – not the chocolates, you understand.'

'The future mother-in-law is irrelevant if the future husband dumps me for being a slut, Al.'

'Don't be ridiculous. He won't mind a bit, I promise.'

'I wish I were so sure.'

'It's all in the past. Trust me, Debs. He won't mind.'

After the call ended, Debbie sat there, gripping the metal hand beside her, her eyes ranging out over the roofs of Florence to the hills beyond. She reflected on what Alice had said and what Flora had said and, for the first time, she dared to hope everything would work out fine, after all. She lost track of time and was miles away when the brass hand against her shoulders gave her an encouraging squeeze. Or so it seemed.

'I was pretty sure I'd find you here.'

It was Dario.

She reached up towards him with both her hands and pulled him down, over the back of the bench, until he landed in her lap. As she did so, she discovered that he was holding a lead in his hand, on the end of which was a very excited black Labrador. As she silenced Dario's mild protests with a long, lingering kiss, Byron charged round and jumped all over them, keen to join in. Finally she let Dario sit up and transferred her attention to the dog, petting him as he rolled happily on the ground at their feet. She glanced across at Dario.

'I'm so sorry about your dad, but I saw your mum and she told me things are looking good for him.'

He nodded. 'I've just been speaking to her and it sounds very positive. She asked me to take this monster out for a walk as he's been cooped up at home.' He caught her eye, suddenly serious. 'She told me you've got something to say to me.'

Debbie dropped her eyes to the ground.

'Yes, I have, and it isn't going to be easy.'

'Why, am I so scary?'

'No, Dario, it's not you. It's me. It's something I've done.'

'Do you feel like talking in the car?'

'Yes, of course, but why? Are we going somewhere?'

'Can you spare a couple of hours?'

Debbie checked her watch and saw it was half past two.

'I don't need to be at the school until half past five or so. I'm teaching at six.'

'Great. Byron needs some exercise and I've got a bit of planting to do if you feel like keeping me company. We can talk in the car.'

–

It was almost three by the time Polly the Panda bumped up the rough track to Dario's house. It had taken Debbie until the outskirts of Florence to summon up the courage to begin to tell him, and she had told him everything, just as it had happened. Gradually, bit by bit, she had managed to recount the whole sad saga. It was difficult to judge his reaction, as she had been distracted by the repeated attempts by Byron to climb over the seatback into her lap, although she distinctly saw the muscles of Dario's jaw tense as she revealed the identity of her lover last August. But she persevered and managed to tell him everything.

She finished her tale just as they reached their destination. He had said little or nothing, concentrating on driving and fending off the dog. When he finally drew up outside the house, he immediately went round and opened the boot. Byron leapt out excitedly and started barking for no apparent reason.

'He always barks when he gets here. I think he's saying hello to the place. Here, can you bring the spade, please?'

He picked up a plastic pot containing a plant and headed for the outcrop with the bench and the magnificent old rose. She followed him, taking heart from the smile on his face, but still unsure how he really felt. When they reached the bench, he wiped it with the sleeve of his jacket and invited her to sit down. He took a seat beside her and the dog charged back to them and positioned himself at their feet. They both gazed down on the splendour before them – a patchwork of olives and vines, with the roofs of Florence in the distance; the Tuscan countryside at its most beautiful, even though it was still wintertime. After a while, he started to speak.

'Debbie, what's done is done. What happened before we met is ancient history and has no relevance to us today. I'm touched, but not surprised, by your wanting to do the right thing by telling me, and by telling Isabella just what sort of scumbag she's about to marry. You're the sort of girl who will always try to do the right thing, and I love you for it.' He caught her eye. 'Sorry, I used the L-word. That's not a word friends use, is it? I should have said that I admire you for it.'

'I don't mind you using it, Dario. I love the fact that you did.'

'As far as Isabella's concerned, I can tell you that she isn't as dumb as she looks or sounds. I'm afraid you're not the first, and you won't be the last of Pierluigi's conquests, but she doesn't care. Claudia's spoken to her about it time after time, but she just says she loves him and she's prepared to accept him the way he is.'

'And are you prepared to accept me the way I am?'

He leant towards her and kissed her softly on the lips.

'I would accept you any way. And, if you need proof, you can help me plant this. I bought it yesterday especially for you. Look.'

He picked up the rose bush in its pot and showed her the label. This described it as a bush rose, attaining a height of between one and one and a half metres, with a medium fragrance and a delicate pink and cream colour.

The name of the rose was *Debbie's Delight*.

'I hope we can watch it grow together.'

Debbie suddenly felt such an outpouring of relief that she started crying. Within seconds, she felt a strong arm envelop her shoulders while a pair of heavy black paws landed on her lap, followed by a big hairy head as Byron added his support.

'What's wrong, Debbie?'

Dario sounded so caring, so concerned, that she started crying even more. He crushed her to him and she felt his lips on her hair. With his free hand he stroked her cheek, occasionally dissuading the Labrador from climbing onto her lap. The dog was clearly concerned for her wellbeing and was making little whining noises. She sobbed into

Dario's chest for a full minute before digging in her pocket for a tissue. Once again, he got there first.

'Here.' She looked up to see he had a tissue in his hand. 'Looking for one of these?'

'Thank you.'

She took it gratefully and set about wiping her face and eyes. The dog, now reassured, decided it was safe for him to leave her in Dario's hands and trotted off on a tour of inspection of the property.

She was about to explain why she had started crying when she heard his voice.

'I'm not a violent man, but when I went round to visit that bastard who attacked you, I came very close to hitting him. I've never done anything like that before and all the way back along the autostrada in Claudia's Porsche, I kept on asking myself why.'

'You shouldn't have gone there. Something could have happened to you.'

'I was fine. Anyway, it all suddenly fell into place a week later when I knocked on your door and you opened it, with flour all over you.' She saw him blink a few times. 'It's never happened to me before. To be honest, at the ripe old age of thirty-three, I'd probably come round to the conclusion that it never would and yet...'

As the tears dried on her cheeks, Debbie felt a smile forming on her face.

'And yet, what?'

'And yet it's happened. Debbie Waterson, I never thought I'd hear myself saying this, but I think I love you.'

'You only think so, do you?'

She was trying to keep her voice light, even though she could feel her emotions bubbling up inside.

'I *know* so. You can't imagine how excruciating the past weeks have been ever since you did your schoolmarm act on me and told me firmly we were only ever just going to be friends. I was the donkey and you were the carrot on the stick, always there, but just out of reach.'

'I'm sorry, Dario, I feel such a fool. It's just that, after what happened…'

'I know and I understand. Of course, that's what I kept telling myself.' He caught her eye. 'And then, today, when my mother told me you wanted to tell me something, I feared the worst. Just as I thought you maybe were developing some feelings for me, you were going to shoot me down in flames. I don't care about Isabella's fiancé, I don't care about anything except being with you.' He straightened up. 'So, is there hope for me after all?'

'Dario, I'm as surprised by the whole thing as you are. We've known each other for such a relatively short time but I can tell you this: I know, truly know, that I've never felt like this about anybody else in my whole life and even if you go off and leave me now, I know I'll never feel this way again. In spite of all that's happened to me, in spite of my firm resolve not to get involved, I've fallen for you lock, stock and barrel.' She reached out and caught hold of his cheeks between her hands. 'I love you to bits, Dario, and I hope you feel the same way about me.'

They kissed for so long that the dog finally gave up chasing rabbits and returned to start pawing at their legs, clearly concerned at their prolonged immobility. Regretfully, Debbie straightened up, but she kept a firm hold of Dario's hands as she looked down at the dog.

'It's all right, Byron. Everything's fine now.'

'Well, almost. There's just one problem.'

Debbie looked up from the dog. Dario was smiling broadly.

'A problem?'

'Yes, I have a feeling the time has come for me to get this place finished. I've got a lot of work to do here.'

'*We*'ve got a lot of work to do here. That is, if you think you can trust your new apprentice.'

'I would trust you with my life.'

'Well, how about starting now?'

'Maybe not *right* now.'

He gently released his grip on her hands and she felt his fingers run up her arms and through her hair as his lips brushed against hers. Her eyes closed in delicious anticipation, but then she sensed his hesitation. Opening her eyes again, she saw him looking down at the big hairy head resting on her knees. She felt an irresistible urge to giggle as she heard him address the Labrador.

'Byron, could you look the other way, please?'

Chapter 20

April was a glorious month in Tuscany. The sun shone brightly for day after day as Debbie and Dario spent all their free time working on the house. It was now warm enough for them to eat outside and the loggia provided welcome shade from the ever-stronger sunshine. Debbie was still very busy at school, but she couldn't wait to come out here whenever she could, loving the house and, of course, the man it belonged to.

The first rooms to be finished were the most important ones: the kitchen and their bedroom. They hadn't got any curtains yet, so they spent their first night there with the shutters closed. It was dark in the room first thing in the morning, so she climbed out of the warm bed and went across to push them open, before slipping back into bed again. As she felt Dario stir beside her, she gently stroked his cheek with her fingers as she stared out of the window and up the hillside towards the tree-studded ridge at the top. Wild flowers were already starting to bloom and the leaves on the trees were increasingly green. It was a time of rebirth and renewal and Debbie felt the same sensation inside herself. Her big gamble, making a fresh start in a different country, had paid off. Her new life was everything she had hoped for, and much, much more.

'Is it time to get up?' He sounded sleepy. She turned towards him and kissed him softly on the lips.

'It's half past seven and we've got thirty people coming for lunch today. Remember, it's our housewarming.'

She felt his hands reach for her body and pull her tightly to him. As ever, she thrilled at his touch. She let one hand run down to his strong, hairy chest as she heard him murmur into her neck.

'I'm warm enough as it is.'

'I can feel that.'

'Besides, it's only twenty-eight people. Don't exaggerate.'

'You're forgetting Byron.'

'All right, twenty-nine. Do we have to get up now?'

She smiled down at him and kissed him again.

'Well, I suppose a few more minutes wouldn't hurt.'

In fact it turned out to be quite a lot longer than that.

Once they finally surfaced, they got to work and it was a busy morning. Dario was going to be grilling meat for lunch so he prepared the fire and the grill. Meanwhile, Debbie threaded grapes and prawns onto cocktail sticks, laid smoked salmon onto little triangles of toast, and made a tomato, basil and garlic mix to go on the bruschetta. Dario opened bottles of Chianti Classico and checked that the Prosecco in the fridge was suitably chilled. They prepared plates, glasses and napkins, along with crisps, nuts and a huge mixed salad, until the kitchen table was groaning with food.

They had told people to come at twelve and, sure enough, a steady stream of cars started to arrive shortly after noon. First to arrive were Giacomo and his fiancée, Anna, along with his aunt, Lina the housekeeper, and her husband. He dropped them off and immediately disappeared again to collect Flora and the count. A few minutes later, Giancarla and Steven arrived in his old Alfa, closely followed by a big taxi containing Rory, Sam, Virginia and Claire, along with their two boyfriends. Three more cars soon appeared, bringing Dario's skiing and squash buddies that Debbie was gradually getting to know and like. Just before half past, the silver Porsche came very slowly and carefully up the rutted drive, with Claudia trying not to damage the underside as she negotiated the potholes.

By the time Giacomo returned with Flora and the count, accompanied by a highly excited Labrador, Debbie and Dario were hard at it, serving drinks, handing round nibbles and preparing the main meal. Rory, accompanied by his now constant companion, Sam, followed Debbie to the kitchen and, in spite of her protests that they were here as guests, they took over the duties of waiter and sommelier.

Debbie managed to get a few moments alone with Rory as he came back in to replenish his glass and collect another plate of nibbles. Well, almost alone – Byron appeared and insisted on having his tummy scratched while Debbie and Rory chatted.

'So, Rory – you and Sam...?'

He grinned. 'Me and Sam, that's right. It's all good. He's coming back to Scotland with me for the Easter break and I'm going to introduce him to my mum.'

'That's great. And trust me, Rory, she'll understand.'

He took a big mouthful of red wine before answering. 'I think you're right. I owe it to her to tell her.'

By now, the sun was beating down hard, and people were soon seeking the shelter of the loggia in order to get some shade. Debbie took a few moments off from food preparation and walked around, chatting and showing those who hadn't seen it what the rest of the house looked like. She was very pleased to find Steven now looking fit again, with colour in his cheeks and a smile on his face. Beside him, Giancarla, too, had a smile permanently on her face. They had been living together now for two months and all appeared to be well between them.

'So, Steven, how do you fill your time now that you're a gentleman of leisure?' Debbie gave him a big smile.

'He's writing a book.' Giancarla was quick to reply on his behalf and the pride in her voice was plain to hear.

'How exciting! What sort of book?'

Steven gave her a wink.

'It's about an English girl who comes to Italy and falls in love.'

Debbie caught his eye. 'So, where did you get your inspiration from?'

He was grinning now.

'All just out of my head. No resemblance to actual persons, living or dead, as they say.' His grin broadened. 'Besides, my girl's got short blonde hair.'

'Ah, well, that's all right, then.' She smiled at the two of them. They looked so happy together. 'Fancy you writing a love story!'

'It's a story about love, and then loss, and finally love again.'

'Well they say you should write about what you know.'

She got two big smiles in return.

Lunch was generally deemed to be excellent by everybody. The dog got the leftovers and looked as though he shared the general opinion. They ate outside under the loggia. The huge table and benches Dario had made out of old oak planks just managed to seat all twenty-eight of them. It was a bit of a crush, but nobody minded. The grilled meat, bruschetta and salad all went well together and the soft pecorino cheese that came afterwards was exceptional. Debbie had managed to get this through Nando at the school, whose cousin was a shepherd, and she knew that she was especially privileged.

As they ate, there was constant chatter around the table and Debbie was pleased to see Virginia and Claire and their two boyfriends having a good time and clearly bonding well with Sam and Rory. The two married teachers had been invited, and although they hadn't been able to come because of family commitments, Debbie was glad she had invited them. Even Claudia's future husband, Piero, began to loosen up as the day went on. It had not surprised Debbie to see him arrive dressed in a suit, collar and tie, but as the meal progressed, first the tie and then the jacket were discarded and Debbie got a view of the cheerful man beneath the formal exterior. He even told a joke about a doctor and a patient suffering from a boil on his bottom that had everybody laughing. He also told Debbie something else that put another smile on her face.

'Have you heard about Isabella and Pierluigi? Their wedding's off.'

'Really?'

Could it be, Debbie wondered, that Pierluigi's fiancée had finally worked out what kind of slimy toad she had been about to marry and had sent him packing? The only people to know about the events of last summer in Cambridge were Dario and his mother, so she affected only slight interest as she prodded Piero for a bit more detail.

'Oh, dear, did something happen?'

'He's been offered a job in Dallas, Texas, and he's taken it.'

'Really, so when's he going off there?'

Debbie was delighted that she and Pierluigi were soon to be separated by the width of the Atlantic Ocean. Since Claudia's party, she hadn't seen any more of him, but she had been living with the looming spectre of having to meet him again at Claudia and Piero's wedding, now only a week away. Piero's next revelation came as a massive relief.

'He's already gone. He left last week. It was all done very hastily.' He lowered his voice. 'To be honest, the administrators, not to mention his colleagues, at Careggi were pretty unhappy about his decision to leave so soon. Mind you, he always was selfish.' He caught Debbie's eye. 'Sorry, of course you don't really know him, but take it from me...'

Debbie nodded, but said nothing.

'Anyway, they've put off the wedding while he goes over to Texas and starts the job. Isabella will go over and join him in a few months' time, once he's got accommodation sorted out.' He caught Debbie's eye. 'Always assuming he doesn't hook up with some American girl while he's over there. He always did have an eye for the girls.'

Once again, Debbie made no comment.

For pudding, she had decided to make a couple of apple pies, following her mother's recipe, and these were accompanied by several tubs of handmade meringue ice cream from a little shop on the outskirts of Florence, recommended by Steven. He had lost a lot of weight over the past few months and looked all the better for it. She noticed that his alcohol consumption had dropped almost to zero, although he accepted a half glass of Prosecco along with a small slice of pie. Clearly, the self-destructive drinking of recent years was now over for good.

Finally, after a coffee marathon involving her coffee machine and several borrowed moka pots, Debbie slumped down at the kitchen table alongside Dario and leant her head against his shoulder.

'I don't know about you, but I'm exhausted.'

'You and me both.'

He kissed her gently on the top of her head and she reached for his hand. As she did so, she felt a cold, wet nose nudging her from under the table and glanced down to find a pair of soulful brown eyes staring adoringly up at her. Removing her hand from Dario's, she scratched the dog's ears.

'So, have you enjoyed yourself, Byron?'

In response the dog grunted contentedly and slid down her leg until he was stretched out on the cool floor tiles, his paws, as usual, waving in the air. She looked back up at Dario.

'Not a bad idea. There's nothing I'd like better than to do the same.'

'Maybe not under the table, but I quite agree.' Dario glanced out of the open door. 'We'd probably be missed if we slipped off to the bedroom – more's the pity. But, as a substitute, how about a little walk?'

'As long as it's short. I've eaten far too much.'

'Come on.'

The two of them got up and slipped away, accompanied by the dog. Dario led her across the vestigial garden, from which the heaps of building rubbish were gradually being cleared, and over to the old rose bush. Although the flowers hadn't come out yet, the plant was a mass of little buds and Debbie had no doubt it would look and smell amazing when they all opened. Together they walked on until they reached the old bench and sat down, side by side, shaded by the big umbrella pine. As she did so, that same warm, cosy feeling of belonging gripped her and she felt like purring, in spite of her tiredness.

The hillside sloped steeply down towards the valley and away to the jumble of rooftops of Florence – the cupola of the Duomo and the bell tower alongside it standing out clearly against the distant horizon. A big grey and white butterfly fluttered past, pausing just long enough by the dog's head for Byron's jaws to open – but before he could snap at it, it flew off and disappeared into the rosemary bushes. The dog relaxed once more and let his eyelids droop. Debbie's eyelids did the same as she rested back against the warm wood of the bench.

Then she felt a movement beside her. Dario's arm, which had been resting around her shoulders, was removed and as she opened her eyes again, she saw he was holding something in his hand.

'This seems like the right time and place to ask.' He looked a tiny bit nervous, but he needn't have been. 'Deborah Waterson.' He dropped down onto one knee. The dog, surprised to find Dario down at his level, jumped to his feet, wagging his tail and nosing him excitedly. Shrugging him aside, Dario reached his hands towards Debbie. 'Will you marry me?'

She stared stupidly at the ring for a few seconds, seeing it sparkle in the Tuscan sunshine. A wave of overwhelming happiness rose up inside her and broke over her. She heard her voice reply as if it belonged to somebody else.

'Yes, of course. Of course I'll marry you, Dario.'

As she extended her left hand towards him, there was a sudden movement and Byron leapt forward, clearly interpreting these hands extended in front of him as an offer of food. Before either of them could intervene, the ring had disappeared into the ever-hungry dog's mouth and down his throat.

'Byron... For crying out loud!' Dario looked horrified. 'Byron, how could you?'

After the initial shock, Debbie found herself struggling to suppress a wave of mirth, but failed. Catching hold of Dario's now empty hands, she dissolved into a fit of giggles. A few seconds later, she felt him squeeze her fingers lightly and opened her eyes, blinking to banish the tears of laughter and joy that now ran down her face. She was vaguely aware of the dog looking at her with an expression of concern, but not contrition, and Dario doing his best not to laugh out loud. He cleared his throat before speaking.

'You'll have to take it from me that it should fit. I measured your finger with a bit of string a few weeks ago while you were sleeping.'

Debbie was impressed, but then concerned. 'The ring isn't going to harm Byron, is it?'

'You've seen the way he disposes of bones? He's got the constitution and the alimentary canal of a goat. He'll be fine. The problem is that you'll just have a wait a while before you finally get to try it on.' He grinned at her. 'And I imagine it could probably do with a wash before you do.'

'I don't need a ring to tell me you love me, Dario.' She took his face between her palms and kissed him. 'Ring or no ring, I've got you, and that's everything I've ever wanted.'